THE MAN WHO WASN'T

Across the strange clearing, Prince Tamino saw the shape of a man—no more than a shadow in a bright cloak. It was tall and erect, and he caught one glimpse of a face. Then it was gone. Had it been a man? Here in these lands, it could have been anything.

He called, but only silence answered. There was no sound in the clearing. Where had the man gone—if indeed it was a man?

Suddenly he heard a harsh roaring sound and felt a hot, scorching wind go past his head. Tamino looked up to behold a dragon looming over him.

In that moment of terror, he noticed only hugeness, with scaled wings. He backed away, fumbling for his bow.

Then the dragon swooped down, a cruel beak striking at his head!

Also by Marion Zimmer Bradley
Published by Ballantine Books:

THE CATCH TRAP

THE HOUSE BETWEEN THE WORLDS

THE MISTS OF AVALON

NIGHT'S DAUGHTER

a novel by
Marion Zimmer Bradley

A Del Rey Book

BALLANTINE BOOKS • NEW YORK

A Del Rey Book
Published by Ballantine Books

Library of Congress Catalog Card Number: 84-91024

ISBN 0-345-30920-0

Manufactured in the United States of America

First Edition: February 1985

Cover Art by Paul Giovanopoulis

PROLOGUE

Of the Halflings of Atlas-Alamesios

IN the beginning was the Serpent, and later it was told among Men that the kindred of the Serpent had come first, and had aided the hands of the Makers in the fashioning of Men. However it was, in those days the Serpent-kin were not known as Halflings, but as Mankind, as well as the Sons of the Ape.

In those early days, so it was said, at the center of the Year, when the Sun begins its returning-round, in the Night of Great Darkness, it was the Serpent-lord who coupled in the Great Rite with the Priestess of the Night. So it was that the blood of the Serpent (so they said in those days) had entered into the kindred of the House of Night and the very blood of the priestesses. The chief among the priestesses, who in those days were called the Daughters of the Moon and Stars, came to be known as the Queen of the Night; or in later days, as the Starqueen.

And since the Serpent-kin had come so close to the heights of thought and sentient intelligence of mankind, in their pride of creation, the priest-kings of the House of the Sun wrought other Halflings. They made the Seal-folk and the Kindred of the Dolphin, to go down into the depths of the ocean beds and bring up oysters for the tables and pearl-oysters to adorn the girdle of the Starqueen and the crown of the Sun-priests; they also herded fish for the nets of the fishermen.

Later they created the Bird-folk in the hope that they would have servants who could fly and bear messages between their towns; but in this they mostly failed, for the Bird-folk were so fashioned and structured that their wings would not bear them. (The Makers had decided that first of all, all Halflings should bear the shape and the semblance of Mankind.) And furthermore, the Bird-kindred were mostly half-witted; some of them had wit enough to be singers and musicians at the courts of Starqueen and Sun-priests, but otherwise that experiment was not a success, and by the time of our tale, few of the Bird-folk remained on Atlas-Alamesios.

They also created Halflings from the Dog-folk, in the hope that they would have servants of the uttermost faithfulness; and in this they were mostly successful, for the Dog-folk were intelligent, but not too much, so that they found their truest happiness in serving those they loved. They also created the Kindred of the Cats, but these were rebellious beyond measure, and fled to the interior, where lay the remains of the People Who Had Gone Before (some said these were the first of the Makers) and there they lived, preying upon the countryside. And they created the Ox-folk who could bear great burdens, and from their labor were built the mighty pyramids and temples which stand to this day in the ruins amid the jungle and tangle of deepest rain forests.

It is not known how long Mankind and the Makers lived at peace with the Halflings. All civilizations have memories and folktales of a Golden Age when all people lived at peace. Perhaps there was such a day, and perhaps not.

But, and it is not known how or why (but rumor

says that it all originated with the Serpent-kin), it became known even to the Makers that all was not well between themselves and the Halflings. Not only did men scorn Halflings, but Halflings who had too little of the true blood of Humankind began to think of themselves as flawed, inferior, lacking what was essential to being human. And in some ways this was true, for, having too little of human intelligence, some of the Halfling-folk were too witless even for servants, far less able to conduct their own lives. Partly because of this, when Halfling interbred with Halfling beyond the borders of their own kind—from innocence or because the priests, in malice or simple curiosity, had ordained it—such a tangle of genetic materials came into being that Men were filled with loathing. The sight of a Bird-Serpent was terrible to them, or a Dog-Ox, or a Seal-Cat. Harmless as these were, they were also useless, and not fitted for survival; their lives often became burdensome to themselves and to their masters.

And those of the Makers who experimented, not only with couplings between ill-mated pairs, but by breeding from germ cells in their hidden vivariums, created more terrible things yet: the dreadful Feathered Serpent, and the Dragons of the Changing Lands, who partook of the nature of Eagle and Serpent, and the Lion-Eagles who ravaged the deserts. And these too, escaping from their hidden places, interbred with one another, and created at last such a confusion of forms that, they say, the gods themselves rebelled at what they had done.

It would take too long to tell of the wars and troubles which followed: of the demand of the people for a King from among untainted Mankind; of the wars between the Sons of the Ape and the Kindred of the Serpent; of the establishment of the Royal House of Atlas, and of the Sun-kings who were their priests. And it was from the House of Atlas that at last the word was given, that the making of Halflings must cease, that no Halfling might be allowed to breed even with his own kind unless he could pass certain Ordeals to prove the worthiness of his blood to reproduce its own kind (and there were few who could demonstrate intelligence enough even to enter these Ordeals), and that the vivariums must be destroyed. Also, they declared that the mating of Mankind and Halfling must cease forever.

And to this last there was some reason. For in the making of Halflings, they had retained (in order that their servants should increase rapidly) the swifter breeding of the Animal-kind. The Halflings looked much like Mankind; but they littered with the swiftness of the Beast-kind, so that one of the Dog-kindred could sow the earth with forty or fifty sons and daughters while only one generation of Man's children, three or four in number, grew to maturity.

And so the priests realized that soon they would be swamped in Beast-folk without wit to learn or to rule, and would have a great multitude without enough intelligence to be anything more than slaves. Nevertheless, though many of the priesthood and the House of Atlas were thus enlightened, there were still those who felt it right that Mankind should rule over all the Beast-kind and Halflings, and that they need have no obligation to treat them in accordance with Law or even common humanity.

Now at this time, there lived in the Temple of Night a great priestess who called herself, as her mothers and foremothers had done, the Queen of the Night; as with all such Queens, her personal name was long forgotten. She had taken, as had many of the Starqueens, a lover from among the Serpent-folk, and to him she had borne three royal daughters. When the word came down from the Great House of Atlas that all mating with Halflings should cease, she was very angry; yet she bowed her head in apparent docility; and even agreed, as the Great Atlas was old and dying, that she should mate with the heir apparent, a quiet and priestly youth known as Sarastro, to bear him an heir who should join in his blood the two royal houses of Atlas-Alamesios, the Great Temple of Mother Night and the Royal House of the Sun.

Although the Starqueen was now almost past the years of childbearing, she agreed to this; the two were married in the Temple of Light, and a year later the Starqueen bore a child, a daughter whom they named Pamina. When this daughter, hereditary Starqueen and heir to the House of Light, came to sit upon the throne of Atlas-Alamesios, then (thought the Starqueen) her daughter Pamina should nullify what the Starqueen considered the weaknesses and follies of the House of Light.

But the truce between the Priest of Light and Priest-ess of the Old Dark Goddess could not last. In the second year, before Pamina was weaned from the breast, Sarastro and the Starqueen quarreled because of her vicious and cruel treatment of her Halfling serv-ants, which she would neither amend nor cease. So the Starqueen fled from the palace of the Sun-kings and took Pamina with her to the Temple of Night. There she vowed enmity forever toward Sarastro and the House of Light. Sarastro was grieved, for in spite of all her arrogance and pride, he had loved the Star-queen with all the strength of his heart, and loved her still. But his father, who detested the woman to whom he had married his son, said, "Let her go; she is an evil creature, and so are all those of that kindred. One day you will marry another wife who will bear you a son without the taint of the Serpent."

Soon after this, the great priest and king of Atlas-Alamesios died, and Sarastro ascended the throne of his forefathers. Still he took no other wife, but bided his time until Pamina should be grown to womanhood, to rule with her mate after him.

And here our story begins.

CHAPTER ONE

*T**HERE** was blood on the moon.*
Princess Pamina, slight and frail, stood on the balcony staring in affright at the dull, blood-colored mist that was creeping across the face of the lunar disk, crawling across the face of the moon. Never had she seen anything like this before. From far below, in the city that was now only patches of greater darkness against the night, she could hear a muffled sound like wailing; wailing from far away, in terror of the red slime that swallowed up the silver chasteness of the night's face. Pamina felt that she too should wail, fall to her knees, and cry out in terror and repentance.

But she was nine years old, youngest daughter of the Starqueen; she had been taught to bear herself in dignity even alone in her own chambers, and one day she would rule over all these people. She could not run and hide within her rooms to weep in fright. Yet the terror was within her. What had gone wrong in the night, and why did not her mother, who was Lady of the Night, right it at once?

Within her chamber, she heard stirrings; then, behind her, she saw the shadowed form of her half sister Disa, eldest daughter of the Starqueen.

"You must come at once, Pamina." It would hardly have been fair to say that Disa's voice was unkind; it was too indifferent for that. "You are no longer a child; did our mother not tell you that at the time of the next procession, you should join us?"

"I did not know that this was a time for processions," replied Pamina, and felt her heart pounding heavily inside her chest. Processions? They were a thing of sunlight and rejoicing, not for this dark night of fear and wailing in the streets.

Yet Disa's words were obscurely comforting, too. Her mother knew of the wrongness in the sky, and was she not Starqueen? Something then would be done to remedy this hideous color on the moon, the dreadful darkness covering the night. She went obediently into her chamber, where her Halfling servant, one of the Dog-folk, a small plump female with soft, lopped-over hairy ears, awaited her with three processional robes flung over her outstretched pawlike hands.

"Which of the robes will my little mistress choose to wear?"

Her voice was something not quite a bark, nor yet a whine, but it held the qualities of both, and to Pamina it was dear and familiar. She knew well that to Rawa she was the very center of the world; she had been cradled in those hairy arms and comforted against that soft body since she could remember. But since she was old enough to know anything at all, it had been impressed on her that Rawa, as a dog-halfling, must not be expected to make choices or decisions for herself; for that, like all Dog-folk, she awaited the word of master or mistress.

Pamina turned to Disa, not knowing what was the right choice for a procession at this unexpected time. Disa, frowning, inspected the proffered garments.

"None of these will do," she finally said, scowling so that the light revealed the narrowly pitted nostrils,

the curious flatness of her face. "Have no ritual garments been provided for night processions, Rawa?"

"I have had no orders," said Rawa meekly.

This answer did not please Disa, who lashed out,
"Witless Halfling!" and struck Rawa across the face.

"Well, there is no help for it, I must fetch you one
of my own robes; it will be too long for you, but you
can girdle it up at the waist, and perhaps, since it is
dark and she will have much else to think of, our mother
will not notice—if you are very fortunate," Disa added,
with a menace that made Pamina tremble as much as
the Halfling woman. Disa paid no attention, but hurried away, turning to fling a threat back over her shoulder.

"As for you, Rawa, perhaps you have been too long
with your mistress and are beginning to take your position as royal nurse for granted! Perhaps a term in the
stables as rat-catcher would restore your proper sense
of humility!"

Pamina went and hugged Rawa as Disa left the room.
The soft body of the dog-woman was trembling.

"Don't cry, Rawa, I'll talk to my mother, she knows
how much I need you. Mother won't let her send you
away," she said. But she was not certain. Her mother
had so many cares and responsibilities, she left the
managing of the residence, where the four princesses
lived, in Disa's hands from one moon to the next. Disa
might indeed put her threat into action before Pamina
had a chance for audience with the Lady.

Rawa probably was not clever enough to think this
all the way through, but the doubt in Pamina's voice
communicated itself to her, and she made a little whimpering sound and clung to the child. But in the next
moment she moved away, sniffling loudly. Pamina,
who knew Rawa's moods as well as her own, immediately reacted.

"What is it, Rawa? What is it, is there someone here?"

Rawa only whined and continued to sniff around the corners of the room. Then she made a swift series of little rushes toward the balcony, and with a harsh barking sound, pounced. There was a shriek, and Pamina called out, "What have you got there, Rawa? Show it to me, at once. Naughty girl!"

The dog-woman only growled through her teeth, "Bad! Bad! Doesn't belong here, no she doesn't," as she dragged in something from the balcony. Pamina hurried to inspect the slightly built form of the Halfling immobilized under Rawa's paws.

This one was no taller than Pamina herself, clad in a scanty green shift which barely covered long delicate limbs which looked so fragile it seemed Rawa's rough grip could snap them in two. Her hair was a soft crest, like feathers of brilliant scarlet and yellow, growing down in silky iridescent layers along her neck and shoulders. Terror distorted her features, but Pamina recognized her. The bird-halfling had been brought in from the city to juggle for her, sing for her, entertain her on her last birthday celebration.

"Let her go, Rawa. No, I mean it," she added sternly as the dog-woman made a little growling sound. Reluctantly, Rawa released the Halfling woman, who scrambled to her feet, squeaking in terror.

"Papagena," Pamina said, taking a step toward the bird-girl. "What are you doing here? No, Rawa, I told you, let her alone, she couldn't hurt me if she wanted to, and certainly not with you here. And she wouldn't hurt me anyway, would you, Papagena?"

The bird-woman was almost gibbering with terror, but as Rawa released her and backed away, she pulled herself to her feet.

"Princess, you were kind to me, and when they

came to take me for sacrifice, I remembered you and came to you.... Don't let them take me! Don't let them take me away and kill me, don't—"

Rawa whined, backing away still further.

"Mistress! Mistress, send her away or we shall all be in trouble—it's not allowed to meddle with the sacrifices, and I smell it on her, the incense—she smells of death! Send her away!"

"Quiet, Rawa," Pamina said again, though inwardly she was quaking. She should have known, the very night smelled of death, with blood on the moon and the wailing in the streets. She knew of the sacrifices and had never before this questioned them, far less believed that they could touch her or anyone she had ever known. That this faraway half-disbelieved terror could reach out and touch the harmless Papagena, who had entertained them all here at court, filled her with a new and unknown emotion she did not know was rage. She only knew that her teeth chattered and there was a foul taste at the back of her mouth. Rawa was still whining and whimpering and growling and for the first time in her life Pamina was exasperated with her servant. But again she reminded herself: Rawa was a Halfling and a dog-halfling at that and they were not to be expected to have any real judgment.

"Rawa, be still, I told you. Disa will be back in a moment, and if she hears you carrying on like this you will surely be sent to the stables after all. Listen to me, Papagena; I won't let them take you for sacrifice, don't worry about that." She did not have the faintest notion of what she was going to do. She only knew that she was not going to let this happen.

Rawa's soft whine alerted her to a step outside; Disa was returning. She pushed Papagena swiftly behind one of the curtains, and turned to face her half sister.

It was not Disa who entered, however, but a half

dozen of the woman guards stationed at the residence,
led by the youngest of her three half sisters. Kamala
was not as tall as Disa, her body was rounder, and,
though Pamina never stopped to analyze it to herself,
she thought that Kamala looked subtly more human.
The guards were clad in smooth dark leather kilts and
breastplates; Kamala, however, was in her processional robes. She frowned at Rawa, who was whining
and growling in excitement, and said:

"She must have come in here. Look at the dog!"

In another moment Papagena was dragged out from
behind the draperies, to stand quivering before the
guards.

"Let her alone," Pamina cried, "you will frighten
her to death! Mother told me that the Bird-folk are not
as strong as we are, and if they are too frightened their
hearts will stop!"

The chief of the guards, a kindly woman with some
intermixture, perhaps of the Dog-folk, said, "Now, then,
little mistress, you needn't trouble yourself about the
likes of her. She's no business coming up here to trouble you. We'll take her back where she belongs, and
never you worry yourself about it. Rawa, you bitch,
what are you about letting this scum get into the princess's room?"

"That one is getting above herself," Disa said, en-
tering with a processional robe flung over her arm.
Pamina cast fascinated eyes on it. It was somewhat
like the one Disa herself wore, soft silk which flowed
like water and sparkled with lights woven into the very
fabric of the robe; never had she been allowed to wear
one of this kind. But as the guard laid hands on Papagena, and the bird-girl gave a terrified screech, Pamina forgot the unaccustomed finery and flung herself
on them.

"No! I promised her—let her go!"

"Pamina, be quiet," Kamala said angrily. "It is not your place to interfere."

"You have no right to take her for sacrifice! I won't let you!"

Kamala moved swiftly to her side, laying hold of her arm. She moved, Pamina thought, like a striking snake. She said in an undertone, "Hold your tongue, you little fool. This is the will of the Starqueen, and neither you nor I have any right to question her decisions. Nothing that happens here is done except by her will; you are a child and that is enough for you to know."

Pamina stared at her, her eyes wide. She felt she had never seen her half sisters before. For the first time it occurred to her: they are Halflings too. She had known all her life that Kamala and Disa and the third sister Zeshi had been fathered by the Great Serpent, but not until this moment had she realized what it meant.

Am I Halfling too, then, and can I too be taken for sacrifice? she wondered. But no; she was the daughter of the Starqueen.

Yet so were they....

"No," she said, though she was so frightened that the words seemed to stick behind her teeth. "I do not believe that. Our mother is kind and just. All my life I have heard that those who are taken for sacrifices are criminals, those who have killed or robbed or broken some other law. Tell me, what law has Papagena broken? What evil has she done to any? If she were a lawbreaker, then, would Mother have brought her here to sing and to entertain me at the festival on my birthday?"

"This is no time to talk of laws, Pamina," Kamala said. "What you say is true for the sacrifices of the seasons. But have you not seen the face of the moon

tonight in its blood? At this evil time all the laws are
suspended, for the blood-faced moon demands innocent blood. And Papagena has been chosen. Stand
aside, Pamina, and let us take her, as it has been ordained."

But Pamina refused to release the trembling Papagena, and Disa commanded, furious, "Let her go or I
will have you dragged away!"

"I won't." Pamina was sobbing and terrified, but
she did not let go of the bird-girl, and at last, in angry
frustration, Disa gestured to the guards. One of them
grabbed Papagena with both hands; another stepped
purposely toward Pamina. Her obvious intention was
to drag them apart by force. Rawa growled menacingly;
there was a howl from the guardwoman and she kicked
out at Rawa, hard. The dog-halfling went down on the
floor, but she was up again in a moment, growling now
in deadly earnest.

"Lay a hand on the princess, will you? I'll have the
flesh from your very bones!"

"Let me," said Disa, every line of her body taut
with threat, and stepped toward Pamina, jerking her
head at the guard to step away. "If the bitch touches
me she will be flayed alive, and she knows it." She
hauled Pamina bodily off Papagena, while Rawa
growled and whined with rage, and Pamina sobbed
angrily, striking out at her half sister.

"I won't let you! I promised her! What does Papagena have to do with the moon?" Between fury and
grief, Pamina was almost incoherent.

Then there was a sudden silence in the room. The
guards went down on their knees with a gasp. Even
Disa and Kamala bent low, while Rawa gave a whine
of terror and backed whimpering against the wall. The
Starqueen demanded, "What is all this commotion?"

Only Pamina was unafraid. She ran to her mother

and demanded, "Don't let them take Papagena for sacrifice! I told them you were fair and just and that you would never allow an innocent person to suffer!"

The Starqueen looked at her youngest daughter, with a momentary, tender smile. "Did you indeed, my precious?" she asked.

The Queen of the Night was a tall woman, and in the flowing processional robe she wore, with its high headdress of owl feathers, she looked even taller. Her features were narrow and austere, her eyes the blazing blue seen only in the very center of flame.

"You won't let them take her, will you, Mother?"

"If you have promised her that she shall not be taken, I will not let them take her," the Starqueen said. "But in future make no such promises without consulting me, Pamina. To do so, you infringe upon my prerogatives; do you understand this?"

Pamina gave a mute nod.

The Queen looked at the guard, who was rubbing an arm from which blood still trickled. She said, "Outside, all of you—this business should never have begun, and having begun, it should never have gone so far. I am not pleased with you, Kamala," she added, in silky menace, and her daughter trembled. "Take the guards outside. No, Disa, you may stay. Papagena, your young mistress has made you a promise. See that you reward her by serving her well from this day."

Papagena fell to her knees and cried, "Always, Lady!"

Pamina said urgently, "Mother! Mother, why—what—you have told me that no one is sacrificed unless they have broken a law. But Disa told me that the red moon demands the blood of an innocent! Why? What has Papagena to do with the moon?"

The Starqueen looked impatient and Pamina flinched. But her mother only said quietly, "Nothing whatever, child. Yet when the moon turns like this to blood, ignorant people are frightened, and they become hysterical and demand a sacrifice. We give it to them because it turns away their wrath from the priests and rulers. Also, ignorant people believe that for some reason these things happen because of their sins. If we make a sacrifice, they can forget whatever imaginary sins are troubling their minds, and go on about their business again."

"That's terrible," Pamina said.

"Indeed it is, my child. But be grateful that you live now and not a thousand years ago, for in those days, when the moon turned red like this or the sun went dark at midday and the stars came out, then only the death of a daughter to the Starqueen would assuage their guilt and terror."

Pamina trembled, for her mother's face had turned stern and remote again.

"Now, Pamina, you have created a great disturbance, and you have made me late for the procession. Disa, I do not hold you blameless in this. You are perhaps not entirely to blame, for we both thought Pamina old enough to attend the sacrifice. She has shown herself still too much a child, and as punishment she shall be forbidden this procession. Go to bed at once, Pamina. Papagena shall stay with you."

"Mother—" Pamina begged as the woman strode toward the door, and the Queen turned back for a moment, her face shadowed with the impatient look Pamina dreaded.

"What now?"

"Mother, don't let them send Rawa to the stables to be a rat-catcher! She would be so unhappy!"

The Starqueen smiled and said, "I promise you Rawa will not go to the stables." Even long after that, when Pamina remembered that smile, it froze her into silence. But the Queen's voice was tender, and Pamina thought she must have imagined that look.

"Go to bed at once, my child."

She never saw Rawa again.

And the years passed...

CHAPTER TWO

"*THE desert stretched away before him, bare and clean, a few low bushes breaking the horizon in the distance. So far away that* it hurt his eyes to focus on it, he could see low hills and some dim outlines that could have been buildings.

Why, Tamino wondered, did they call this deserted wilderness the Changing Lands? It would have been more accurate and descriptive to call them the Unchanging Lands.

He had been traveling now for the best part of a moon; when he had set out upon this journey, the moon had been full. Now again the moon rose in a pale circular disk at the edges of the night, and he did not know whether he was yet in sight of his goal.

Tamino looked at the pallid face of the moon and remembered that he had eaten nothing since the early morning. He set down his pack, and rummaged inside it. Little remained of the provisions with which he had set forth: a few bites of dried fruit and a strip of dried meat, final scraps left over from his last hunting—the body of some small desert animal, no larger than a squirrel but unlike any squirrel he had ever seen in his entire life. Perhaps tomorrow he could hunt again—if any game of any kind could be found in this howling wilderness.

Carefully, he untied the waterskin at his waist. To-morrow, at the latest, he would need water too. He thought briefly of building a fire, for company—the sight even of sparks against this deserted and silent waste would be friendly. But there was little to burn, only the dry and woody stems of the barren plants. And such as they were, dry and inhospitable, they were the only living things he could see, and he was reluctant to take from them even the little life they possessed without real necessity. Tonight, then, he would sit in the dark.

He sipped a few mouthfuls of water and chewed thoughtfully on the dried fruits.

A year ago, a moon ago, he had never believed that he would find himself in any place like this. He wrapped himself in his shabby traveling cloak—it had been fine and new not long ago, but since then it had served him for blanket, garb, and shelter in all weathers, and it had aged. Like I myself, Tamino thought.

Until a bare moon ago, Tamino had been no more than the pampered younger son of the Emperor of the West and had known no hardship and little exertion, except for games with his companion and some hunt-ing.

Then he had been sent forth, knowing only that it was the will of his father, the Emperor, that he should travel to the great Temple of Wisdom in Atlas-Alamesios—of which he knew only that it was about a month's journey distant—to undergo the Ordeals. During much of this journey he had wondered about the Ordeals, when they would begin and if this journey were, indeed, the first of them. In accordance with the instructions given him, he had traversed the mountains which bordered the Empire of the West, crossed the Great Waste which separated that Empire from the lands of Great Atlas, and entered upon the Changing

Lands, which, so far as he could tell, did not change at all.

Yet now, as he lay beneath the distant stars, shivering a little—for the night was cold and his cloak had been intended for the warmer climate of his father's lands—he began to wonder if, indeed, this wilderness and this journey had not wrought a change, at least, in himself. He was perhaps not exactly the same Tamino who had set out thirty days ago from his father's place. For one thing, he was thinner. Never before had he missed a meal, and on this journey he had missed a great many. Many of those he had eaten, in fact, he had had to provide for himself by his skill at hunting.

Nor had he ever known what it was to be alone, or to be afraid. Not that the journey had been unduly perilous. But it had been solitary; never before this had Tamino lacked for counsel or for companionship. There had been none to advise the better road, the safer path on steep crags, none to guide his hand or arrow when he shot for game. He had had no guide but the rough instructions he had been given to follow the rising sun; no adviser; no company but himself, no counsel but the memory of his childhood's advisers— and now he was all too aware that he had made all too little use of that guidance.

Yet he was no longer, as he had been earlier in the journey, afraid. He no longer felt the want of someone to talk to, nor the need of anyone to guide him. Not only was his body harder, but it seemed to Tamino that his mind and determination as well were more firmly muscled, more self-reliant. When he notched an arrow and let it go, he knew it would fly swiftly to its target and strike. This was no longer a game, no longer a competition to prove his superiority, where at least half the time the companions chosen by the Emperor for his son would hesitate to best him in the game.

Here in the desert, if the arrow went wide he would likely go to sleep supperless, and must hunt, as well, for an errant bolt, since there was no way to replace one.

No, he thought, I am still Tamino, but a stronger Tamino, perhaps—the thought was hesitant, almost shamed—more worthy to be called prince. Even if nothing further came of this journey, if he should come to the edge of the very world and find nothing but the barren sea, the Ordeals no more than a delusion, so that there was nothing for him to do but turn around, retrace his steps and go home again, he would not regret the journey nor think it wasted.

He lay looking at the stars. In his father's palace he could not remember ever having taken any more note of the stars than of the brilliant ornamental lanterns which adorned the palace ceilings. Rather less, in fact, for it had sometimes been necessary for him to order the lanterns changed or replaced. Since he had come on this journey, he had seen more of sunrises, sunsets, moon, sun, and stars than in his whole lifetime before this. He had come to rely on them; clear sight of sun and sky telling him that he could travel without losing his way, clear sight of moon and stars that he could sleep in the open without needing to seek the shelter of cave or overhang or even a convenient thicket or bush. At home he had slept through the sunrises, insulated by silken curtains, and if a hunting party kept him abroad long enough to see a sunset, he thought of it only as a tiresome delay before the evening's revelry. Here for entertainment he had only those same sky and stars.

Lying now and looking up at the clear desert sky, he remembered. Years ago when he was still in the schoolroom, he had had a tutor who had tried to teach him the lore of the stars, but Tamino had hardly listened, always eager to get out to his pastimes and companions. He could have learned all the wisdom known to mankind, become familiar with the influence of stars, sea, tides, and clouds, all the things which he should have known before he ever came on this journey. Instead, he had had to learn all these things painfully by studying them and discovering for himself how they affected his progress.

He had not been trained to rule. That had been for his elder brother, the crown prince. Yet he had been provided with a good education; it was not the fault of his father that he had made no use of it.

Well, tomorrow would be another day of travel, and perhaps it would bring him a little nearer to his unknown goal. He took a final frugal sip from his waterskin; his mouth was dry and he could gladly have drained the skin, but he had made that mistake, too, early in his journey, and had learned to conserve his last water until he was sure where he could next replace it. Carefully, he retied the neck of the waterskin, thrust it beneath his neck for a pillow, and slept.

The first light wakened him. The sky was flushed crimson, an ominous color; he had learned on this journey that it meant rain or storm. Yet there had been no rain in the desert in ten days of crossing this waste. Was he about to see rain here, then, or did a crimson sky in the desert mean something other than crimson at sunrise in a more hospitable territory? It seemed he was about to learn something more about weather.

A few sips of the stale water from the waterskin, and the last few bites of his dried fruit made an unsatisfactory breakfast. Perhaps, when he reached the Temple of Wisdom where he was to undertake the unknown Ordeals, they would let him have at least one good meal first.

But here and now there would be no meal at all, good or otherwise, unless he provided it for himself, and in this wilderness it would probably be otherwise. There was little game here—he had seen none of the peculiarly shaped squirrel creatures for several days— and even less vegetable food that could be eaten. His most crucial need at the moment was for water. Only a little, and that dank and musty, remained at the bottom of his waterskin; he had learned enough of the torture of thirst that he was unwilling to repeat that particular lesson.

He looked around to try to get his bearings. To the east the sun was just rising from a sea of crimson cloud. The horizon was broken by some squarish shapes which might have been rock formations or possibly—Tamino's breath caught in his throat—buildings. If so, this would be the first human habitation he had seen since he left his father's city.

But they were very far away, at the very edge of the horizon of his sight. A month ago he might have made the error of thinking them closer than an hour's walk, deceived by the clear desert air.

Now he knew they were a day's walk, and perhaps even further away than that. Excited though he might be at the thought of once again encountering men, first it was imperative to renew his supply of food and water; after, there would be time enough to think of the build-ings—if they were buildings at all, and not strange formations of rock. Once before he had been deceived, thinking he saw a city where there were only cliffs and spires of rock.

Dismissing the thought of the buildings, he turned about to assess the other directions, to see if there was in his immediate surroundings any chance of renewing his supply of food and water. He had seen nothing the night before, but he had walked until dark and might have missed something in the twilight.

He turned round to gather up his cloak, which had served as his blanket, then stopped and rubbed his eyes. Last night, of this he was certain, he had slept in the open; he could remember lying and looking up at the stars. Surely he had not been deluded, had not been actually looking up at them through the branches of a tall tree?

No, for he remembered, just before sleep had taken him, that he had taken note of the lack of all vegetation except for the dry and spiny bushes. Yet now, above the crumpled cloak which still bore the creases and impress of his body, the tall corrugated stem of a date palm swayed; and the thick golden brown bunches between the leaves were surely clusters of ripened golden dates.

Tamino blinked and rubbed his eyes again. This marked the return of one of his earliest fears during the first stages of his journey: that the solitude might drive him mad. A date palm, and furthermore a date palm laden with ripe dates! Yet, when he went to sleep—right under it, by the evidence of his eyes— there had been nothing of the sort.

But the thick rugose trunk was solid beneath his fingers, and when he climbed, it supported him. He thrust one of the fresh soft dates into his mouth. It was not like the elaborately prepared sweet dates, sticky with syrup and stuffed with sweetmeats, he had eaten at the Emperor's table, but it still seemed good enough to him for an imperial banquet. He ate several more of the fresh dates and thrust a bunch into his pack.

Food, then, was supplied, unless—and he did not seriously think so—this was a bizarre dream born of hunger and solitude and he was still lying in his sleep of fatigue under the dry and barren desert bush.

His hunger satisfied, he turned to the even more pressing problem of water. Date palms did not usually grow in the bare desert. He had heard that they grew only in oases. Had he then been moved while he slept, his body carried to an oasis of date palms with the usual springs at the center? Alas, no; the solitary date palm under which he seemed to have slept without knowing it was alone in the barren wasteland. It was a riddle he could not read.

He was certainly awake. The only possible solution, and that was as mad as all the other ideas, was that the dry and spiny bush had somehow been changed, while he slept; changed to a date palm where no date palm could grow. Was this then why they called this barren waste the Changing Lands?

The dates were real and wholesome; at least they felt so to his palate and to his stomach. What a pity that they had not somehow transported their oasis with them.

Slightly to the north stood a boulder; not very high, but when the terrain was so flat, it could perhaps provide a vantage point from which he could spy out whether there was any break in the rough and barren country, any sign of an oasis or even of vegetation of the kind which might signal the presence of water. Tamino climbed the rock and turned slowly in all directions. The sun had now risen, and the view to the east was obscured with light. Tamino, squinting his eyes against the cruelty of the sun, now saw not only the low horizon, broken only by the distant shapes he had seen on arising, but, roughly halfway to that broken line of horizon, the rising green of palms and a glint that might well be water.

On the face of it this was as unlikely as the scrubby bush which in the night had become a palm loaded with bunches of ripe sweet dates. Was it a mirage? Ten days in the desert had taught him something of that danger, too. Yet he had breakfasted well on the impossible dates; it was at least worth the possibility that he might quench his thirst at the equally impossible oasis.

It took him no more than a moment to gather up his possessions: the pack which now held only a few scraps of dried meat and the miracle dates; his cloak, which rather than wearing he now tied carefully about his waist; his bow and a few remaining arrows; and the short sturdy knife he carried about his waist, less weapon than utilitarian tool for skinning game or cutting firewood.

He set off in the direction of the oasis. After thirty days he was a hard and tireless walker, and set a steady pace. The dry and thorny bushes tore at his legs, though he had wrapped them in scraps of an old tunic, and impeded his walking. Strange that there were now so many of them; the day before they had grown as sparsely as all other life in this desert. He looked down curiously. They were thicker and not as spiny as they had been—a new plant with thorns rather than spines, and bearing leaves. Leaves, green leaves in this barren desert?

Yes. Leaves, green leaves with prickly undersides and ragged toothed edges. And rather than the low spiny bushes, they now grew on trailing reddish vines which were—Tamino stopped, wondering again if his eyes played him false—laden with ripe blackberries.

He tasted one. It tasted like any other berry, perhaps a little sweeter than most, or was it only that he had gone so long on short rations? He went on pushing his way through the thickening tangle of thorny bushes, filling his hands with the ripe berries, which also quenched his thirst.

There was a crashing sound through what had become, almost swiftly, thick underbrush. Before Tamino's startled eyes, a gazelle leaped across a clearing before him and disappeared while he was still staring.

He blinked and went on, scowling. He should have had his bow at the ready, but he had not expected anything like this in the desert. But was it a desert now? When he had surveyed the country round the rock, it had been the same barren desert in which he had gone to sleep last night. Now it seemed to have taken on some of the qualities of a jungle. Definitely, the ground was softer under foot, and after a time he heard a soft and definite squelching sound beneath his boots.

The Changing Lands?

Long before he reached what had been an oasis when he surveyed the ground, he reached a small pool fed by a crystal spring. He rested there for a time, bathing his parched face in the water and drinking his fill for the first time in many days.

He was still not free of the fear that this was all a mad dream. He had lived for twenty years and never before had he encountered any territory where date palms appeared by magic or desert changed to bog without any intervening transition—or, more accurately, lands which he had seen as desert were discovered to be bog. But then he had never traveled, before this, in the Changing Lands.

A rustle beyond the pool alerted Tamino. He snatched his bow from his shoulder, strung it swiftly with one hand, almost in the same motion fitting an arrow to the notched string. At the far side of the pool, bending to drink, were a small herd of antelope, shoulder high to a man, with long curving horns.

He paused for an instant before loosing the arrow. Although after a month of short rations the smell and taste of fat roasting haunch of antelope was already in his mouth, yet if he reached his goal in a day or two, he could not eat that much meat. Was it right to kill for so little, and waste the rest?

Or—he looked again—was it an antelope? His eyes must have deceived him; it was a small gazelle, not much higher than knee-high to Tamino, who was not particularly tall. This much he could certainly make use of. With swift decision, he let the arrow fly.

The gazelle fell soundlessly to the earth, shot through the heart.

CHAPTER THREE

QUICKLY, Tamino hurried toward the spot where he had seen the gazelle fall. He stumbled over roots and vines that he had not seen before (had they been there?) and when he looked round he saw no sign of the dead animal.

This was as mad as anything else that had happened this morning. Yet he persisted. He was no longer starving, for he had eaten his fill of the dates, but he had lived far too long on dried foods, and was hungry for the taste of fresh meat. He looked carefully for the gazelle's body. Had he missed it, after all? No—he had seen the arrow strike, and at this distance he could hardly have missed clean. Moreover, he had seen the creature fall.

He kicked restlessly at the underbrush. It was not as tall as all that, not enough to hide a full-grown gazelle.

His foot encountered some obstacle. With astonishment, Tamino saw that it was one of his arrows. He bent and lifted it. It was stuck in something, and when Tamino lifted the arrow to free it, he found that he had indeed shot something through the heart.

But it was not a gazelle; it was, instead, one of the small and peculiarly shaped squirrels which had constituted his last previous meal of game.

Thoughtfully, Tamino picked up the animal. This was even stranger than the other things that had been happening to him. He had seen an antelope, and forborne from killing it because he felt he could not eat so large a beast. Whereupon it had conveniently turned itself into a gazelle, and he had shot it. And when he found the carcass it had undergone yet another metamorphosis into a squirrel.

Maybe, he thought, he had better cook and eat it at once, before it underwent some other change and shrank down into a sparrow or a cricket!

He returned to where he had left his possessions, watching carefully to be sure they did not change into something else. If his skinning knife, for instance, were to become a fishhook or a spinning reel, it would be troublesome to get his meal ready. But everything was reassuringly the same. He sat down cross-legged and skinned the squirrel—carefully not taking his eyes off it—gutted it and cut a dry stick to spit it; then he built up a fire and set the carcass over it to roast.

Soon it began to sizzle and sent out the most appetizing smell. While it was cooking, Tamino rinsed and refilled his waterskin, and, stripping to the skin, plunged into the pool to refresh his dusty and sunburned body. He washed his soiled tunic and his leggings and hung them to dry on one of the thorny bushes. Again he drank from the sweet water of the pool. After so long in the desert he had begun to think he would be thirsty forever.

Half naked, he sprawled on the bank, munching the roast squirrel. The flesh had a strange taste, as if the beast had fed on some oddly astringent berries, but it was meat, and filling, and Tamino enjoyed the first really satisfying meal he had had in many days. When he had finished, his tunic and leggings were dry, and he went to reclaim them from the bushes. The sun was warm by the pool, and he delayed a little before putting them on again.

In the pool there was a ripple and splash, and a small furry face, whiskered and inquisitive, peered up at Tamino. Although at first he thought it some small water animal, perhaps an otter, he realized quickly that there was human intelligence behind the dark eyes: a Halfling! He had heard of them, even far away in the Empire of the West; but never before had he actually set eyes upon one. Although he had known that many years ago such creatures had been brought to the Emperor's court as curiosities. There was a story of an ape who had played at chess with the Empress, Tamino's mother, and had beaten her at the game.

The otter-halfling crawled slowly up the bank. In form it was a small furry woman, the face so round and bewhiskered that only by seeing the small paired breasts down her belly was Tamino certain that the Halfling was female. She had fur all along her back, too—though there was less of it on her breasts and belly—and her arms and hands were abnormally, almost grotesquely short, ending in stubby clawed fingers. The legs were short and clawed too, rather than footed, and less than half the length of the torso. Tamino looked at her halfway between fascination at her strangeness and revulsion for this parody of the human form. A real otter would have pleased him, and an encounter with a real woman, after so many days with no sight of a human creature, would have been more than welcome. But he was not at all sure that he wanted to encounter this curious being. She watched him so intently that Tamino was suddenly aware that he was all but naked. He reached for the tunic and pulled it quickly over his head. Why should he be so self-conscious in the presence of an animal? Yet as he looked at her he discovered that he was very conscious of her femaleness, as he would not have been in the presence of a real animal. He was very much aware that this was not an animal but a woman, and to be treated as such.

Small splashes in the pool revealed three or four smaller furry faces, replicas of the Halfling woman: her babies, surveying him from the safety of the water. They made small chittering sounds. He wondered if the Halfling had human speech, and if it would be useful to ask her the way. He took a step toward her, and she slithered swiftly down the bank and into the pool, swiveling an inhumanly supple neck almost all the way round to look cautiously at Tamino. Could she possibly think that he meant her any harm?

He coughed self-consciously and said, "I won't hurt you."

There were small squeaking sounds from the furry babies; but the otter-woman only stared, the brown eyes fixed on him with curiosity and skepticism. She was after all a woman, though a very strange one; perhaps she had reason to fear strangers encountered in the wild like this. He had not been sexually aroused by her, but somehow he was conscious, without knowing how he knew, that other men perhaps had been so, that she had reason for her fear. She went on looking at him, and that intense dark gaze gave Tamino a chilling sense that merely by being, as he was, human unadulterated, he had somehow wronged her, and that made him angry. He was not to blame that he was a man and a prince of the West.

"I only wanted to ask you," he said stiffly, "what is the way to the great Temple of Wisdom, the palace of the Sun-kings?"

Silence, while the Halfling woman stared at him with her great dark eyes, then the furry babies chittered softly. He wished, if she was capable of speaking, that she would do so.

Quickly, she pointed to the northeast with one stubby arm; then, in a splash and a ripple, submerged, leaving nothing but fading circles on the surface of the pool. In four little splashes, the babies dove after her.

Tamino stood staring for a moment, watching the ripples remaining in the pool, before turning away. Well, he had encountered now the first of the strange things he knew that he must face in the Changing Lands, and he was sure he would see stranger things than this while he was in the country of the priest-kings of Atlas-Alamesios.

He gathered together the remnants of his meal and was about to bury them in the leafmold near the pool; then he wondered if otters were meat-eaters. He supposed, being pool-dwellers, that they lived mostly upon fish, but in case they liked meat, he left the scraps for them. If they chose not to eat them, he thought crossly, wondering why he was annoyed, the bugs and insects near the pool would do away with them soon enough. He took up his bow and his few remaining arrows, gathered up his cloak and tied it around his waist, carefully extinguished the last coals of his fire, and strode away.

He took the path to the northeast, as the otter-woman had directed him, but the character of the land had changed, and he found himself traveling now through thickly forested country. It was almost impossible to see very far ahead or behind in any direction, for there were trees and tangled vines and heavy underbrush, and sometimes they grew so thickly that he could hardly see the sky. He found it incredible that only the night before he had slept in a barren desert; surely, if this forest had been here, he would have seen it somewhere on that deserted skyline. Here and there in the overgrown forest, which was rapidly becoming a jungle, he glimpsed great ruins and overgrown buildings, and more than once he heard the snarling cry of a predatory jungle cat.

Gradually, as he moved, he grew hotter; even his thin tunic was too heavy. He started to take it off, then remembered that he was no longer alone in an untenanted wilderness. Where there was one creature with sentience there might well be others, and he might at any moment encounter the inhabitants of this place. And if he must, he preferred not to do so with the disadvantage of near-nakedness.

There were now many sounds in the forest and after the silence of the great desert, they seemed to press in upon him. Birds called in the trees overhead, small things scurried away under his feet, and from time to time, glancing up, he could see some creatures moving swiftly through the branches. As yet, though, none of the sounds were specifically human sounds. Not unless some of the beasts he could dimly see sharing this wilderness with him were, in truth, Halfling, partaking in some small measure of Humankind. And he still found that hard to believe.

All that morning and well into the afternoon he walked. At one period he heard the beast-sounds, high overhead and under his feet, fall suddenly silent; then there was a short, swift, violent shower of rain. Even in the shelter of the trees he was drenched, stunned by the sudden wind stirring the leaves and whipping the branches. He huddled under the trees, shivering, letting the wind roar over him, and the rain was like knives cutting his skin.

Then the rain stopped, as swiftly as it had begun. The sun came out and gleamed through the rifts in the branches; silvery drops tilted and fell shimmering on his head. A bird screamed in the high foliage overhead and Tamino saw a flash of brilliant yellow and crimson swooping above. Almost at once his soaked tunic dried in the heat.

He was beginning to think about looking for a place to rest for the night, and of another meal from the cooked remnants of the squirrel when the forest opened into a clearing. At one time this had been a settled place where men lived, for great masses of stone rose overhead, high pillars and half-fallen walls. When he looked down he was treading on small bright stones set in a mosaic; there were curious shapes, beast and bird, human and half-human, a woman with the horned moon set above her brow, a great coiling serpent who yet bore the shadow of human-form. But even the colors of the stones had faded. He wondered who had lived here, and how long ago it had been?

Even as the question crossed his mind, he saw across the clearing the shape of a man, no more than a shadow in a bright cloak. Or had it been a man? It was tall and erect, carrying his head proudly, and he caught one glimpse of a face, high-bridged nose, sharp arrogant chin, then no more; there was something inhuman in the swiftness with which it moved. But Tamino had seen it only for a second or two before it disappeared behind the great ruin which stood at the far end of the clearing. In memory it looked something less than human. Another Halfling? He retained the image in his mind of a profile that was both noble and melancholy, and without thinking he called out, if indeed it was a man:

"Hey, there! Hello! Won't you come and talk to me? I am a traveler from the Empire of the West—" and, remembering how the Halfling woman had feared him, he added—"I don't mean you any harm, I only want to talk to you!"

Silence. Tamino realized that his heart was pounding against the walls of his chest. Was it only excitement at the thought of encountering something human after a full month of solitude? Or was it fear? There was no sound in the clearing except for the rustle of grasses and insects underfoot. In the distance a bird chirped and there was a merry little whistle—Tamino could not tell whether it was a bird, or some human sound. It did not sound entirely birdlike, but seemed to have some purposefulness behind it.

Where had the strange man, if indeed he was a man, gone? The clearing was empty; it seemed that now even the birds fell silent.

Then there was a harsh roaring sound and a hot scorching wind past his head and Tamino looked up to behold a dragon looming over him.

In that moment of terror he noticed only hugeness, scales, and wings, a suggestion almost of feathers, a cruel beak striking at his head. He backed away and fumbled for his bow, stringing it swiftly; but the dragon swooped down and Tamino ducked and went sprawling on the ruined mosaics and grass of the clearing. Almost automatically his fingers notched an arrow into place and let it fly.

It must have found a target somewhere, for he heard the creature scream with rage as it struck down again to the kill. It was too close for his bow to be any use now. Somehow he had his knife in his hand, but he was all too conscious that it had never been intended for a weapon. He was all but unweaponed against the worst menace he had ever seen.

He thrust blindly upward. The dragon's wings were all round him, blurring away sight. The monster's evil breath was hot against the back of his neck as he turned blindly and began to run. Fighting was useless; no single human could hold his own against such a beast.

He cursed the fates that had sent him out unweaponed and felt a desperate regret that his journey should end here, regret for all the new things he would never see or know, even for the Ordeals he would now never have a chance to attempt.

He whirled about desperately and struck up again with his knife. He would at least die fighting, not let himself be carved up and clawed to bits from behind. He wished there would be someone to carry news to his father of how he had died, and he found himself wondering wildly if there was anything after death or if this would be the end. The roaring of the dragon was loud in his ears. His knife found a target again; he ripped at it and dark foul-smelling blood showered over him, but the dragon was still fighting, he had not even seriously wounded it.

Then, in the dark nightmare of blood and stench and effort he heard high voices, women's voices. He saw the sharp points of metal spears piercing the dragon, saw, disbelieving, that it fell away and died. Above him were women's faces: three women clad in leather armor with high moonlike crescents on their armor. They looked, he thought in a last flicker of exhaustion, like the moon-crowned women in the mosaics beneath his feet. Was this a dream, were these the guardian spirits of this place? Were these only the last dying fancies of his brain, had the dragon killed him after all?

Exhausted, he fell a million miles into starless dark.

CHAPTER FOUR

*D*ISA kicked the dead body of the dragon; then bent to tug it away, signaling to her sisters to help her. Zeshi bent to the task, but Kamala remained motionless, staring down at the face of the unconscious youth.

"Can he really be a prince? His cloak is so shabby—"

"He is the second son of the Emperor of the West, and his name is Tamino," Disa said, "but unless we move away the body of this dragon we cannot release or revive him."

Reluctantly Kamala took her eyes from Tamino's unstirring form and hauled, with her sisters, at the dragon's body. As she hauled she said resentfully, "What kind of work is this for us? I never heard that there were dragons in this place."

"These are the Changing Lands," Zeshi said. "You should know as well as any that you are likely to find absolutely anything in the Changing Lands, and whatever you find, it will not be what you found there before."

"I suppose so." Kamala straightened her back, and looked down at Tamino again. "How handsome he is!"

Zeshi nodded, and slid her tongue over her lips. "There are no men in the Temple of Night to compare with him.

Look at his shoulders, his thighs, his hands. His eyes— are they blue or are they dark? His lashes are as long as a maiden's. I am sure he could give great pleasure. I wonder if in his faraway country he has a lover, and if I could make him forget her? I wonder—"

Disa laughed. It was not a kind sound. "Your body is hot for any new young man, Human or Halfling, no? I do not think he is intended for you, nor yet for me, Zeshi. Forget for once the pleasures of your pillows, and put your mind to the task the Starqueen has given us."

"And do you think you are better, Disa? There are stories I could tell from the Temple of the Bull—"

"Be quiet, both of you," Kamala interrupted with authority. "When the Starqueen bade me leave the guards and come here into this wilderness, she ordered me to protect the youth—and now that we have done so, our next task is to tell her that her wishes have been carried out. I do not think that she wants him for her pleasures either."

"We were ordered to protect him," Zeshi argued, "and there might well be dangers in this place. I will stay and guard him while you bear this news to the Lady."

"If there is guarding to be done," Kamala reminded them, "the Starqueen put me in charge of her guards, so that task would be mine. And you, Zeshi, have other duties to the Halflings. Go, then, and tell the Queen, and I will guard him—"

"And who will guard him from you?" Disa jeered. "He will be safe enough here alone. Come, then, and let us tell the Starqueen. She has enough to trouble her," she added in a gentler voice, "must we quarrel among ourselves? Especially now, when she is so distraught?"

"You are right," Zeshi agreed, and Kamala laid a hand on her sword.

"If only my guards and I could lay hands upon that monster—first I would tear his eyes from his head and cut away his manhood, and then when I had done I would fling the remnants to the crows!"

Disa nodded grimly. "He is mad with power. And it does not help our mother, I suppose, that Monostatos, our half brother, the son of our father, the Great Serpent, has defected to the monster and taken himself away to the temple of the priest-kings. Yet one would think the Starqueen cherished no hatred even against him!"

"She has room now for only one hatred," said Zeshi, "and it is not for Monostatos. Perhaps she has sent for this prince to help her."

"With all her allies among Halflings and men, why would she turn to a stranger from a distant land?" Kamala asked, and she looked scornful.

"She might well," said Disa, "for a prince from a distant land would have no loyalties already given among us. But I remind you, my sisters, it is not our work to question her, but to carry out her wishes. Come, let us be on our way."

Kamala cast back a wistful look at the motionless body of the young prince, but she did not protest. She followed her sisters from the clearing.

Tamino came slowly to his senses, hearing the sound of a whistle. Slowly, he sat up. His head felt bruised, and as he raised his hand to touch it he felt slimy evil-smelling blood on his tunic.

Now he remembered. He had fought a dragon. He looked around; its lifeless body lay at a short distance. He had not killed it. These were the Changing Lands; had it turned conveniently into a dragon's corpse, as the antelope had turned first to a gazelle and then to a squirrel? But he was not lying where he had fallen. Someone had dragged the dragon's body off his own, and propped him up against a tree. His knife lay nearby; Tamino retrieved it, and stowed it away in his belt, then looked about for his bow and arrows. He found the bow lying still strung where it had fallen; no arrows were to be found. Well, now he was once again among the dwellings of men, he might be able to get some more.

But who had saved him?

Now he became aware that he was not alone in the clearing. The whistle he had heard earlier sounded again, and he saw a strange-looking man moving about near the edges of the trees.

He was slenderly built and small-boned, and for a moment Tamino thought he had green hair—no, he had green feathers on his head! No, that was not quite right, either, but his hair was an odd color, greenish yellow, and it grew down along his neck in layers which did indeed give an impression of feathers. His nose, too, was just the suggestion of a beak, or so it looked at a quick glance, though at a second look Tamino realized that it was a perfectly normal nose, though somewhat sharper and beakier than any nose Tamino had seen. There was something odd about his hands, too, though he used them deftly enough. He raised them now to his lips and blew on a small set of pipes, which perfectly imitated a birdcall. Then he whistled engagingly, and at the sound a half dozen small birds flew down into the clearing, pecking up something he had scattered there. The strange man made a movement with his strange hands, so swiftly Tamino could hardly follow it with his eyes, and four of the birds were squawking and fluttering between his hands. He thrust them into a wicker cage that Tamino had not noticed on the grass at the edge of the clearing, and whistled again.

As he watched, Tamino realized what this strange creature must be. He looked like a man who had been partly transformed into a bird; or like a bird who had somehow taken on human characteristics. And that meant he was a Halfling.

Another Halfling. But the Halfling he had met before had not been nearly so human in manner, had not worn clothing, had not spoken. This Halfling wore a coarsely woven green tunic trimmed with green and yellow feathers—which struck Tamino as being in poor taste, as if he himself had worn a belt of babyskin. But perhaps he did not think of it that way, or had not the wit to think of it that way, or whoever owned the bird-man thought it a pleasant japery to dress him in bird feathers and set him to catching birds.

The previous Halfling, the otter-woman, had not been able or willing to speak. But she had indeed given him directions by gesture, so she must at least have understood human speech.

Tamino got up and hesitantly approached the bird-man, who went on unconcernedly whistling to coax the birds from the trees.

"Excuse me, friend—" he began.

With a great flutter of wings and shrill cries, the birds took wing, and the Halfling turned. He saw Tamino, started and frowned.

"Look what you have done! Now they've all flown away," he scolded.

"What were you doing with them?" Tamino asked, startled and yet pleased that the strange creature could speak.

"Catching them and putting them into cages. Couldn't you see that? Are you blind?" He sounded cross, and Tamino wondered if he had made a mistake, if this were after all an ordinary man and not a Halfling after all.

"Why were you catching birds?"

"It's my work; I get fed for it," replied the stranger. "I catch birds, and in return they give me cakes and wine and good fruits. Don't you do any work? What kind of idler are you then?"

"I am no idler, but a traveler," Tamino said, then was annoyed at himself for being drawn into irrelevancies. "Who are you—I mean, what are you?"

"A man like yourself, a man like any other man," said the bird-man crossly. "I really think you must be blind after all. And what are you doing here? There are not supposed to be any strange men in these parts, and the Starqueen will be angry when she finds out."

"Who is the Starqueen?"

"You really are very ignorant," the bird-man said. "Don't you know anything about anything? She rules these wilderness lands. How did you get here anyway without her leave? Why, she might send a dragon after you, or something like that!"

"I think that's just what happened," Tamino said grimly. "Did you kill it?"

"Kill what? I was joking," said the odd little Halfling, with a comical grin. "There aren't any dragons in these parts."

"That was what I thought," Tamino said, and pointed. The bird-man jumped, shrank back in terror.

"Oh, help! Is it dead?"

He edged around behind Tamino, looking out fearfully at the corpse. Reassured by its continued silence, he sallied out, and stood over it in a swaggering attitude.

"Hah! You don't think a fellow like me would be afraid of a dragon," he said. "Not a little dragon like that! Why, you should see some of the real dragons around here!"

Tamino tried to hide his grin. Now that he was safe, he could see that the dragon was not as large as he had believed when he had been fighting it; but it was larger than anything he had ever fought in his life, and larger than anything he ever wanted to fight again. He was still not sure that it had been real, rather than an illusion of the Changing Lands. Yet the corpse looked real enough. He had not killed it, either; but he was perfectly sure that this comical Halfling had not done so, either. The Halfling was slender and so slightly built, Tamino would not have wagered on him to win a cock-fight, if the cock was a real fighter.

"You killed it, then? What sort of weapon did you use?" he asked, laughing.

The bird-man looked at his belted tunic, where the only things even resembling weapons were a tiny knife which would hardly have trimmed a quill pen, and an implement for braiding wicker or vines—probably the birdcage he carried had been made with its help. He touched the hilt of the little knife and Tamino could almost see him debating whether he would be believed if he claimed to have used the knife. Instead he bragged, "I don't need weapons! Can't you see the power of my arms and fists?"

Tamino was almost shouting with laughter now. How absurd the little fellow was. If a human being had told such lies, Tamino would have been repelled, but this little chap could not be expected to have human standards and ethics.

"Tell me about all the dragons you've killed," he said, still chuckling. "Does the Starqueen collect them as she does the birds in your cages?"

The bird-man's eyes widened at the mention of the Starqueen. "Oh, no," he said, his eyes wide. "She would rule over all the dragons as she does over all of us! She is great and powerful—and I, Papageno, am her chosen companion, catcher of birds, killer of dragons and her wisest of councillors—"

"Oh, are you indeed?" Tamino chuckled. "Then perhaps you can direct me to some friendly inn around here where a traveler can be fed, and have a bath and perhaps a jug of good wine, for I've been traveling for thirty days, and I'm in need of some gracious hospitality!"

"There are no inns in these parts," Papageno said naively, "or at least I don't know about them. I haven't seen many travelers. It must be terrible to be hungry! I'll tell you what—soon there will be some pretty ladies, come to collect my birds, and they will bring me fruits and good wine and a loaf of fine bread. They always do, because I'm such a charming fellow—after all, the Starqueen's chosen champion. There's always more than I can eat and you're welcome to anything I can share with you."

"You are very kind," Tamino said sincerely. The little chap might be a silly and comical braggart, but he had a kind heart.

There was a soft call from the edge of the clearing. "Papageno!"

The bird-halfling quivered, and again tried to hide himself behind Tamino. Again the soft insistent call, in a woman's voice.

"Papageno, naughty fellow!"

"Are those the pretty ladies you told me about?"

The bird-man nodded miserably as the call came again for the third time: "Papageno!"

Tamino looked around for the speakers, and saw three women coming into the clearing.

"Who are those ladies?" he asked.

"They are the ladies of the Starqueen," said Papageno, trying again to hide behind Tamino. The prince looked at the women.

All three were tall and imposing, with dark hair and dark eyes, strong-featured, with high foreheads. Tamino, who had seen no woman in a month of travel, looked at them with interest. One was dressed as a warrior, in a kilt and breastplate of black leather and high boots about her shapely calves. The other two wore robes of pale woven material, and their brows were crowned with a kind of headdress bearing a crescent moon. Somehow Tamino felt that he must have known them somewhere before. Yet to his certain knowledge he had never set eyes on any women like this, they were certainly nothing at all like the delicate, fair-haired, fair-skinned women of his own country, clad in silks and soft stuffs; not one of them would have considered bearing weapons like this.

He was about to come forward and speak to them, but their attention was entirely on Papageno.

"Papageno," one of them said with silken menace. "Today I bring you from the Queen, instead of fine bread and fruits, only a basket of empty hulls and husks." She raised the basket and emptied it over his head, laughing gaily. Tamino was startled; the young woman looked too kind and gentle for such rough teasing. Papageno stood uncomfortably brushing away the husks from his head and off his rough clothing.

"My lady Zeshi, what have I done? Look, my birds— how fine they are, what beautiful colors, not a single tail feather missing—" he babbled.

"And from her Graciousness I bring you no sparkling wine, but a jug of muddy water from the pig trough!" The speaker was the warrior woman with the sword; and as she spoke she threw the water over Papageno's head. He emerged soaked and miserable, shaking the featherlike layers of greenish hair from side to side and muttering, "Lady Kamala, I beg you—"

Tamino, shocked, moved out of range. The third, who was the tallest and most imposing of them, said sternly, "And for your lips, lying and bragging to an unsuspecting traveler, I bring a liar's bridle to still your untruthful chatter!"

"Oh, Lady Disa—" Papageno moaned, but he was quickly seized between the two smaller women and the gadget fixed over his mouth.

He shook his head, mumbling, but all he could say was, "Ummm-ummm-ummm!" Tamino was troubled and distressed. They were laughing. They were playing with the Halfling. It was only a game to them; he could tell they did not mean to be cruel, but why should they treat the poor little fellow so harshly?

But they had finished their fun, and while Papageno cowered, the tallest and most imposing of them advanced toward Tamino.

"Prince of the Empire of the West," she began, while Tamino wondered how she had known his name. "Good fortune awaits you. Your name and purposes in traveling here are known to our great Queen, and she bids you to her palace, where you shall be an honored guest of her Graciousness."

Tamino hesitated only a moment. He had been commanded to seek the Temple of Wisdom, yes, and request admission to the Ordeals; but he had not been forbidden to undertake such adventures as might befall him on the way. This Queen was evidently a person of local importance, and she might well be able to set him on the correct path. If he could encounter the dangers and difficulties of the road, there was no reason he should not also undertake and enjoy such pleasant encounters as came his way.

"I should be delighted," he said.

"Papageno, you come too," said the woman warrior. "You shall wait on the prince. You have spent too much time among the birds, if you think that they have qualified you to brag of dragons." She gave Papageno a half-kindly, half-stern push in front of them, but he could not speak. He made a few helpless grimaces and grunts, but with the bridle fixed over his mouth he could not utter a word. Tamino went with them, and as they left the clearing he saw in the distance dark towers rising over the wall of a great fenced enclosure.

"There lies the palace of the Starqueen, the Lady of the Night," the warrior woman Kamala said. "There shall you be an honored guest, and with the coming of darkness shall the Queen of the Night receive you into her gracious presence."

CHAPTER FIVE

THE walled enclosure was a city of broad streets, where men, women, and Halflings both male and female mingled in the squares and streets, along the narrow alleys and before the houses that Tamino saw everywhere. The people of the city were of two distinct stocks: tall, dark, and aquiline like the Starqueen's ladies, or fair-skinned with blond or reddish hair, not unlike the folk of the Empire of the West. Intermingled thickly in the streets and gardens were Halflings of all kinds; many looked dirty and neglected, half-starved and filthy, in greater squalor than any animal.

There were also many like Papageno, obviously servants of some noble house: well fed and sleek, they mostly wore collars, chains, or fantastic costumes which seemed to be a kind of livery. Most of them looked ridiculous so gotten up. They might, Tamino thought, have been attractive, and even had their own dignity, had they been treated either as animals or human beings. But there seemed no middle ground; either dressed-up pets like complicated toys, or slaves, with the disability of being only half human, or dirty neglected animals. Animals, thought Tamino, would have been better treated.

There was no sign of squalor or neglect in the palace,

though he did see one disconsolate creature who looked half ox, half man. His shoulders were enormous, like the muscles in chest and arms; he had thick, coarse hair which grew down over a low, broad forehead, bulging suggestively as if horns were budding. He looked unhappy and stupid; there was not in his face any of the quickness Tamino had seen in Papageno's.

He wore a rough garment of leather, which struck Tamino as being the same kind of tastelessness that clothed Papageno in feathers. His hands were clumsy, the fingers thick and covered with calluses like horn. He was dragging a heavy broom along the corridors, clumping on feet as horny and stumpy as hooves. The hairy, thick-set body was manlike enough except for huge genitals bulging the leather apron. Wrists and ankles were burdened with fetters. Tamino wondered what the bull-man's offense had been, whether he had displeased someone as Papageno seemed to have displeased the Queen's ladies.

The women conducted him to a suite of rooms.

"Pray, make yourself at home; if you want for anything, Papageno will make sure it is brought to you," Disa said. "Papageno, serve him well, and perhaps the Queen will be gracious enough to free you."

Papageno bent humbly to the ground, making the mumbling sounds which were all that he could utter.

When the ladies had gone, Tamino explored the rooms. There was a luxurious bath, which reminded him that he had been traveling for many days and that after a long time in the desert, he had washed only sketchily in the forest pool.

"I'd like a bath," he remarked aloud, then became aware of Papageno crouching nearby, making his inarticulate sounds.

"I'm really sorry, my poor fellow; I honestly think

they were too harsh with you," he said. "Turn round and I'll see if I can get you out of that thing."

Papageno shrank away; evidently the thought of displeasing the ladies was worse to him than the pain of the device. He pushed Tamino into the bathroom and made signs to him to disrobe, and in a little while a couple of furry Halflings—who made Tamino think of the otter-woman he had met in the forest—came into the room and with many frolicsome splashings filled the bathtub and guided Tamino into it. The water was warm and pleasant, though not hot enough to be enervating. Tamino scrubbed the dirt of his journey from his body with pleasure, aided by the otter-creatures, who frisked round him in the bath, making it obvious to him that he could give them no greater pleasure than to use their bodies as sponges, brushes, and towels.

Towels indeed, large and dry and fuzzy, they provided when at last, reluctantly, he dragged himself from the water and made it clear that while they might serve excellently well as sponges and washcloths they were no use at all as drying towels. The room was flooded with soapy water and suds, and Tamino could not, in fact, imagine more pleasant bath companions than a couple of friendly otter-people. He was really almost embarrassed by their obvious sensuous enjoyment of the whole process, but they were as innocent about it as a couple of huge friendly dogs, and he supposed that if they were trained as bath attendants, there was no reason they should not enjoy their work.

But the bath was finally done, and Tamino returned to the main room of the suite to discover that his dusty and travel-worn clothing had vanished. In its place were tunic and breeches of finely spun silk, deep crimson in color, and girdled with a heavy belt reinforced with plates of copper. There were drawers and stockings of soft cotton, and his boots had been cleaned and rubbed to a high polish. A cloak fastened with a silver chain, in a gray as subtle as the very silver itself, completed the outfit, and Tamino felt once again like the prince he had been.

Papageno looked at him with mute admiration, and gestured to a pair of Halflings, of the same stumpy leather-clad breed as the chained man he had seen pushing the broom. They went away and came back with a succession of silver trays, laden with all manner of delicious food and drinks. There was also a good-size jug of wine. Papageno made mournful chirping moans as he set out the fine food and poured Tamino a glass of the sparkling pale yellow wine. It was heady, with the sweet perfume of many mingled fruits, and after a second glass Tamino felt as if his fortunes had definitely taken a turn for the better.

He lounged at ease on a couch padded with silks and pillows, eating slices of the fine-textured bread, of finer grain than he had ever tasted in his homeland, savoring the platters of roast meats, and the cakes of honeyed fruit. When he had finished his meal, the attendants brought him his bow, which like his boots had been refurbished, rubbed and polished and fitted with new strings and a supply of finely crafted arrows.

Whatever could be said for the way the Starqueen's attendants treated her Halfling servants—and the lady herself could hardly be blamed for that—her palace could certainly not be faulted for luxury and hospitality.

Suddenly there was a sound like a great rushing wind. The doors of the apartment swept open, the bull-halflings who were clearing away the meal made mournful bellowing sounds and hurried away, their hooves shaking the floor. The windows swung wide, opening on the night and the stars beyond the balcony.

Then the three ladies were once again in the room. They too had changed their attire: all of them, including the warrior woman, wore dark robes that glittered as if they had been washed in moonbeams and stardust. Shimmering crescents crowned their brows, and it seemed to Tamino that their eyes in the pale lamplight shone with the very glimmer of the evening stars that were beginning to shine outside.

Kamala whispered—Tamino knew her voice now— "She comes, our Lady of the Darkness and Queen of all the Stars!"

"She comes! Do her honor!" commanded Disa's imperious voice. The rushing of wind beyond the doors grew almost to hurricane proportions, so that the windows rattled and the curtained hangings flapped and rustled like wild birds.

Then silence, utter and entire. The last of the lamps flickered into darkness. Tamino could hear a little clicking sound. Papageno's teeth were chattering, and he heard the painful chirping moan which was the only sound the Halfling could make with his bridled mouth.

In the darkness there was a faint glow like the moon rising within the room. Abruptly, with a thunderclap, she stood before them, crowned with the moon and gleaming in a mantle of a million million stars: Queen of the Night.

Tamino fell to his knees, awe-struck before her beauty and majesty. The glow dimmed. Suddenly the candles in the room were burning again, Tamino never knew how, and the awesome figure of the Starqueen had dwindled. Now she was nothing more, or so it seemed to the overawed young man, than a fragile, aging woman, small in stature. Her face, lined and careworn, still held the remnants of great beauty. She came softly toward him, her steps as noiseless as cloud;

like cloud, too, was the pale misty wrap about her shoulders.

She said, and her voice was as soft as a night wind through the branches of the trees, "Do not be afraid of me, my son. I know that you are strong and honorable, and I know with what courage you have met the hazards of the journey."

Tamino opened his mouth, but could not speak. He wondered if this fragile little lady were any more real than the overpowering vision of the Goddess of Night. Which was her real semblance—or was her true being something completely other than either of these?

The Queen went on, her voice a sorrowful and faraway murmur, "You see before you the unhappiest of women. My daughter, the child of my old age and the comfort of my solitary life, has been stolen from me by an evil fiend named Sarastro, and I tremble for her fate. You are wise and strong, and Sarastro would have no power over an uncorrupt youth like you, a stranger to these lands... I can ask no help of my own people, for he has exerted his evil will over all the folk of this countryside."

Fingers as delicate and unsubstantial as mist pressed something hard into Tamino's palm. "Here," the voice that was like the twilight whisper of a wind through an oasis, "you will see the likeness of my daughter. Does she find favor in your eyes? Your courage and strength, and your high station as the son of the Emperor make you her equal, and worthy of her. If you will undertake her rescue, you shall be rewarded. She is not married nor promised in marriage, and her dower—" The Star-queen paused. "—is the very kingdom of the Night. Have courage, and restore to me my daughter—and you shall rise higher than you could ever have dreamed."

Tamino found in his hands a small hard flat object

like a mirror. Gazing out from the surface of the mirror
was the fair, tear-stained face of a lovely young girl.

She could not have been more than fifteen years
old. Her features were delicately made; he could see
not the slightest resemblance to the Starqueen, neither
to the awesome Goddess—if that had been anything
more than illusion—nor to the dark, aging woman who
stood before him in her shrouding veils. The girl in the
portrait—or was it some kind of magical mirror?—was
very fair-skinned, her eyes deep-set in a fringe of long
blond lashes, her brows almost too pale to be seen.
Tears stood in the violet eyes, tears smeared the delicate cream of her cheeks, tears tangled the long eyelashes. Her robe of white silk was cut modestly high,
but he could just see the swell of young breasts.

"She is beautiful," he whispered. "What is her
name?"

There was a soft answering whisper in the room,
"Pamina," but he hardly heard. His eyes seemed to
have been trapped by the lovely breathing face.

Then there was another thunderclap; lightning flared
through the room and he was alone, clutching in his
sweating hands the mirror, on which the lovely face
of a young girl stared magically out at him.

Papageno was still whimpering in the corner. The
magical darkness was gone; Tamino realized that outside the room it was barely sunset. Night and darkness
had been an illusion, created by the Starqueen.

He stood perfectly silent, wondering if he had fallen
into a bizarre dream. But the face of the young girl in
the mirror was real, though magical.

And surely she was no more than a part of that
magic? The Queen had first appeared as awesome and
terrible; then she had revealed her true self, a sorrow-
ing mother. Tamino thought of his own mother. She

had died when he was very young and he could hardly remember her face, though, now that he thought of it, she must have looked something like the Queen. He told himself that he would have helped this unhappy and deeply wronged woman, even if her daughter had not been beautiful and even if she had not promised him her daughter's hand and dowry.

He looked again at the lovely face of the weeping girl in the portrait. She was not crying now; she looked angry and frightened, and in the darknesses of the magical mirror it seemed to him that he could see a shadow behind her. The shadow of the evil sorcerer, her kidnapper?

Sarastro, that was the name; a man accursed, if he would tear a daughter from her mother for his own evil purposes. What could he possibly want with the girl? Tamino told himself that he was naive: what could that corrupt priest want with the girl, except to make her one of his deluded disciples, and perhaps take advantage of her youth and beauty?

Papageno was still making his pitiable mumbling chirps when the Starqueen's three ladies came into the room.

"Papageno," Disa said, and the bird-man cringed. Tamino could almost hear him wondering what new cruel frolic they had devised for him as their butt. Instead she beckoned him to her, and he went forward slowly, reluctantly, more afraid to disobey than of whatever treatment he might receive.

"Her Graciousness, Queen of the Night, has instructed that you are to be forgiven," Disa said, turned him briskly around and whipped the bridle from his lips. "Now beware of lying and bragging, naughty fellow!"

Papageno, capering with delight, made haste to go to the table where the remnants of the luxurious meal brought for Tamino were still lying on their trays. He caught up a handful of fruits and cakes, then looked fearfully at Tamino.

Tamino gestured to him to help himself, and Papageno crammed the goodies into his mouth. The ladies ignored him.

"Prince Tamino, have you resolved to accept the Queen's mission?" Disa asked.

She spoke with a solemnity that was almost ritual. He answered in the same tone.

"I have, lady."

"Then take this," she said, and extended to him a long leather case. From the shape, Tamino thought it might be a sword, and was grateful; he had, after all, expected this journey to be religious in nature and had brought nothing in the shape of a weapon. With eager fingers he unwrapped it.

But it was not a weapon. It was—what was it? A long hollow reed, varnished and painted with curious symbols; along its length were a series of holes, each one a little smaller than his fingertip. Tamino wondered if he looked as confused as he felt by this curious gift.

"Do not be disappointed," Kamala said. "I, who am a warrior, tell you this is a weapon I have long coveted, and would give you my sword, spear, and bow for it. What do you think it is?"

"It looks to me like something one of my father's musicians would play," said Tamino, wondering if she had meant her offer and if he ought to take her up on it, and if the Queen would be offended if he did. "I should tell you, my lady, that while I have some small skill with music, I know but little of playing the flute. I was reared as a hunter and a warrior, not as a minstrel or entertainer."

"You will be able to play this flute," said Disa, "for it has magical qualities. And within Sarastro's realm it will be of more value to you than any other weapon, or all other weapons together; for it has some powers over his deluded slaves. And, make no mistake, of these he has many, for he has forced his delusions on all the people in the surrounding countryside. You may even find that he has bent the princess to his will; she is very young and she may even have come to believe Sarastro's pretense of noble purposes. She may not wish to leave his realms."

"I will make certain she knows the truth," Tamino promised.

"Papageno," Zeshi said sharply. "Where are you going?"

Tamino turned around and saw that the Halfling was trying to sneak inconspicuously out of the chamber, his hands filled with cakes and sugared fruits.

He mumbled, "Back to my little hut in the forest, ladies. This place is too fine for me. Please excuse your humble servant, and I wish you all good night. And my gracious compliments to your lady the Queen, and to Princess Pamina, and to the prince, and to all of you fine ladies, and sleep well, and pleasant dreams. Good night to all of you, good night." He gave a soft, pleasant whistle on his little birdcall, turned and stepped toward the door.

"Come back here," Disa said. "I did not tell you, but it is the will of her Graciousness that you shall go with Prince Tamino on his quest, to guide him and serve him well."

"Oh, no, my lady, oh, no!" Papageno stared at them in dismay. "Oh, no, I am your humble servant, but truly I must decline such an honor! Why, Sarastro would tear me to pieces and feed me to his buzzards! The prince deserves a—a better and braver servant than I am. Why, I'm such a liar and a braggart, you said it yourself, Lady Disa, I'm a very unworthy person. Why don't you send one of your warriors to guide him?"

"Because Sarastro would know one of my warriors at once," said Kamala. "And with you he is unfamiliar, so you will be safe within his realm. Don't be afraid; Prince Tamino will protect you, and if I hear that you have not served him well, you will have to reckon with me!"

Papageno looked back and forth between Tamino and Lady Disa, not able—Tamino could almost hear what he was thinking—to decide whether he was more afraid of the unknown Sarastro or of the ladies, and what they would be sure to do to him if he defied them. Tamino was sorry for him, but at the same time not at all unhappy that he was to have a companion on his quest.

He put his arm around the Halfling's shoulders.

"Cheer up, friend Papageno," he said. "I'll look after you. In fact, you know more about this part of the world than I do; we'll have to look after each other."

"Why, you don't think we'd let our gallant champion go without his own weapon?" Zeshi said good-naturedly. "Her Graciousness has sent a gift for you as well, Papageno." She handed him something wrapped in a cloth. The bird-man unwrapped it with curious fingers. It was a small frame on which little bells were fastened, with a finger-brace to keep the bells from sounding until they were touched. Papageno's fingers reached out to touch it, but Disa gestured to prevent him.

"Not until it is needed," she said, "for this is a marvelous weapon indeed; it has power over some of Sarastro's people. Tie it round your waist, Papageno, and use it only when danger threatens. And now it is time for you to be on your way."

"Now? In the dark?" Papageno's tone was plaintive,

and Tamino wondered if he went to roost at night like other birds. To tell the truth he felt much the same; after a month's journey he had looked forward to sleeping in a proper bed.

"But I don't know the way to Sarastro's realm," he protested, but even as he spoke the palace walls seemed to melt away, the ladies were gone, and he was standing on a dark road at the edge of a forest. He wondered if the whole bizarre episode had been a dream. No— for Papageno was standing beside him, trembling in the darkness, though it was not cold, and in his hands was the magical flute.

"What are we to do now, friend Papageno?" Tamino asked.

The Halfling whistled on his pipes. He said, "I should have thought to bring some more of those cakes and a little of that nice wine with me. But I didn't know we were going to start off again on our travels so soon. What to do? Well, the ladies gave you some kind of magical weapon, didn't they? You could try playing it, and see what it does. If it helps, that's fine, and if it doesn't, at least a tune might cheer us up a little."

"That's an idea." Tamino couldn't imagine what good it would do, but on the other hand he didn't know anything about magic. He found himself wondering if this encounter had been the first of the unknown Ordeals he had traveled so far to undergo. When you traveled into the magical realms—and this certainly felt as if it were part of them—he had always heard that you must be prepared to face the unknown.

He unslung the flute and put it up experimentally to his lips. He blew softly into it, expecting an unpracticed dissonance, but he heard a soft, piercing melody, surprisingly sweet. Astonished and pleased, he went on playing; he had always loved music, without having very much skill at making it.

Suddenly there was a faint golden glimmer in the air. Tamino blinked; in the darkness of the path before him there was a glow as of fireflies, and then three creatures stood before him.

He could not tell whether they were boys or girls. They were too human to be Halflings; but they were slight and golden-haired—or was that only the golden glow that surrounded them? He blurted, "Who are you?"

"We are the Messengers of Truth," said one or were they all speaking together, a soft blended sound, almost like the music of the flute at his lips? "What do you ask of us?"

"Well, if it's all the same to you," Papageno said. "I wish I had some of that supper I never had a chance to finish in the Queen's palace."

"Papageno!" Tamino reproved gently, but one of the Messengers raised his hand—her hand?—with a little gesture, almost, but not quite, as if snapping half-invisible fingers. He said in that soft singing voice, "To each is given according to his needs of the moment." In his hand appeared a golden goblet and plate piled high with cakes. "Satisfy your hunger, my little friend. Wisdom may not reside in a full stomach, but it is certain it has never lived in an empty one. And you, Prince Tamino, what is your will?"

Tamino watched Papageno gobbling the cakes. He thought of the tree loaded with dates which had appeared out of nowhere in the Changing Lands and decided this was not such a bad country after all.

"At the moment," he said, "what I need more than anything else is a guide into the lands ruled over by a wicked magician whose name is Sarastro."

"Who told you about Sarastro? And why do you call him a wicked magician?" the Messenger asked—or were they again all speaking at once?

"A cruelly wronged woman made her complaint to me," Tamino answered.

Papageno whispered, "Tamino, these are good people, at least if I can judge by their food and wine. How would they know the way into any wicked sorcerer's house? Isn't it insulting even to ask them such a thing?"

"If they object," Tamino said reasonably, "they can always tell me so. And if Sarastro has extended his influence over all the people around here, as the Star-queen told us, certainly they would know it." He looked hesitantly at the Messengers.

"Can you guide us to Sarastro?"

"Certainly we can, and we shall do so," said the Messenger, or perhaps all of them, for try as he might Tamino did not see their lips move nor could he tell which one of them was speaking. "If you follow us you shall certainly come before Sarastro, and you will have an opportunity to confront that which we serve: the Truth. Have you finished your meal, little friend?" He reached for the empty goblet, tossed it into the air, where it vanished in a golden, firefly glow.

Papageno asked, "How did you do that?"

"Be careful what you ask," answered the Messenger, "since to ask a question involves you in a search for the answer; more than the answer—for the Truth which lies behind the answer. Are you sure you wish to know?"

Papageno only blinked, but the Messenger was evidently waiting for an answer. At last he said, "I don't know. I haven't got a very good head for riddles."

"Honestly answered," said the Messenger. Tamino was almost sure it was the one at the far right who was speaking this time. "Have you this much honesty, Prince Tamino?"

Tamino looked at the three glowing figures. He said at last, "I don't know either. But I'll try."

"Very well," said the Messenger. Now he looked like a very young girl. In fact, their figures and features seemed to shift and change. "That answer will do to begin with. Follow us, then."

They turned about, and Tamino followed the glowing figures along a path—he would have sworn that the path had not been there a moment ago.

"Come along, Papageno," he said, "and don't be frightened. I don't think they mean us any harm, and if they are the Messengers of Truth, I suppose they were telling us the truth when they said they would take us to Sarastro."

"It's dark," Papageno said, trembling.

"There's nothing there in the dark that isn't there in the light," Tamino said. He remembered his nurse telling him this when he was very small and asked for a nightlight. To tell the truth he felt no braver than Papageno; but fate had given him the harmless Halfling to look after, and he should set Papageno a good example.

Trying to sound braver than he felt, he whistled softly and they walked after the glowing figures of the Messengers, into the dark path between the trees.

CHAPTER SIX

*H*E *was there, and spying on her again.*
Nervously, Pamina drew the sheet round her body. She had never really liked Monostatos, not even when she had known him distantly, as one of her mother's faithful servants. He frightened her. It was not only that he was peculiar in appearance, akin to the Serpent-folk. But it seemed that whenever by chance he encountered her, his colorless eyes seemed to cling; so that she always wondered if somehow she had encouraged him to stare.

And here in this strange house, among strangers, and away from all familiar things and patterns of life — even the Halflings here were presumptuous, speaking without being spoken to, taking license as if they had never been beaten — Monostatos seemed to expect she would turn to him as to an old friend.

Only the level of friendship he seemed to offer was strange, troubling, over-familiar. All too often he appeared within the suite of rooms Sarastro had put at her disposal, trying to seem as if he were on the best of terms with her servants, and more than once, as now, she had sensed that he was spying upon her when she was in her bath or being dressed. In her mother's house he would not have dared to intrude upon her, and her mother's servants would have swiftly thrust him out the door if he had tried. But here in the strange household of Sarastro, how could she tell whether this intrusion was something Sarastro had willed?

She wrapped her robe around herself more tightly and called the Halfling servant to bring her garments. "And draw the curtains closed," she commanded. "I feel eyes upon me."

But would they obey her, if Monostatos here enjoyed the privileges he seemed to claim without even thinking about it, if he was, in truth, closely allied to the unknown and frightening Sarastro, who had seized her and brought her here?

But they drew the curtains without protest, and she gave orders to have herself dressed. Should he override her commands, she preferred to face him fully clothed; his eyes, it seemed, never left her, but if he must stare, she preferred that he confine his staring to the outer layers of her clothing.

But at least, now, if he wished admission to her suite, he must ask entry in the ordinary way, and Pamina took what comfort she could from that fact.

"Does my lady wish food brought to her here?" asked the dog-halfling who waited upon her, a woman who reminded Pamina poignantly of Rawa. She had not thought of Rawa in years and was annoyed at herself that she felt so secure and comfortable with this woman, who was after all one of Sarastro's corrupt and deluded slaves.

"Yes, I suppose so." There was, after all, little else to do here, unless she wished to look into some of the scrolls Sarastro had left for her, and she supposed they were full of Sarastro's hateful philosophy. He had asked her to read them, and that was enough to turn her against whatever apparent or pretended wisdom they might have contained.

It was not that he had been cruel to her, or inhuman.

In their one brief interview, Sarastro had treated her with gentleness; had, if anything, seemed kind, though detached. But Pamina was remembering the terror of that day—how long ago had it been? She had lost count of the days—a handful of days, at least—since she had raised her eyes from her favorite seat in the orchard with Papagena to see strange Halflings approaching her without her permission. When she cried out to them in outrage—who were they to intrude upon the daughter of the Starqueen?—she had seen the strangely dressed priest. She knew now that he was one of Sarastro's debased priesthood, but then she had only seen the curious and unfamiliar emblems on his clothing, and had been too frightened to listen to any reassurances.

Princess Pamina, no one will harm you, but you must come with us quietly, without any outcry.

She had at once screamed out loudly for her mother's servants. But she remembered nothing more, except a muffling cloak over her mouth, a sense that she was falling, dying. Then she had awakened here, among servants wearing Sarastro's livery, who assured her again that she would not be harmed, and had provided her with every luxury except the one thing she really wanted—to be returned to her mother.

My poor mother. She will be in terror for me, her heart will surely break.

Everyone else, Pamina knew, was afraid of the Starqueen. Pamina alone knew her softer side; to her alone, her mother was invariably tender and yielding. Why should Sarastro have chosen now to resume their old warfare?

She knew nothing of Sarastro except this: that he was the Starqueen's enemy. There was some old grudge between them; Pamina did not know its cause, but she knew her mother to be a just and virtuous ruler; if

Sarastro set himself against the Starqueen, Pamina was sure she knew where the truth must lie.

When food was brought she ate reflectively. She felt like crying again, thinking of her mother's distress. But she had done too much weeping. She must put her mind now to something useful: escape, or at least how to keep her own integrity among Sarastro's people.

"Lady," said the dog-halfling, whose name she had not troubled herself to ask, "Prince Monostatos humbly begs that he may be admitted to speak with you."

Really, Pamina thought, *Prince* Monostatos! And who conferred royalty upon him, I wonder? She was tempted to tell him to go away again, proudly refuse to speak with him. But Monostatos was at least halfway familiar, he was—or once had been—one of her mother's trusted servants, and if he too had defected to the hateful Sarastro she could at least reproach him with his treachery. She had no great desire to sit and talk to Monostatos. But what else was there to do, except sit and stare out of the window? Sarastro had exquisite gardens, but Pamina was tired of looking at them. That, or torment herself with thinking of her mother's despair.

"Let him come in," she said.

Monostatos, son of the Great Serpent, was tall, his skin dark and sallow; but the features were not unhandsome. There was, Pamina thought, a faint resemblance to Disa, whom she had always thought beautiful. He moved gracefully; almost, it seemed to Pamina, he glided. His eyes, though, were unpleasantly quick, bright, and gleaming.

"Ah, lady, does our hospitality please you? Have you been made comfortable? Are your servants serving you well? Have you been brought everything your heart could desire?"

Pamina drew her brows together in a frown and said, "Monostatos, my mother trusted you. And you have deserted her for Sarastro. How dare you come into my presence like this?"

"Had it never occurred to you that wherever you are is where I wish also to be, Pamina?" he asked her, and stood so close to her chair that she got up and moved farther away from him, frowning.

"Do you think I am eager for gallantries from you, Monostatos? Certainly not! Either give me a sensible answer as to why you are here, serving Sarastro when you are honor-bound to serve my mother, the Star-queen, or go away again and don't come into my presence at all!"

"You speak like a child, Pamina," he said. "You are even too much a child, I think, for me to call you lady or princess. But I will give you a truthful answer. I have come here to undertake the Ordeals of the Temple, and thereby gain my birthright."

"Your birthright?" She shook her head, confused.

"My father was the Great Serpent and I am his only son and heir; there have been great men and great priests among the Serpent-kin of Atlas-Alamesios. Among them I intend that the name of Monostatos shall be written. I intend also that the son of the Great Serpent shall be considered when Sarastro shall give the hand of his daughter in marriage—for he has no son, and therefore to the husband of his daughter shall pass the power of the crown of Atlas-Alamesios."

"If Sarastro has a daughter," Pamina said, "then he should have some compassion for my mother; and if not he is no man but a monster. Is his daughter known to you?"

"Perfectly well," said Monostatos.

"I should like to see her sometime," said Pamina.

"Nothing is easier." Monostatos crossed to the

dressing table, while Pamina watched in indignation. How dare he meddle with her belongings? He picked up her silver mirror, bowed deeply and handed it to her.

Pamina flushed angrily and struck the mirror from his hand. "What mockery is this?"

"No mockery at all," said Monostatos. "Has the Starqueen told you nothing of this, daughter of Sarastro?"

"I think you must be mad," Pamina said.

"Nothing of the sort." The pale smooth features were taut, as if repressing some emotion—anger, scorn? "I am certain your mother intended, one day, to tell you who fathered you, daughter of Sarastro; but perhaps she thought you too young to understand that between a man and a woman who once loved, various causes may arise for contention."

"How did you find that out? I cannot believe my mother would have confided in you, of all people," Pamina said, lifting her lip in contempt, and Monostatos let his features tighten still further.

"Beware, Pamina," he said, "I wish to be your friend; perhaps I am your only friend here. I would be your lover, your husband. But I will not be mocked this way. Sarastro is the power of this place, and I shall be high in his favor when I have undertaken the Ordeals and hold all the power of the ancient Serpent-kings. It would be wise for you to remain my friend."

"If that is my only alternative," Pamina said, feeling her mouth curl in distaste, "I am resigned to being friendless here. Before I would have you for lover, or for husband, I would take a vow of chastity and hunt forever for the Sacred Antelope in the band of the Maidens of the Moon."

Monostatos laughed, a curiously mirthless sound. He said, "You are truly a child, Pamina. You are heir to the Starqueen; do you truly believe that she would allow you to waste yourself in that way? The Divine Polarity must be manifested in her child as well, before you assume your heritage. I intend that when you are given in marriage, the hand you take shall be mine."

"Given in marriage to the Son of the Serpent?" Pamina cried out in mingled horror and scorn. "Never! I cannot believe my mother would give me to you—"

"You dare say so, when your own sisters, the children of your mother's own body, were fathered by the Great Serpent, my father? If the mother accepts the father, shall the daughter refuse the son?" The sallow features now were almost flushed.

"Yet when she wished a daughter for her true heir," Pamina cried out furiously, "mark it well, Monostatos, she turned not to the Great Serpent, your father, but to a priest-king of Atlas-Alamesios—if what you say is true and I am in fact daughter to Sarastro! If my mother thought your father so high-born and so fit for her consort, why did she not then choose him to father her heir?"

"I say again to you, Pamina, beware," he said, and now she was really afraid of him. He advanced on her with his fists clenched, his eyes glittering. There was a swiftness about his movements that suddenly terrified her. She backed against the wall, covering her mouth with her hands.

Then suddenly he relaxed and smiled. He lowered his clenched fists, saying genially, "You are really only a child, Pamina. When the day comes when I have conquered the Ordeals and taken all my birthright, then, I dare say, when Sarastro lays your hand in mine, you will be ready to have me for your true mate."

"Never!"

"Well, we shall see," Monostatos said, laughing softly. "And in earnest of that day, give to your promised husband your first kiss, Pamina." He strode forward toward her; she shrank back against the wall, putting out her hands mutely to stop him. Laughing, he grasped them in one of his own, pulled her against him, almost roughly, and with his free hand pulled her head forward, crushing his lips against hers. She jerked her head away, frantic, hating the heat in his lips. His breath was not foul, but nevertheless she twisted her head away in disgust.

"How dare you? You—you *snake*! You *Halfling*!"

His face went pale. He jerked his head away from her and said, in a voice whose very low evenness terrified her worse than the touch of violence, "Someday I shall make you regret those words, Pamina." He turned on his heel and strode out of the chamber.

Left alone, terrified, the girl let herself fall into a chair. She covered her face with her hands, and sobbed. Oh, for the safety of her mother's house, where nothing like this could ever have happened, where such as Monostatos knew their place, and Halflings were not so presumptuous!

Her mother, in the strength of her wisdom, might choose such consorts for her amusements as she would; she could do no wrong. Pamina knew well that Disa, at least, and probably her other sisters as well, chose male Halflings as lovers now and again, and her mother, if she did not precisely approve, at least forbore to interfere. But she had warned Pamina against doing the same, in words the girl could not mistake, telling her that when the time was ripe she would have a consort worthy of her.

Her mother would never have given her to Monostatos. But here in Sarastro's realm, where she could not trust anything or anyone—that would be exactly the kind of thing the debased priesthood of Sarastro might consider suitable.

But Sarastro was her father—or so Monostatos had

said, and would he dare to tell a lie that she could uncover by asking a single straightforward question?

Yet here among the priest-kings of Atlas-Alamesios—so her sketchy knowledge of this realm went—she had heard that women had no power to choose their consorts, but that their husbands were allowed power over them. This, she had once guessed, was one reason for the enmity between the Starqueen and Sarastro, that he did not accept the great truth, that the Queen of the Night was Lady and Mistress of all the lands. And now she was in the power of this corrupt and wicked man who dared to deny the powers of the Starqueen and to assert dominion even over the Starqueen's daughter. Yes, she could even believe that Sarastro might attempt to give her over to the Son of the Serpent in marriage!

She dared not take that risk; dared not remain here. This time, Monostatos had stopped with a single kiss, and even as inexperienced as Pamina was, she could tell that it was a kiss, not of passion, but of conquest, even of contempt. But if he was firmly resolved to have her— Pamina's skin crawled, feeling that if Monostatos touched her again her very flesh would crawl off her bones. She did not know why she felt such revulsion; it was simply a fact, a reaction she could not control.

She had heard her sisters talking of their lovers, heard them compare the strength of a bull-halfling with ordinary men, had seen presumptuous Halflings punished. Never in her wildest dreams had it occurred to her that anyone, human or Halfling, would touch the daughter of the Starqueen against her will. Now, thinking of the old rivalries between Sarastro and the Starqueen, she wondered if Sarastro had brought her here to humble her. Pamina resolved that she would die first.

"Go," she said suddenly to the dog-halfling who served her, cast a swift look at the plate containing her abandoned meal, and said, "Bring me—bring me another cup of wine, and some of those little cakes."

The Halfling woman, evidently delighted to be asked spontaneously for something, hurried away. Pamina went quickly to the clothespress in the corner of the chamber and drew on her old cloak. Sarastro's minions had furnished the room with an elaborate wardrobe of silken garments of all kinds, but Pamina disdainfully refused to touch them. Now she pulled the cloak over her head and stepped out of the garden window, hurrying down the path toward the distant gates.

As she hastened through the line of cypress trees, her heart beating fast, she actually believed she might succeed in slipping away unobserved. It was high noon and the priests, she knew, would be in the temple for the celebrations.

Abruptly Monostatos, surrounded by a half dozen Halfling servants, stepped out of the concealment of the trees.

"I thought you would," he observed with satisfaction. "Take the princess back to her rooms."

Pamina struggled wildly as they seized her, with an agonizing sense that this had happened before, that this was simply a repetition of her kidnapping, that it was destined to be repeated over and over again, that it was some terrifying trap of her destiny, to be seized and flung back into her imprisonment.

"You had better come with dignity," Monostatos said quietly. "If you do not, I will license them to treat you with force, and if you do not yield to them I will drag you with my own hands."

Pamina sank down, weeping, on the path. She hardly knew when they lifted her and carried her back to the suite of rooms.

CHAPTER SEVEN

*W*HEN *Pamina came to her senses again, she* was lying on the silken couch in the suite of rooms placed at her disposal by Sarastro, and at the side of the couch stood Monostatos.

"Pamina, you have displeased me," he said, "and you have displeased Sarastro, since it was by his will that you were confined to these rooms. Will you give us your pledge not to attempt escape again? Or will you force us to restrain you physically, with bonds? It would be a distressing sight—a princess in chains!"

His face looked pale, stern, unbending. It frightened her more than any grimace, any menace or threat. Would he really dare? Looking at that pallid face, Pamina decided that he would.

Nevertheless, she refused to beg or plead with him. Nor would she give a parole to Sarastro. Even if he was actually her father, and this not just another of Monostatos's abominable lies.

"I will certainly not promise you anything of the sort," she said, staring up at him angrily. "I am the daughter of the Starqueen, and I have nothing to do with Sarastro, or with you. I do not admit that you, or he, have any right to imprison me, and if I can escape I shall certainly do so."

"Pamina, you will force me—you will force us to put you in chains!"

"Don't you dare to say it is I who will force you, or your master either," she retorted, at white heat. "If you do such a thing, you will do it out of your own wickedness, rather than because of anything I have done."

"You will force me to it," he repeated, and his colorless eyes, curiously flat, stared down at her without blinking.

Suddenly as her eyes were held by his she realized what he was doing, he was trying to frighten her, as he did with the Halflings, to intimidate her so that she could neither look away nor move without his consent. Furiously, she sprang up and faced him.

"Get out of my sight! Don't come into my presence again! If Sarastro wants something of me, tell him to come himself instead of sending you! If my mother could not trust you to be faithful to her, what makes Sarastro think he can trust you to be faithful to *him*?"

For a moment, then, she thought she really had goaded him too far, that this time he would strike her. Time seemed to stop, to freeze around her, she could see the draperies softly moving in the wind from the open window, see a Halfling—an unfamiliar bird-halfling—who had just come through the door of the room, her cloak where someone had hung it on a peg, the faint flicker of Monostatos's eyelashes in his otherwise unmoving face. Then he said, in a sibilant whisper, "You will truly push me too far, Pamina, believe me," and spun round on his heel as if to stride out of the room. He came face to face with the bird-halfling; for a moment they stood face to face, the bird-creature hypnotized by Monostatos's eyes. Then Monostatos roared, "Get out of here!" The bird-man uttered a smothered screech and fled in the opposite direction.

"Yes!" Pamina shouted after him. "Go frighten Half-lings with your yelling, frighten them into fits—it's all you are good for, you are big and brave against those who cannot fight back, are you not? Now make haste to run to your master, you vile toady and apostate, go lick Sarastro's boots and beg his leave to put a helpless prisoner in chains!"

But when he had gone, her bravery deserted her and she fell sobbing on the couch again. Perhaps for once Monostatos had told the truth, and Sarastro had indeed given leave for her to be chained and imprisoned this way. Even the company of one of the Halflings would have been a comfort, but the dog-woman who had been sent to wait on her had fled, too, before Monostatos's wrath, and she felt very frightened and very much alone.

"My lady—Princess Pamina—?" said a hesitant, musical voice behind her, and Pamina raised her head.

"Yes?" she asked without much interest, then blinked. It was the Halfling who had come face to face with Monostatos and run away. "Aren't you afraid?" she asked. "He is likely to come back any minute; he said he would put me in chains."

"Then all the more reason we had better get out of here at once, Princess Pamina, before he does come back," said the bird-halfling. "I have come here from the Starqueen to rescue you."

"Mother! You did remember!" cried Pamina, and this time she wanted to cry again, but for joy. She had not really believed her mother would abandon her to Sarastro's devices—or had she? But now she was certain. Though surely this funny little fellow was an unlikely messenger for the Starqueen.

"What is your name?" she asked.

"Papageno."

She found herself wondering if he knew Papagena,

who had served her faithfully for so many years. This was no time to ask him, of course. Then she hesitated; Sarastro's house was filled with strange creatures, presumptuous Halflings, tricksters and liars like Monostatos. She picked up her cloak, looking at him fearfully.

"How do I know that you are not one of Sarastro's evil spirits come to delude me?" she asked.

"There's nothing wrong with my spirit at all," he said valiantly. His eyes, wide and dark, met hers, and twinkled, and Pamina could not believe that there was any harm in him. "Let's go," he said, and led her out, not through the door but the window. Swiftly they crossed the garden; then Papageno reached for her and roughly pulled her down into a depression of dry grass. She was about to cry out in protest—had she been mistaken in him, was he about to attack her?—but he chirped and pointed.

"Look!"

Monostatos, with a file of slaves, was hurrying into her chambers; some of them bore ropes and chains. Pamina gasped; he put his hand gently over her lips to silence her, but the touch was gentle, almost deferential.

Monostatos had found the rooms empty. She heard the terrified whining of the dog-woman, Monostatos shouting in rage. Pamina and the bird-man crouched closer together; after a time the slaves scattered from the front of the building, fanning out in all directions.

"But they're not likely to look so close, here in the garden," Papageno said. "They'll expect us birds to fly away. So we wait here till it gets a little darker, then we start out and look for the prince."

"The prince? What prince?" Then, suspiciously again, "Not Prince Monostatos—that's what's he's calling himself these days."

Papageno's eyes were rounder than ever. "Him?

Oh, no, Princess. That's right, I didn't mention the prince, did I, and I should have told you about him the very first thing. After all, it's his job to rescue you, but we got separated. He went up toward the front gates and I came round this way, and you see, I was the lucky one. No, this prince is very young, and very good-looking, and the Starqueen was very taken with him, I must say, she gave him a magic mirror with your picture in it. And the minute he looked in it, he fell in love with you right away!"

"What a romantic notion." Pamina laughed, but secretly she was pleased. A handsome young prince, who was in love with her, and with her mother's consent . . . she felt enormous curiosity about him.

"What is his name? What does he look like? Is he kind and well-spoken? You said he saw my picture—did he think I was pretty?" Pamina stopped her flow of questions with an effort. Papageno was looking at her with great sadness.

"What's the matter, Papageno?"

He sighed. "For the princess there is a prince, just as for every king there is a queen. But for Papageno there is no Papagena. I once heard of a girl by that name, and I wondered if she was like me, but no one would tell me anything about her."

"Poor Papageno, are you lonely?" At first it had sounded comical to her, and her question had been almost careless. But the seriousness of his glance made her ashamed of her own flippancy.

"Very lonely," he said in a quiet voice. "There is no one at all like me, and it seems that I am fated to live alone forever. I spend my days catching birds, all alone, beautiful feathered birds to make robes for the Starqueen. I have harmed no one, yet I am mocked and laughed at by everyone."

Now Pamina knew who he was; she had heard her

sisters speak of him. But, she thought, and was momentarily shocked, any of her sisters could have told him about Papagena! Why had they never done so? It would have cost them little effort and it would have made him so happy.

Pamina felt suddenly very confused. Everything in her childhood told her that this man was only a Halfling, no more than an animal, to be used for her convenience without worrying about his feelings. Of course Disa or Zeshi or Kamala would not have bothered to tell him anything about Papagena, why should they? They were the daughters of the Starqueen, why should they concern themselves with a little Halfling's happiness? How they would laugh—why, she herself had been close to laughing—at the thought of a Halfling pining away for love! How absurd and how presumptuous, just what she would expect to find here in the abode of Sarastro—but this was a messenger from her own mother. Pamina felt dreadfully confused. Her own sisters would not rescue her—but this Halfling, who had no reason to be grateful to her family or to the Starqueen, had come to try and do so.

"Never mind, Papageno," she said gently, and touched his warm bony small fingers. "Someday we will find you a Papagena, I promise you that."

The girl and the Halfling lay side by side in a grassy depression, silently waiting for the sun to set.

Meanwhile, Tamino, who had lost sight of Papageno soon after the Messengers had led them through a set of front gates which could have been those of the Imperial Palace itself, was wandering in darkness so thick that he could not see a hand's span before his face. He shouted once, aloud, for Papageno, but the echoing of his own voice reverberated as if he were locked inside a vault, and he could see nothing. The sound of his own voice actually intimidated him.

He was silent, fumbling his way through the darkness. Where had Papageno gone, and how had they lost one another? For a moment he considered taking out the magical flute again to resummon the Messengers. But they had given him, he considered, such help as had been ordained; surely they would have known that he was lost and separated from his traveling companion. Again it occurred to him that this might well be one of the mysterious Ordeals of which he had been told so little. If so, he must somehow surmount it. When he had been genuinely in danger from the dragon, help had been at hand. He must simply trust that someone or something was watching over him.

Slowly the darkness began to lift. Tamino, as his eyes accustomed themselves to the twilight gloom, made out that he was within a great, overvaulted space; dim, pale looming shapes rose in the distance. His feet made soft noises as if he were walking on stone or even metal as he groped his way forward.

As he moved forward, a pale light, like an approaching sunrise, began to glow in what he supposed was the east. By the time he approached the nearer of the great looming shapes, he could see that it was an imposing facade: a great doorway leading between two great pillars, one black and the other white. Over the door, in a script Tamino could barely read, was written

Enlightenment

I could use a little of that, in this darkness, Tamino thought, advanced toward the door and raised his hand to knock.

Immediately a great chorus—or was it only a single

voice, reverberating as the echo of his own voice had done—rocked the vaulted space like thunder:

"Stand back! It is death to seek here unworthily!"

Involuntarily, Tamino recoiled, as if fearing that to touch the door would blast him with a thunderbolt.

Just the same, he thought, it wouldn't have hurt anything for the unseen voices to enlighten him a little bit about why he had been led here, if they were only going to turn him away again so rudely. Anyhow, he had been told that the point of undergoing the Ordeals was to attain Enlightenment.

What now? He stood for a moment surveying the facade from which he had been warned away. If it was death to seek here unworthily, how did he become worthy?

After a time, as the light grew somewhat in intensity, he looked around and saw the outlines of the other two buildings. He went slowly toward the second. Over its pediment was written the word:

Wisdom

If he couldn't have Enlightenment, Tamino thought, this would be the next best thing. There was a great knocker; he stepped forward, a little gingerly, and was about to grasp it.

"Stand back! You are not yet worthy!" thundered the invisible voices.

Tamino stopped in his tracks. Nevertheless, he thought, it was something of an improvement. This time the voices had said nothing about death. All the same, he was not a bit better off. He was still lost and alone, with nobody to help him.

Well, there was still a third door. Although, considering how uncooperative the people in this neighborhood seemed to be about answering their doors, perhaps it would be a waste of time to try knocking.

He approached the third door, which was considerably smaller and less pretentious than the others. Above the entrance, in the growing light, he could just barely make out the word:

Truth

If he could not have either Enlightenment or Wisdom, Tamino thought, Truth might be a fair substitute. Hesitantly he put out his hand and knocked.

Silence. More silence. Tamino wondered if it had been somehow symbolic; nobody home in the abode of Truth, as a sign that truth was hard to find!

Then he began to hear a little scraping sound, not unlike the rustle of mice behind the door. At least they had not angrily warned him away. He waited. The light was growing now; but if it was sunrise, certainly the sun would now be above the horizon; and there was something about the light that did not quite look like the sun.

At last the great handle began to lift from inside, and slowly, slowly, the door began to open. Finally it stood just wide enough to admit him, and paused as if waiting for him to come through.

With a mental shrug—they hadn't told him to come in, but at least they hadn't told him to stay out—Tamino went through the door. It scraped noiselessly shut behind him; Tamino remained for a moment in darkness. Then, as before, the light began slowly to increase.

In the light a form appeared, as if taking substance from the air. Tamino wondered, so silent had been this manifestation from nowhere, if this was the wicked magician Sarastro himself? But no; surely he would have no place in a temple devoted to Wisdom and Enlightenment. And in a temple devoted to Truth, at least he could get—he was sure—some straight answers.

Before him stood the venerable form of a man in late middle-age. His gray hair was covered with a hood, on which the emblem of the rayed sun was inscribed in gold. He wore robes of silvery gray, and once again the sun's rays were inscribed on the breast of his garment. His features were nondescript, but he looked mild and even kindly.

"Well, young man," he asked, "what do you want?"

Tamino stood silent for a moment. Now that he was inside the place, after three tries, what did he in fact want?

"The truth," he said at last, "that's what your notice out there tells me."

The old man smiled. He said, "There are many different kinds of truth, you know. It may not be that simple. And even if I were to speak the truth, you might not be able to hear it, so that whatever I said, it would sound like a lie to you."

"I'll take that chance," Tamino said, and then it occurred to him that the Messengers had answered Papageno's question almost in that way, as if he was not capable of understanding the simplest thing.

Well, he was a stranger here and it made no sense to be offended by their peculiar customs. He had never before had an otter as a bath attendant either, and that had been an interesting new experience. Maybe this would be no worse.

He might as well tell the exact truth about what he wanted.

"I am looking for a wicked magician called Sarastro," he said.

The old man—Tamino imagined he must be some

sort of priest—raised his eyebrows; his look was mild and kindly.

"What do you want with Sarastro?" he inquired.

If, Tamino thought, this was the Temple of Truth—with, he noticed, Wisdom and Enlightenment thrown in—they must know what kind of evil Sarastro had been doing in their territory. He said, "I came here to rescue a helpless girl that this evil man has in his clutches."

There was not the slightest change in the priest's kindly and benevolent face. His expression showed only mild curiosity. "Who told you that?" he inquired.

"The victim's mother!"

"And," continued the priest in his gentle voice, "how do you know that what she told you was the truth? The world, my son, is filled with those who have no respect for the truth."

"Well, is it true then?" Tamino demanded belligerently. "Did he kidnap Pamina, or didn't he?"

"As I told you, my boy, there are many kinds of truth. On one level, what you say is true; Sarastro took Pamina from her mother's care."

"And you dare to admit it!"

"You do not know Sarastro," the priest observed, "and his motives are not known to you. How, then, can you stand there and judge him?"

"I may not know Sarastro," Tamino said, and in spite of himself he felt indignation surging up into his voice, "but I know what he has done. And I know right from wrong!"

He stepped back a little as he spoke, so sure was he that the ancient priest would immediately contest him. But the serene old face remained calm.

"Do you indeed? Do you indeed?" Incredibly the ancient face broke into a wide smile. "Well, then, my son, you know more than any of us here, and we ought to roll out the velvet carpet and canopy reserved for the gods!" HIs smile was so purely benevolent, so devoid of malice, that in spite of his anger and confusion Tamino found himself wanting to smile in return.

Then the priest said, "I wish you would refrain from judging Sarastro—or anyone else—until you are certain of the truth. It is not as simple as it sounds."

Now Tamino was angry again. He said, "Every malefactor can find some good excuse for what he has done! The facts speak for themselves. What excuse can there be, for tearing a daughter from her mother's arms?"

"I am not here to make excuses for Sarastro," said the priest.

"Oh, aren't you? I thought that was exactly what you were doing," said Tamino, conscious that he was being rude, and not caring.

"Let me ask you a question in turn, since you have asked me several," said the priest. "Who appointed you judge of Sarastro's deeds and motives?"

Now Tamino felt on surer ground. He said, "I am a stranger in this land and I do not know your customs. But in the country where I was born, when the man of nobility hears of an injustice, it is his duty and privilege to correct it and to right a wrong. Otherwise he is no better than the worst of churls."

"Then we are agreed on one thing at least," said the priest, "but you do not know the whole story. If Sarastro were here, I am certain he could make himself clear to you, if he chose to do so. Until that time, a stranger would do well not to judge between rival causes until all the truth is known to him."

"Then," Tamino said, "how am I to learn all the truth?"

The priest's smile spread until it seemed to glow all over his gentle face.

"At last," he said, "you have asked a question to which I am permitted to give you the answer. The truth will be made known to you when you have successfully passed the Ordeals and been admitted as a sworn member of our Brotherhood."

Abruptly the light vanished; the priest was gone, and the temple around him, and Tamino was standing alone in the great vaulted space before the three temples, with the sun rising behind him.

CHAPTER EIGHT

*T*AMINO *wondered if he would ever get used to the way in which people around this place kept appearing and disappearing.* It was still dreadfully dark, although the sun should soon be surfacing over the temple.

And he had not been able to answer the old priest. A dozen answers, arrested on his tongue, were still crowding his mind; things like, "What makes you think I would have anything to do with your Brotherhood, when a creature like Sarastro is at the head of it?" From the way in which the old man had defended Sarastro, he supposed this man was another of Sarastro's deluded creatures, hypnotized by the wicked magician. He remembered the tears of the Queen of the Night; how could anyone doubt that she was a great woman, and a much-wronged one?

Yet in spite of himself Tamino found his mind returning to the vicious mockery with which her three ladies had treated the harmless Papageno. If the servants were reasonlessly cruel, how could he believe in the goodness of the mistress? Perhaps, he thought, and was ashamed of himself for his doubts, he should hear Sarastro's reasons for what he had done.

But meantime he was lost in the precincts of an unfamiliar temple; and if the temples here were anything like the ones in his home country, then one thing of which he was sure was that the priests would soon be about for the sunrise observances—supposing, that was, that they had anything so civilized and predictable, here at the end of the world. And if he were found here—well, Papageno had been afraid of Sarastro and what Sarastro might do if they were caught here, and Papageno knew more about this part of the world than he did.

Of course, Papageno too was a servant of the Queen of the Night, and his attitude toward Sarastro would be what he had learned from his fellow servants— Tamino broke off that thought angrily. Why had he begun to doubt the Queen, that lovely and grieving mother?

It was still dark; why was the sun not rising? Where was Papageno? He started to shout again; then thought better of it. He could hardly hope to remain unobserved in Sarastro's precincts, if he went around shouting at the top of his voice. And even if, as that old priest had said in his riddling manner, he had been expected here for those mysterious Ordeals, Papageno was a strange Halfling and afraid of Sarastro. And he had brought Papageno here; he was responsible for the funny little bird-man, and that responsibility would hardly be served by letting Papageno fall into the hands of Sarastro's priests.

And how, he wondered irritably, could he possibly be about his real business, which was the rescuing of Pamina, when he had to stop and worry about taking care of Papageno? And the wretched Halfling had gotten himself lost, too. What a nuisance!

His hands fell on the bamboo flute tied at his waist. Perhaps, with the help of the flute, he could manage to attract Papageno's attention without shouting. He put his lips to the flute, and began to play.

There was a flickery of firefly golden light before him, and he saw the faint gleam of the Messengers who had brought him here.

"We are glad to see that you turn to the flute when you are in darkness," said that strange voice that was like a blend of many voices. "That is the power of the flute: to bring Enlightenment to those who walk without the light."

Tamino suddenly thought, through the sounds of that curious voice, that he could hear something like an echo of that mighty chorus which had warned him away from the first two doors.

"Why is it so dark in here?" he asked. "Surely the sun should be rising—"

"The darkness in which you wander is not only the absence of the sun's light," replied the Messenger. "The Light you seek is the Light of Enlightenment."

Tamino clapped his hands to his head; made a grasp at the flute to keep it from slipping through his fingers. "Doesn't anyone here ever talk in anything but riddles?" he demanded angrily. "For all the talk about Truth here, there seems to be damned little of it around, at least when it comes to giving straight honest answers!"

"If you ask complicated questions to which there are no simple answers, we can hardly give you simple answers," the voice of the Messenger—or of all of them—answered. Tamino was trying to focus his eyes so that he could really see the shifting forms. He could only see the movement of draped limbs, never a whole face but only the momentary flicker of an expression, a moment's amusement or humor or compassion, a movement that suggested wings—or a bared muscular arm? Or was it only the sweep of the draperies? He wished they would stay still long enough that he could really see what or who they were.

He said, "You said something like that to Papageno. He's a Halfling and he's not very intelligent. But if you give me an answer, I think I could understand it. It seems to me that a question like *How long will it be till sunrise?* is simple enough!"

"This I can answer," said the Messenger. "If the darkness does not soon give way to light, then you will wander forever in darkness which will never lighten." The voice was like a great chorale, and it was not for a moment that Tamino realized what he had actually heard.

"Another riddle," he said in disgust. "To a perfectly simple question!"

"What makes you think it is a simple question?"

To that, Tamino found no immediate answer. He said in a rage, "Well, here is a question that perhaps you will find simple enough! Tell me, riddlers, is Pamina alive, or has Sarastro done away with her?"

"Pamina is alive, and unharmed," said the Messengers. "You need know no more than that at present." The insubstantial forms flickered again, and abruptly vanished. With them vanished the light; once again Tamino was alone in the dark.

That answer had been unequivocal, at least. But he had had other questions to ask; chief among them was, "What is Sarastro's true nature? Who then had been telling the truth—the Queen of the Night, or the old priest?" But he supposed that if he had had a chance to ask the Messengers, they would have answered him in more riddles, and he had had enough of those for one day—or one lifetime.

He had learned one thing, at least: Pamina was alive and, presumably, well. No, he had learned a second thing: the flute was the instrument of his own enlightenment—though, at the moment, he felt more muddled and in darkness than ever. Though, by now—so long he had delayed talking riddles with the Messengers—the sun was really rising. It hardly seemed, here in these precincts, the same sun he had seen crossing the desert, that hard, brazen, blazing disk; here it seemed a gentler sun, soft light streaming with mist.

He wondered if the riddling Messengers would consider that a symbol for enlightenment as well? Or did it simply mean that the sun was rising, as it did every day in the world outside, as it did, presumably, even in the realms of the Queen of the Night. In any case, it made the question of locating Papageno, and getting under cover, even more urgent, for in the light the priests of this place, whether or not they did civilized things like sunrise observances along with their main business of talking in riddles, would soon be out and about and alert for intruders.

If he should begin to play the flute again would the Messengers reappear with more of their conundrums? They had vanished of their own accord, presumably because they thought he had had enough enlightenment for one time. So now, presumably, if he played the flute it would be to look for enlightenment without their dubious guidance. Or even, he thought cynically, for a totally mundane purpose, such as making music or attracting the attention of Papageno, who would presumably hear it more easily than if Tamino started shouting. Or would the Halfling think it simply one more birdcall in this strange place?

Whatever happened, he would try the flute. If the Messengers took it into their heads, or whatever they had in place of heads—he had certainly never gotten a good look at their faces—to appear again, he would simply ask them where Papageno was, and again try their ability to give simple factual answers.

He set the flute to his lips and began to play.

Tamino had always been fond of music. One of the

things he had missed most, on this journey, had been the evenings in the royal palace when his father's musicians would play, sing, and dance to a variety of instruments. From childhood he had had good teachers, and could even play one or two instruments. The flute had a singularly soft tone, sweet and reedy; it was evidently the work of a master craftsman. Quite apart from any magical qualities it might possess, it was itself a treasure. As he improvised a simple pastoral melody of his faraway homeland, he lost track of everything else, thinking only of the music.

There was no sign of the Messengers, to Tamino's relief. But after a little while, as he played, he noticed one of the temple doors quietly opening. Soft bulky forms, indistinct in the half-light, stole down the steps of the temple, moving quietly toward Tamino. The melody faltered; at once they were motionless, and Tamino could see that they were men—or were they? Surely they were bears, thick fuzzy hair on their bodies, noses so long they surely qualified as snouts, their hands deformed—or clawed? He had never seen bear-halflings before; had not known they existed. A tall rangy man who could have been a horse? His ears stood up at the side of his head, his hair was long and coarse and jet black, swept back along his skull and down his neck. A small furry man came and nestled against Tamino's arm: a beaver, a rabbit-halfling? And still they came, and listened, and hovered, while Tamino played, in a marveling wonder.

He would never have believed there could be so many kinds of Halflings. Even seeing, he did not really believe. The larger ones frightened him, especially the bears, they pressed so close and were so huge. What troubled him most was that none of them uttered a sound. Had they any human speech, or were they dumb, flawed, made without voices by the folly or uncaring of their makers? And the smaller ones upset him too. Why should anyone have bothered to make Halflings in this purposeless travesty of Humankind? What use could they possibly serve? He found himself petting the small rabbit-thing as it snuggled against him, and had to remind himself that this animal, this pet, was a sentient being with, he supposed, something resembling human consciousness and a human soul and he should somehow manage to treat it—no, him, or perhaps her—as a fellow human.

But how? It was one thing to treat someone like Papageno, who was at least human in form, and had human speech, as what he looked like, a fellow soul in an animallike body. Tamino could treat him as he did one of his father's subjects who was not particularly intelligent. He had not been educated to reign, but he had been brought up knowing that, as their prince, he was, in a very real sense, responsible for every soul in his father's kingdom and Empire.

But what, in the name of all the gods he had ever heard of and a few he hadn't, did one do with a rabbit-halfling? He could hardly treat the poor thing like an equal, for it wasn't. That in itself didn't bother Tamino—few men were. He had early been taught how to act toward his father's subjects, and had never abused that position since a long ago day when he had beaten one of his playmates simply because, as the Emperor's son, he knew the other child could not fight back. He had quickly learned that this was an offense too grave even for a beating in turn by his tutors. The Emperor himself, gray and terrifying, called his younger son to him, and in words Tamino was never to forget, forbade him ever to repeat the offense.

But his father had never had a rabbit-halfling for a subject. He could not even speak with the poor thing, since it had no speech. He had been taught that if a man was ignorant, he should be educated. How did one educate this creature? He supposed it could be trained like a housepet, a cat or dog or an idiot. That did happen. Regrettably some children were born idiots and must be as well treated. But idiots were created by the gods for some unknown purpose of their own. Man, sentient man, had created these creatures. Tamino's head throbbed. Why?

His lips trembled on the flute, and the music stopped. The creatures made soft sounds of disappointment, but Tamino had no heart to continue playing.

He thought, bitterly, of what the Messengers had said; the flute would bring him enlightenment. But he was more confused than ever. Why? What had prompted the men of Atlas-Alamesios to create these folk?

An ape who could play chess with an Empress, and even win—yes, perhaps there was some reason for that. Even a bird-man who could be put, as a delicious jest, to dressing in bird feathers and catching birds to be made into ritual robes when they were not made into potpies. But what place was there for a rabbit-halfling in the society of court or temple?

The common excuse for misery was that people who were poor and hungry did not work hard for their food and sustenance; that they were lacking in industry, application or skill, and would not take the trouble to better themselves. But what could a bear-halfling do with his clumsy paws? He could not even till the land, yet he had been made partly human and his skills at hunting were little good to him, even supposing his human masters would allow him to hunt and kill for his food. For every one of the Halflings there was some such deficiency, and why had not the folk of Atlas-Alamesios thought of this before creating them? And now that they were there, crowding the steps of this sacred place, what could their makers do about them? They could not be killed in cold blood, and they had done nothing to deserve death.

He put the flute away with hands that shook. The Halflings crowded around him made soft sounds of discontent, growls and mutters and whines, but none of them menaced him.

"There, there," he muttered, "that's enough for now. Maybe I can give you folks another concert one of these days." He could do nothing for them; he could give them pleasure with his music, but that was doing nothing for their basic trouble, which was that they had been made human, but not quite human enough.

One by one the Halflings stole quietly away. Last to go was the odd furry little rabbit-halfling, who lingered to rub his soft fuzzy body against Tamino's, and look up wistfully with his pink eyes. But at last he too scampered away with his odd hopping gait, and Tamino was alone.

Was it, could it ever be justified, to create such havoc for the sake of a few devoted servants such as the dog-halflings? Tamino was ashamed of being human; no other race would have done such things.

Yet, having met Papageno, would he wish this charming and comical man had never existed? Tamino struggled with his own feelings and came to no conclusion. And at that moment he heard the sound of Papageno's pipes.

Theoretical questions about Papageno's existence could be forestalled for another time. Now, he and Papageno were in similar case, lost in the hostile environs of Sarastro's Temple—and if Sarastro had been responsible for creating these Halflings, he hated the man more than ever—and he was responsible.

"I am here, Papageno," he called, and began to run in the direction of the sound.

CHAPTER NINE

WHEN *Monostatos had gone away, Pamina* got up cautiously, and beckened to Papageno to follow her. Carefully they skirted the garden, seen only by a harmless dog-halfling who was scouting the edges of the planted lawns and chasing down small rodents; not, Pamina thought, one of Monostatos's flunkies.

She followed Papageno at a little distance, taking care to move quietly. Her mind was full of the prince he had mentioned. She had never wasted much thought on the fact that one day she would find herself interested in some young man; the casual loves of her half sisters had repelled her, rather than encouraging her to do likewise. And this youth was actually one her mother had chosen to rescue her. Her thoughts were filled with rosy romantic images, while on quite another level she was aware that she was thinking of the prince to keep from confronting her thoughts and fears about Monostatos. The prince, so far, was merely a pleasant daydream; Monostatos was a very real threat.

If he had been telling the truth when he said that Sarastro destined her for his consort, she must somehow get away from here, entirely away, without a moment's delay. Would the prince, then, restore her to her mother? Her heart sang at the knowledge that,

before very long, she would be in the familiar surroundings of her mother's residence.

Sarastro would be disappointed in her. If he was
truly her father—but Monostatos had lied about everything else. Why should he have told the truth about
that, either? On the other hand, why would he lie about
it—except out of pure vicious cruelty, to hurt and
frighten her?

For the moment, though, they were out of reach of
the hateful Monostatos, prince, son of the Great Serpent, or whatever he was calling himself now. Whatever he called himself, all she wanted of him was to
keep out of her sight. And, if Sarastro chose Monostatos for his assigned messenger, she wanted nothing
to do with Sarastro either, father or not.

She ran toward the edge of the garden, now aban-
doning her caution and hurrying to the path which
wound outside the hedges. She was not sure of her way,
but even if she lost herself in Sarastro's realm, that
was better than being imprisoned in some luxurious
suite, treated as an honored guest while, in truth, she
was as much a prisoner as if she were wearing the
chains Monostatos had threatened. Sooner or later,
she, or Papageno, would find a way out, and be safe
again in the security of her mother's familiar rule.

Papageno, behind her, touched her shoulder.

"We can't simply go blundering around," he whispered. "The prince must be somewhere near. We lost
each other on the way in—he should have had the
sense to stay close to me," he added petulantly. "I
would never have allowed myself to do anything so
silly as getting lost."

"I'm sure you wouldn't," said Pamina gravely. It
was full daylight now; any passerby could see them.
"But he did lose himself, and somehow we must find

him before we get out of here. Have you any ideas?"

For answer, Papageno put his little whistle to his lips and played a cheerful birdcall. From a distance came an answering note-aflute.

"It is the prince. Come this way," Papageno urged. They hurried in the direction of the voice, momentarily forgetting caution—and ran directly into the arms of a dozen Halflings, bearing ropes and nets as if for hunting. One of them shouted, "There they are! Don't let them get away!"

Helplessly, Pamina tried to run; but they already had hold of Papageno, and two more seized her.

"Let me go!" she cried out. "You'll be punished for this!" She simply could not believe what was happening. In her mother's house—in any properly regulated place—the Halfling who laid hands on any unwilling human would have been flayed alive. Their rough paws on her terrified her; she felt dizzy and light-headed, and was suddenly feared she would fall to the ground; yet pride would not let her cling to a Halfling for support.

"Don't touch me! Take your hands off me! Papageno, help me!"

"Do you think that he can help you? Oh, no, Pamina," said the familiar, hateful voice of Monostatos. "No one can help you now, except me; and you have refused that help. They are acting by my orders. Take her," he commanded the Halflings, who were hanging back a little. "Bind her."

Still unbelieving, Pamina felt one of her hands seized and bound with cords. Monostatos himself grasped the other.

"Come, Pamina, my little sweetheart, don't make me do this to you," he murmured, and bent close to her. "Now that you know you can't escape, resign yourself. Nothing will happen to you, if you recognize that you are designed for me; do you believe I would let them harm my promised wife? Come, give me a kiss, and let's be friends again."

His lips touched hers; she wrenched away with desperate strength. Her fingernails raked down his cheek; he sprang back, cursing angrily.

Papageno, struggling furiously, flung off the Halfling who was trying to hold him. His fingers fumbled at his waist for the bells given him by the Queen's ladies. The Messengers had told him to ring these when he was in danger. Maybe they were like the flute Tamino had been given, and would summon help. His fingers moved swiftly on the bells.

Pamina heard the sound, a merry and sweet jingling, and wondered what could possibly be in Papageno's mind; music at a time like this? But Monostatos, at the sound, dropped her hand and let her go; he looked away from her, and, while Pamina watched in utter astonishment, he began to dance. Not looking at her, not looking at anything, he described a curious gliding circle, his upper body weaving back and forth, while the dog halflings circled round him, jigging crudely in time to the bells. Papageno blinked, moving his own body gently in time to the sound, but he kept on playing.

Pamina had heard of legendary control devices which had power over the Halflings. She had never seen one before this. Nor would she ever have believed that Monostatos, for all she had flung the word *Halfling* at him for an insult, would have been affected. Papageno continued to ring the bells; to tell the truth, it was all Pamina herself could do to keep from dancing!

One by one the Halflings formed into a line and danced away.

Papageno kept the bells ringing until they were out of sight, then cautiously slacked off. Pamina was filled with a thousand questions. Where—and how—had he come by the bells? What had made Monostatos and the rest react this way? Why had Papageno himself been immune? But none of these questions were important now. What was important was to get away.

And then she heard a sound that froze her with terror. It was the sound of the royal trumpets which preceded the procession. Sarastro, and his priests enroute to the sunrise observances, were on this road. She froze in her tracks; it was too late to run, she could see the glitter of the rising sun on the priestly ornaments they wore. And some of them had already seen her.

Papageno, his hands busy stowing the bells in their skin at his waist, looked up to see her look of consternation.

"What is it, princess?"

"It is Sarastro and the priests," she whispered, clutching at the last remnants of her courage. Papageno stood shaking, with all the feathers on his crest twitching in dread.

"Sarastro," he moaned. "Oh, what will he do to us? What will we say to him?"

Pamina was nearly as afraid as the Halfling; but she had been trained never to show fear or dread, even at the sacrifices, and her training stood her well in place of courage.

She said resolutely, "We will tell him the truth." She stood her ground, waiting for the priests to come up with her.

The first of them had nearly reached her when Sarastro, walking in procession with his trusted favorites, saw Pamina and looked at her—in surprise, Pamina thought, and displeasure.

Of course he is angry, she thought, I have tried to escape from him. But if what Monostatos did was at his wish, I want to know it now.

Sarastro stepped toward her, gesturing the priests at his side to remain where they were.

"Pamina," he said, not unkindly. "What are you doing out here at this hour? I can hardly imagine that you intended to attend the sunrise observance. Perhaps you—"

He stopped abruptly as a great commotion broke out behind them. Monostatos, surrounded by the dog-halflings, was dragging a prisoner toward them; a young man Pamina had never seen before. She knew from Papageno's face that this was the prince. He was richly dressed, in finery a little the worse for wear—he had evidently put up a tremendous struggle before they captured him—and handsome, with fine features and troubled eyes. He had come to rescue her—and this had befallen him. Pamina felt, even knowing that it was irrational, that she was to blame for his predicament. "Let him go!" she commanded, so imperiously that the Halflings who held him had released him before they knew what they were doing. She went swiftly toward him, and held out her hands.

"You are Prince Tamino," she murmured, looking into his eyes.

He grasped her hands in both of his own and drew her toward him, returning her gaze as if there were nothing in the world but the two of them. For a moment, for Pamina, there was not.

Then the rough hands of Monostatos grabbed them both and pulled them apart, and Pamina was gazing up into the mild blue eyes of the priest-king Sarastro.

The sunrise observances had been turned over to another of the priests. Pamina sat beside Sarastro on a couch, and he gestured to her to help herself from a tray containing fruits and wine and cakes made with dried fruits and honey.

She said nervously, "You won't let any harm come to poor Papageno, will you? Or to the prince?" Then, fearing lest he should misunderstand, she added quickly, "Prince Tamino, I mean, not Monostatos." She took a dried fig and nibbled at it, though it felt like wood in her dry mouth.

"I don't know what you have been told about me, Pamina," Sarastro said, and his voice sounded kind. "But I assure you that I intend no harm to Papageno, and still less to Prince Tamino, who has come here as my honored guest, for the purpose of undertaking the Ordeals."

"I was your honored guest too," she observed a little bitterly, "and I found myself your prisoner."

"Pamina—" Sarastro sighed, then leaned his chin on his hands. He said, "It is no part of my purpose to rehearse all the differences I have with your mother. I had hoped you would never hear of them, but I suppose that is too much to ask."

"May I first ask a question, sir?" she asked, and the priest nodded at her.

"Here you may ask whatever you will, and I pledge to you, whatever answer you receive will be the truth."

"Monostatos told me that you are my father. Is that true, then?"

"I'm afraid so, Pamina," Sarastro said. "Does it displease you as much as all that?"

He was looking at her kindly; his eyes seemed to twinkle at her. Surely there was nothing intolerable about acknowledging this serene and kindly man as her father. But then perhaps the other things Monostatos had said were also true. She demanded, "Did you promise me to Monostatos as his wife?"

Sarastro's serene face betrayed a certain surprise. "Why, no," he said. "Did you want him as a husband? It is true that I told him that if he successfully passed all the Ordeals, and if you liked him, he might have permission to ask you to marry him; no more than that. Did he tell you that, Pamina?"

"Why do you think I was trying to run away?" she demanded.

"I was hoping you would tell me that." Sarastro did not take his eyes off her; they held a quiet watchfulness she did not yet understand. "I gave orders that you were to be well treated, and to be given everything you asked for. Did anyone violate these orders?"

Was it possible, then, that Sarastro did not know the truth? She said, and to her dismay she heard her voice shaking, "I tried—I tried to escape because I was afraid of him—of Monostatos. He threatened me; he told me that you had destined me for his bride, and I was afraid—afraid it was the truth. He—he spoke with such conviction, and he treated me as if—" again she paused, searching for words—"as if I were already pledged to him as his wife."

Sarastro bent his eyes on her face; Pamina hung her head, frightened, afraid that she could cry, fighting against tears that threatened to escape anyhow. Then she felt Sarastro's hand, gently turning her face up till she met his eyes.

"Pamina, is this the truth?"

"I don't know what you do here in this place," she flared at him, in sudden anger, "but I would never stoop to lie about it!"

He sighed. "That is true; you do not know this place, nor do you know me," he said, "and you cannot be blamed for that. Well, Pamina, let me ask again; would you repeat this accusation before Monostatos, if I should ask you to do so?"

"With the greatest of pleasure," she said emphatically. "And if the damned Halfling can look in my eyes and deny it—" She stopped; her whole body was throbbing with indignation, and Sarastro reached out and took her hand.

"I can see the truth in your eyes, my child. I can only say that I regret, more than I can say, that you were subjected to such an ordeal. I was mistaken in Monostatos; I thought that as the son of the Great Serpent, who was once my friend and a sworn Brother of the Temple, he would behave honorably. Anyone can be mistaken; I only regret—well, no matter now."

Sarastro sighed heavily, then went on, "As for Prince Tamino, I have made him the same offer that I gave to Monostatos; if he successfully completes the Ordeals, he may court you for his wife. And if I have properly read your heart, you will not be offended by this as you were when Monostatos took his success for granted." His eyes twinkled at her again, and Pamina blushed, that he had seen her holding Tamino's hands and defending him.

"Tamino—Prince Tamino," she amended quickly, "is a noble young man. I—I would willingly hear him, if he should make an offer for my hand."

"He is indeed noble, and he seems kind and courageous as well," Sarastro said encouragingly. "For this purpose, my dear, I summoned him from his own country, in the hope that he would meet with your approval."

He patted her hand again, so kindly that Pamina cried out suddenly, "Oh, Father—if you are really my father—won't you let me go back to my mother? It is not that I am unhappy here, now that I know Monostatos did not—did not come after me with your consent and approval! I am sorry I misjudged you. But won't you let me go home? My poor mother—she will die of grief!"

Sarastro sighed deeply. He said, after a moment of silence, "I am sorry, Pamina. I cannot. You do not know your mother as well as I do . . . she is a heartless woman, cruel and domineering. In her hands you too would become heartless and wicked. I cannot expect you to know what I know; I only ask you to trust me for the time being. Somehow you have escaped the taint of bitterness and cruelty which lies within her; but you were a child, with a child's unconsciousness of wrong and evil. Now that you are a woman, I must see you guided in the pathways of truth and of light. Your mother—"

"She is my mother," Pamina said with quiet dignity, "I do not want to hear anything against her."

Sarastro put down the honeycake he had taken up, untouched. He said, "I cannot fault you, child, for believing in your mother. I wish you would trust me, but I suppose I have yet to earn your confidence. Let me now deal with Monostatos, and with the prince."

"And Papageno?"

"No harm will come to him," Sarastro reassured her. "He tried to help you escape, but I do not hold him responsible for that, since he too was misled, and did not understand what he meddled with. I propose to allow him to enter the Ordeals—what do you know of them, Pamina?"

"Very little."

"In time you shall know all; but, in brief, should he be found worthy, he will be given a wife, and allowed to mate under the protection of the Temple. When I took you from your mother, I also had your faithful servant Papagena brought here. The priestesses who deal with the female Halflings have spoken with her, and they tell me she is truthful, kind and virtuous for what she is. Bird-halflings are few, especially those who are gifted with sufficient intelligence; and I was hoping I could find another who was worthy of your good Papagena. This Papageno seems to fit that description. You have observed him; what do you think of him?"

"I like him, Father. And I am glad to know Papagena is safe." She felt troubled to realize that without knowing it, she had been afraid her mother would visit her wrath on Papagena because she, Pamina, had been taken when Papagena was with her.

Then she felt disloyal again. Was she accepting Sarastro's evaluation of her mother? She looked away from him, picking up a handful of sweet dates and eating them quickly.

He gestured to a priest who had remained at the end of the room, out of earshot of their conversation. Raising his voice, he said, "Bring Prince Tamino to me, and Monostatos as well."

Pamina finished her dates, dipped her hands delicately in a basin of water and at once a dog-halfling who reminded her a little of Rawa was there, offering her a small perfumed towel. She had not thought much of Rawa in years, and now she knew, with a sudden wave of dismay, why she had been afraid for Papagena. Afraid, and suddenly very much ashamed of herself, she realized that what she felt was relief, because Sarastro had refused to send her back to her mother.

She had been afraid for Papagena. But what she was really afraid of, she now knew, was her mother, and what her mother would say to her.

After a moment, a great assembly of priests, servants, Halflings, and others entered the chamber. Ceremoniously, Sarastro gave her his hand and escorted her to a chair somewhat lower than his own. Then he raised his hand, and Monostatos rushed forward.

"My lord," he cried. "In your service I found this intruder in the precincts of your temple!" He gestured to the servants to drag Tamino forward. Sarastro shook his head and they released Tamino; he motioned Monostatos toward him.

"Be assured," he said, "you shall be rewarded as you deserve."

Monostatos grabbed his hand, kneeling and covering it with kisses. "My lord, you overwhelm me, I am not worthy—"

"You have well deserved this reward," said Sarastro sternly, snatching his hand away, and said to the priests, "Take him away and give him a sound beating!"

"My lord!" Monostatos cried in indignation as they laid hands on him. "You promised to me that I might undertake the Ordeals!"

"Why, so you have, and failed the first of them, which disqualified you for the rest," Sarastro said harshly. Pamina had not realized that the gentle voice could thunder with such wrath. "I trusted you, Monostatos, with my daughter Pamina, and you failed the test."

"Lord Sarastro, I protest! She tried to escape, and look, she is here, safe again in custody; I have not failed you!"

"But you have," Sarastro said. "For that was the first of the Ordeals; and when you laid hands on her, and lied to her, you betrayed the trust I had reposed in you. Take him away," he added sternly, and Monostatos struggled fiercely, howling curses, as the priests dragged him out of the room.

Sarastro motioned to Tamino to approach his chair. He said, "Is it still your desire to undertake the Ordeals, my young friend?"

Tamino could not keep his eyes from Pamina. He said, "For this purpose I undertook the journey from my homeland, sir." He looked at Pamina, seated beside Sarastro and evidently quite content to be there; she smiled at him.

"Then, if that is your will," Sarastro said, "let it be so." He smiled, and Tamino felt the smile warming him with kindliness.

"Take him away," he said to the priests, "and let him be prepared to enter the Ordeals, and tested as our laws decree."

His eyes were still on Pamina; he held out his hands to her. As if in a dream, she rose from her chair and approached him; but Sarastro shook his head, and the priests took Tamino by the shoulders; not roughly, as they had done with the struggling Monostatos, but with firm purpose.

"Not yet," he said, with surprising gentleness. "You are not yet worthy of one another. Take him away."

Tamino bowed, and went with the priests without resisting. Sarastro held out his hand to Pamina.

"Don't be afraid," he said, "they will not hurt him, I promise you, my child. I have confidence in him. And now—" he gestured to a tall, sweet-faced woman in the robes of a priestess—"you, too, are to be tested, Pamina. But first, if you wish, you may see Papagena and reassure yourself that all is well with your faithful servant." He kissed her gently on the forehead.

"I will see you again at the proper time, my child. Take courage; I have confidence in you, too. I see already that you are brave and truthful; call upon your mother's strengths and not her weaknesses, and you will succeed in your testing. For now, daughter, go and be prepared for what will come. There is nothing to fear, and nothing will be demanded of you except that you be your own best self, I promise you that."

He bowed to her, with a curious ceremoniousness, and went away between attendant priests. Pamina stood staring after him, still not sure what was going to happen, until the tall priestess touched her on the shoulder.

"Princess Pamina, come with me," she said gently, and Pamina, still staring at the place where Tamino had disappeared, let them lead her away.

CHAPTER TEN

TAMINO stood in the darkness, a blindfold fastened over his eyes; though it seemed to him that even if the blindfold was removed, it would be dark, for through the folds he could make out only darkness.

His hands were tied behind his back with a soft cord that did not chafe his wrists. In spite of the strangeness, he was not afraid.

When he had been taken away between the two priests, and Sarastro had spoken of testing, he had been a little frightened. Sarastro seemed kind and well spoken, but he did not know what to expect; anything might be a part of the Ordeals. Yet he had been reassured by Sarastro's unsparing treatment of Monostatos; whatever his preconceptions about Sarastro, the priest-king had been just. And Pamina trusted him. So he was prepared to suspend judgment about Sarastro. It seemed Pamina was in no immediate need of being rescued, after all. He might as well go on with the Ordeals, which were, after all, what he had come here for. Perhaps a day would come when he would know all the truth, even all the truth about the Queen of the Night. There would be time enough for that.

Sarastro had told them to take him away for testing, and he had not had the slightest idea what to expect.

He was led first to a building which was, the priest told him, the dwelling place of the younger priests. His clothing—the luxurious finery given him by the Queen of the Night, which had been cut and torn in his struggle with Monostatos's men—as taken from him, and after he was given a chance to bathe in a pool of cold water, he was given a plain white robe like the robe worn by the younger priests.

Soon they brought him a meal—flat cakes of bread, butter, and a jar of honey, boiled eggs, some fruits and a jug of cool milk. He supposed this was priestly fare. It was, despite its simplicity, all very good and plentiful. When the old priest came back to take away the tray, he also took away the flute. Tamino began to protest, but the old priest smiled kindly at him

"You do not need this here," he said, "and although the one who gave it to you had no right to bestow it, for it was not hers to give, let me assure you that if you prove worthy to bear it, it will be returned to you at the proper time." He added, "Wait here, Prince Tamino, and meditate until moonrise, when you will be sent for."

Left alone, Tamino had tried to meditate, but Pamina's eyes, the memory of how she had watched him when they took him away, kept coming between him and his own thoughts. In the end, he actually dozed off, and only woke when the darkness fell in his cell. At moonrise two priests had come, and without speaking to him, they had blindfolded him and bound his hands. But before they touched him, he had seen that one of the priest was the old man who had first welcomed him in the Temple of Truth; so he simply assumed that this strange and inhospitable procedure was some part of the introduction to the Ordeals.

He stood in the dark, and all round him he heard soft sounds, the rustle of robes, muted shuffling of feet, a man's cough in his darkness. Hands tugged at him and led him forward; he was pushed to his knees.

Then through the bandages over his eyes he saw a glow of light, and Sarastro's voice, deep and strong like some great organ, spoke his name.

"Tamino," Sarastro said. "Is it still your desire to undertake the Ordeals and achieve your own enlightenment and wisdom?"

"It is for that purpose I came into this country," Tamino said, "and I am still resolved that I will do so."

"I know you have courage," Sarastro said, "even though it is, as yet, untempered with wisdom. Tell me, Tamino, are you able to put aside prejudice and examine all things before judging?"

"I will try," said Tamino.

Sarastro said in the dark, "Brothers, any of you has the privilege of interrogating him, if you choose. If you would prove or test his fitness before he is admitted to the Ordeals, speak now or forever after keep silence."

A voice said, "Prince Tamino, you are of royal birth. Tell me, what does it mean to you to be a prince?"

Tamino answered what his father had told him, once, when he asked that same question.

"More has been given to me," he said, "and therefore more is demanded. I must set every one of my father's subjects an example of what a man should be, and never demand of any man what I am not willing to exact of myself."

Yet another voice, this one rough and deep, said, "Prince Tamino, you are a prince of the Empire of the West. Can you greet as a brother, whatever his birth, any man who has passed the Ordeals and is sworn to Brotherhood in our Temple? For within our Order, the only distinctions of rank are not of birth, but of merit and virtue alone."

Tamino did not answer at once. Finally, he said, "If a good reason is given me why I should do this, I will."

Silence. At last Sarastro asked, "Are there any further questions?" Further silence. Finally, Sarastro said, "If nothing further is demanded of him, let us proceed. Which of you will guide him?"

"I will." It was the voice of the old priest who had welcomed Tamino into the Temple of Truth. "I will consider it my privilege to guide him toward the Light."

Sarastro asked, "Tamino, will you accept his guidance, and obey him through the testing?"

"If he doesn't ask me any more riddles," Tamino said, and there was a little ripple of masculine laughter that echoed in the spaces of the great hall. Sarastro himself sounded as if he was trying to keep back a chuckle unsuitable to this solemn interrogation.

"Will you obey him without question?" he asked.

Tamino stopped to think that over. At last he said, "I'm not sure. That sounds like a trick question. Suppose he should ask me to do something I know is wrong?"

"Wrong by whose judgment?" asked Sarastro. "I understand that you told our brother that you understood the difference between right and wrong. How will you judge whether what he asks of you is wrong?"

Tamino bit his lip. He said, "I'm not—not trying to set myself up as a judge. But how do I know he won't ask me to do something wrong to test me, so that if I obey him I'm doing something wrong, and if I don't, I have broken my promise to obey?"

To his surprise there was a murmur of approbation. Sarastro said, "Good. Let me ask that question again; will you obey him, provided he does not ask you to do anything which is against your conscience? And if you are not sure one way or the other will you listen to his counsel and judgment before you act?"

"Oh, yes," said Tamino, relieved, "I'll promise that, of course."

"Then, Tamino," said Sarastro in his deep voice, "I accept you as a candidate for trial in our Order. Surround him, now, my brothers, and let us pray that he will find courage and strength for the Ordeals which he now must face."

In the darkness Tamino heard the rustle of robes round him again. He felt hands take his—he could not tell whose hands. Another pair of hands touched his forehead in blessing. Then hands were touching him, laid on him as if to heal or bless. He was surrounded, touched everywhere with this laying-on of hands. Then, in the darkness, there was a sound of voices. Sarastro's voice, a strong and resonant bass, led the voices in a mighty, blended harmony of sound.

This was the hymn:

> You Gods of Light, you awesome powers,
> One stands before your doors today;
> Be with him now, through these dark hours,
> Help him to tread the Pilgrim's way.
> Guide him, on paths of Truth progressing,
> Help him to find true Wisdom's blessing;
> Grant that he seek not Power, but Right,
> And find the great eternal Light;
> Guide him to Truth's eternal Light.

When the hymn had ended, there was a moment of silence. Then Sarastro said softly, "Go forth on your way, Tamino; and may your own courage and wisdom serve you well. You come before us blindfolded and bound, in token that you are still walking in the darkness of the world's ways and know nothing of the greater Light; you are bound, not by external bonds, but by your own ignorance. Yet you have signified a desire for true freedom. Therefore, let him be loosed from the bonds of ignorance."

The cords tying Tamino's hands fell away.

"Take him away," Sarastro said. "Let him be tried."

The blindfold was removed abruptly from Tamino's eyes. It was very dark; but Tamino could tell, from the echoes round him, that he was in a high vaulted chamber, and beneath his feet was stone. Soft echoes were all round him. There were no lights in the room; nevertheless, as his eyes accustomed themselves to the darkness Tamino could see Papageno, blindfolded like himself, in the custody of a strange priest.

The priest ceremoniously removed the blindfold from Papageno and said, "Let your eyes be freed for the Light of Wisdom."

"Light? What light?" grumbled Papageno. "I can't see a thing."

"The Light will come when you are worthy of it," intoned the priest. "Your first test is silence and obedience."

"I'll be sitting in the dark forever, then," Papageno said sullenly.

Tamino's guide touched him lightly on the shoulder.

"Remain here until you are sent for, Tamino, and meditate on the mortal end of mankind."

Tamino started to return a polite acquiescence, then remembered that Papageno had just been admonished to be silent, and an answer might be interpreted as disobedience. He contented himself with a courteous bow.

There was a faint flicker of light as the door opened; in that pallid gleam they could see the robes sweeping behind the forms of the priests as they went out.

Tamino heard a discontented chirping sound from Papageno. The little bird-man hunkered down on the floor, his skinny arms wrapped round his knees.

"Tamino, why are we sitting here in the dark?"

He had been told to be silent. Nevertheless the Halfling sounded frightened, and Papageno was his responsibility; he had brought the little bird-man here.

"Because we were told to," he replied gently, "and
even I, a prince, must obey."

A sudden flare of lightning blinked through high windows; Papageno flinched. The lightning was followed
by a crash of thunder, and the Halfling cried out with
fear, crowding close to Tamino in the dark.

"Hush, Papageno, it's only thunder; aren't you
ashamed to behave so like a coward?"

"I'm not a prince. I don't have to be brave!" Papageno sat shivering, his arms wrapped about his body,
trembling at every flash of lightning as the storm rose
to its height.

Tamino went to one of the windows and looked out
into the night. This was the mysterious realm of the
Starqueen, and he had come here at her bequest. But
everything seemed to have reversed itself. The wicked
magician Sarastro seemed, after all, to be an honorable
and benevolent man, and Pamina, the maiden in distress, seemed to be quite content and in no need whatever of being rescued. Moreover, Sarastro was actually
in charge of the Ordeals. Tamino felt that all his cer-
tainties were being challenged.

By the intermittent flashes of lightning, he could
make out that the room where they waited was an
ancient crypt. Niches in the walls held sarcophagi,
inscribed with runes in languages so antique that Tamino had never heard of them. Atop one pillar was a
skull, inlaid with jewels which shone with a pallid lus-
ter; but in the colorless light Tamino could not even
make out what kind of jewels they were. He had never
known of any society or people which so treated their
dead. Who had they been, these strange long ago peo-

ple, and what had become of them, that now Sarastro's folk held their rites in their burial chambers?

Whoever they once had been, now their names were known only to the dead. And one day, Tamino thought, my father's Empire and Sarastro's people, and all of us, will be no more than this. He supposed this was what the priest had meant when he told Tamino to meditate on man's mortality, and secretly he felt a little pleased with himself.

But Papageno shivered and fretted on the floor, staring around in terror, and Tamino fancied he could hear the Halfling's teeth chattering.

"What a horrible place this is! If they can't find a better place than this to keep the candidates for their Ordeals, it would serve them right if nobody came at all!"

"Hush, Papageno; you were told to be silent and meditate on mortality."

"No, it's you who were told to do that," Papageno said. "It's bad enough to have mortality without having to meditate on it. Anyhow, I wouldn't know how to meditate."

Tamino was hard put to keep from smiling. He said, "They meant you were to think about it very, very seriously."

"Then why didn't they say so?" demanded the Halfling.

Tamino gave up, and began to study the runes on the sarcophagi. The fitful lightning came and went. Papageno was still muttering in discontent, but Tamino ignored him. Time went by, crawling on noiseless feet. As his eyes accustomed themselves to the dark, he examined the momentoes of that dead civilization, feeling at last that he, and his father's Empire, and all the current races of men, were all very small against the grandeur of Time. Did it matter, would it ever matter to anyone if one small prince called Tamino, from an ephemeral Empire on a tiny speck of a world lost among the stars, lived or died? Whether he passed the Ordeals in triumph and married Pamina? Or whether he died here among the lost remnants of a people who had once lived and suffered and died and now were no more? Did any of it matter? Why was he here, after all, pitting himself against unknown Ordeals?

He had pledged himself to do so. But was that reason enough? All those people in those lost centuries had pledged themselves to unknown purposes, lost and forgotten causes, which now meant nothing to anyone, whether they had kept their promises and lived with honor, or whether they had died forsworn and forgotten. In the fullness of Time, would it matter to anyone whether or not he succeeded, or failed, or whether he had ever lived or died?

Dizzied, swaying with the awareness of Time and the lost, he pressed his aching head against the cold of the stone. Why had he ever come here? If the door had been open, he might have run away.

He was no longer aware of how long it had been, but he was recalled to the present by the light of a lamp and the sound of an opening door, and the two priest-guides entered the room.

"Prince Tamino," said the first, whom he thought of as "his" guide, "have you resolved, then, to persevere, whatever may come?"

Tamino drew a long breath, sensing that at this point his resolution was being tested. For a moment it seemed to matter no longer. Still, he had made a promise and he would keep it.

"I have," he said quietly.

"So be it; the Ordeals shall begin. For the first; you shall wait here till sunrise, or until I myself come to take you elsewhere. It is forbidden in this place to speak to any woman. I warn you, as well, that although you may see Pamina, you may neither speak with her, directly or indirectly, nor may you touch her. Do you understand me? Whatever happens—not a word or a touch. Otherwise—" his voice deepened with menace—"she shall be lost to you forever. Will you obey us in this?"

Tamino swallowed hard. It all seemed foolish to him. But who was he to judge these priests? They must know what they were about. "I will."

"May the gods grant you keep to your resolve, my son," said the old priest. "Give me your hand."

The other priest, a short, bald, nearsighted man with a small and scruffy beard, bent over Papageno. "And you, my son," he said. "Will you endure the Ordeals, even though they should lead you to the very edge of death, and fight against evil wherever you should find it?"

"Well," said Papageno, waggling his feathery crest in an indecisive way, "I'm not a fighting man. And I'm not very brave. Maybe we'd better forget the whole thing."

"Will you work hard for wisdom and enlightenment?"

"Me? What for?" Papageno demanded. He then swallowed and said, "Excuse me, I mean, no, thank you very much."

"Tell me," said the priest, and Tamino was surprised at the gentleness and patience in his voice, "what do you want out of life, my son?"

Papageno stood up, moving restlessly around the room. "Well, I like to have enough to eat and drink, and a comfortable place to sleep. I don't mind working hard, but I don't have any wish for more than that. But I'll tell you one more thing I want. I would like a wife, a friend, a mate; I'm tired of living all alone. And that, good and reverend father, is all I really want out of life. I haven't any wish for wisdom, or enlightenment, or any of those things. Oh, please, I don't mean any offense, I'm sure they are all very good things, but to tell the truth, I don't think they're for the likes of me."

"But," said the priest, "Sarastro has already chosen a wife for you; she is very much like you, even to the color of her feathers. But you will never see her unless you persevere in the Ordeals."

"I have a feeling I'd do better to stay single," said Papageno, but he looked up curiously at the priest. "She has feathers, too?"

"Exactly like yours."

"I certainly would like to see her," mused Papageno. "I've never known anyone just like me. Is she young?"

"Young and pretty."

"And you say I can't even see her unless I undertake the Ordeals—"

"Absolutely not."

"Well, in that case—" a great clap of thunder interrupted his words and Papageno clapped his hands over his ears and cried out in dismay, "I'd better stay single!" Then he asked, "What is her name?"

"Papagena."

"I really would like to see her," Papageno said, but his teeth were chattering. "Just out of curiosity."

"You may see her," said the priest gently, "but you may not speak to her. Do you think you can control yourself enough to keep a bridle on your tongue, and speak to no woman here?"

"Well, it wouldn't be the first time I've had a bridle on my tongue," said Papageno. "I'll try."

"Excellent," said the priest. "Give me your hand." He took Papageno's hand in a firm and friendly grip. "Remember: it is forbidden to speak to a woman here."

"I'll do my best."

"That is all we ask," the priest said, and withdrew.

Tamino sat on a stone bench, hearing the sandals of the priests on the stone floor. One of them said softly to the other, and it seemed to Tamino that he could almost see the headshake accompanying the words, "Sarastro himself could not make an Adept of that one!"

"How do you know that is intended?" asked the voice of Tamino's guide. "There has been no Adept from among the Halflings since the Great Dragon. Yet he may endure the Ordeals as well as is demanded of him; it isn't for us to say."

So they are talking of Papageno, Tamino thought, half ashamed of himself for his relief. Had he really believed they were talking about him? Did that mean they were confident of his own ability to face the Ordeals without doubt? This first one seemed almost idiotic; what difference could it make, after all, whether or not he spoke to a man or a woman?

He supposed they had their rules, and he would do his best to obey them, whether they made sense to him or not. Whatever their purposes, he was sure that he could no more understand them than Papageno could understand Tamino's ideas and designs.

In any case there were no women here, and it seemed unlikely that any could get into this crypt, guarded as it was by the priests. For that matter he couldn't imagine anyone coming here unless he had to. Tamino was tired of looking at skulls and reminders of death and mortality, time past and ruins of past nations. He stretched out on one of the stone benches, deciding that since there was nothing to see and no one to talk to, he would try to sleep for a little. They had told him not to talk, but they had not said that he must stay awake.

Afterward, he never knew whether or not he had actually dozed a little. He was roused by a terrified screech from Papageno, and a glare like lightning—but it was not lightning. It seemed that the stone floor suddenly gaped wide; torches flared and suddenly the three ladies of the Starqueen stood in the room.

"Prince Tamino," cried Disa. "The Queen is angry with you! You have fallen under the evil spell of Sarastro, and you will surely be punished by the furies of her wrath! What have you to say for yourself, you who swore to our Queen that you would rescue her daughter?"

Tamino opened his mouth, ready with swift protest, self-justification; but before the first syllable escaped his lips, he remembered the old priest:

It is forbidden to speak to women here....

So this was the reason for the warning. He wondered if the Starqueen's ladies were actually here, or whether it was some trick of the priests to make him believe they were here, simply part of the Ordeals. He was again pleased with himself for apparently seeing through their tricks, and turned away from them and said nothing.

"What! Have you nothing to say for yourself, Tamino? What will you say to the Queen when she demands her daughter?" Zeshi cried. "You were sent forth and armed with magical weapons, and you sit here listening to the counsel of a trickster!"

Tamino did not speak. After a moment they whirled on Papageno.

"Papageno, what do you think the Queen will say when she hears that you could have rescued Pamina, that the princess was actually in your hands, and you turned her over to Sarastro's minions?"

"I didn't exactly have any choice, Lady Disa—" Papageno began.

"Be silent, Papageno! Remember your vow!"

"If you listen to his advice, you are lost, Papageno! But you are the faithful servant of the Starqueen, and she has sent us here to bring you back," said the one Tamino had heard him call Kamala.

"Look here, I never wanted to come here at all," Papageno said, "but you made me come with the prince, and now I think I'll just stay here, after all."

"Papageno—" Tamino said, moving toward him; perhaps he could help the little Halfling to remember his promise. "Be silent, friend."

Zeshi demanded, "Papageno, why would you stay here? What do you think Sarastro can give you?"

Papageno said, "Sarastro has promised me a wife."

"Oh, if it is a woman you want," Zeshi said, and her voice had a soft, cooing quality. She came to Papageno and wound her arms round his neck; her slender, long-fingered hands caressed him, smoothing down the feathers along his head. She rubbed his face against hers. Papageno stood motionless, and Tamino thought of a bird he had once seen fascinated by a snake. Zeshi's slim, graceful body pressed against Papageno's, and the bird-halfling began to sway against hers, to move against her own. She smiled and made a soft purring sound.

Abruptly Papageno thrust her away with both hands. He said, "This isn't the way you treated me in the Starqueen's house! I think this is a trick, Lady Zeshi." He retreated, hastily, and Zeshi hissed with rage. Kamala raised her spear, menacing him, but Papageno stood his ground, almost shouting.

"I don't think you can hurt me here! I think if you could hurt me here, Lady Kamala, you'd have done it already!"

There was a fearful thunderclap; the torches went

out, and the place where the three ladies stood was bare and empty.

Papageno collapsed to the stone floor, moaning.

"Oh, woe, oh woe!"

Tamino reflected that the little Halfling had broken his vow; he had not been silent, he had driven them away with words. Yet it had been successful, after all. Were the Ordeals different for Papageno than for himself?

"Papageno, what are you doing?"

From the darkness of the vaulted room came a small, tremulous, determined voice.

"I am lying in a faint!"

CHAPTER ELEVEN

*P*AMINA *lay in the silence, staring out through
the drawn-back curtains at the sky filled with
stars—her mother's realm.* She had never questioned her mother before this. The knowledge that Sar
astro was her father had filled her, first with disbelief
and dread, and then with confusion.

He was not the ogre she had been brought up to
believe him. He was not a monster at all. Living as
she did in the residence of the Starqueen, she had never
once thought of wanting or needing a father, save in
the purely physical sense. But now that she had seen
and spoken with Sarastro, she decided that if she must
have a father, Sarastro was certainly the one she would
have chosen. The question beat in her head: why had
her mother lied to her about Sarastro, why had she
chosen to portray him to his daughter as an evil sorcerer?

Perhaps it was only that she loved me so much,
Pamina thought. She did not wish to share me with
anyone, not even with my father. But try as she might
she could not make herself believe it was only that.

Now she was in Sarastro's house and she was committed to undertake the Ordeals—why, she did not
know, but Sarastro had told her that it was a necessary
preliminary to all that he had in store for her; the study

of wisdom, her marriage to Tamino. She thought, shyly, of Tamino, and the moment of their brief touch, the meeting of their eyes. She had never seen him before. She felt as if she had known him for a hundred thousand years and a hundred thousand lifetimes.

It was enough that Tamino was obliged to undertake the Ordeals; she was willing and glad to share them with him. But she had no idea what they would entail. The priestess who had given her a ritual bath, taken away her fine silken garments and left her with a coarse, white, shapeless tunic which, she said, was a neophyte's robe, had told her that they were different for everyone. So that whatever trials she must face, they would be different trials than for Tamino. She was sorry for that. She would have liked to face whatever it was that he must face.

Yet, when she had questioned about when they would begin, the priestess had told her nothing; only that everything would come in its time, and that for the moment all she need do was to obey. Questioned further, she said gently:

"Princess Pamina, the nature of the Ordeals must be unknown, or there would be no virtue in facing them. Remember only this: nothing will be demanded of you except that you behave always in accordance with your own best self." Then she told her to go to bed and sleep, embraced her in a sisterly way—no, Pamina thought, none of my own sisters were ever so kindly to me, for I always knew that they were jealous of me as Mother's heir—and left her alone in the darkened room; she took the lamp with her when she left.

Obediently, Pamina tried to compose herself for sleep. But the face of Tamino was in her mind, and the brief moment when their hands had touched. She should not be thinking of Tamino now, but of the Ordeals. Would they be very frightening, would they involve enduring pain, or tests of courage or endurance? She had never been taught any of these things; she was sure she would find herself inadequate. After a time she fell into an uneasy doze.

She was wakened by a footfall and a shadow falling across her bed. At first she thought it must be one of the priestesses, come to awaken her for the first of the Ordeals. But this was no woman's face or form in the shadows; a stocky, wiry man's body bent over her, and in a moment of horrified revulsion she made out the form of Monostatos.

His hands gripped her shoulders; his face pressed down on hers, his lips covering hers so that she could not breathe, in a long, violent kiss. Pamina struggled, trying weakly to tear his hands away, but his lips clung; the weight of his body came down over hers, and she realized, with horror, what he was trying to do. She struggled, trying to bring her knee up into his groin; but he was enormously stronger than she was. She managed to twist her body aside, gasping for breath as she freed her mouth.

"Sarastro will have you flayed alive for this!"

"Are you so sure, my little one? Perhaps, afterward, you will not be so dissatisfied. In any case, Pamina, I have already had one beating for your sake, and I am going to have more than a kiss for my pains this time! Why not make it easy for both of us?"

"No!" she gasped, struggling, resolved that she would be killed, if she must, before she was ravished by this—this creature! But however she struggled, he held both her hands easily with one of his own hands, like a cord of leather, while with his free hand he fought to tear away the coverlets and the white novice's robe.

She screamed, "Help! Help! Rape! Murder!" But she knew that she had been left alone, as candidates for the Ordeals were always left alone, her servants

having been sent far out of range of hearing. Would
no one come and help her? She would rather let him
kill her. If die she must, she would then die defending
herself from this repulsive thing in the shape of a man.
But her throat hurt with screaming, and her heart
pounded in her chest. She knew her struggles were
growing weaker, and thought she would vomit, as he
tore the white robe from her, and paused to look down,
gloating.

There was a sudden flash of lightning, dazzling her
eyes, and Monostatos was ripped off her as if by the
very lightning itself. She heard him cry out, a wordless
shriek of pain and fear, and she saw him crouching on
the floor in the lightning glare. Over him, in the cold
light, was the face of the Starqueen.

"Mother!" she cried.

The Starqueen's face was pallid and cold beneath
the high ritual headdress of owl feathers; her eyes glittered like the distant stars themselves. Pamina flung
herself, sobbing, into her mother's arms, and felt them
tighten briefly, possessively, around her. Then she felt
she must have imagined it, for her mother's voice was
cold and detached as ever.

"Has he hurt you, Pamina? Or only frightened you?"

Shaking, Pamina pulled herself upright. The white
robe was torn from her throat to her knees. Her wrists
felt sore, and her mouth was bruised; she felt sick and
defiled at the touch of his lips, at his gloating eyes on
her bare body. But she was not seriously hurt.

"Only—only frightened," she said, and heard her
voice shaking.

The Starqueen looked, frowning, at the torn white
linen robe. "That is not fit for you to wear, my love,"
she said, and though the words were gentle, Pamina
flinched from the scorn in them. "Find yourself a whole
garment and cover yourself decently. I have many

things to say to you. Even in the house of Sarastro, though," she added with biting contempt, "I had believed you would be better guarded than *this!*"

Pamina started to say it was not the fault of Sarastro, who had, after all, had Monostatos flogged for offering unwelcome advances to her; but under her mother's eyes thought better of it. In one of the chests, she found a loose silken robe, and pulled it about her body. She felt better clothed; even under her mother's eyes, in the torn linen she knew herself naked and vulnerable.

"Now come here and listen to me," said the Starqueen, "for there is little time. You can see"—she moved her head, the faintest possible gesture of disdain, toward the crouched figure on the floor—"what will become of you *here.*"

Pamina opened her mouth in protest, surely this was none of Sarastro's doing, but suddenly, under her mother's eyes, she was no longer certain. Perhaps this had been the first of the Ordeals destined for her? Obediently, as she had done in her childhood, she sat down on the edge of the narrow bed, looking up at her mother with her hands clasped in her lap.

"Where is the young man I sent to rescue you?"

"He awaits the Ordeals at the hands of Sarastro's priesthood."

"It is worse than I thought," said the Starqueen grimly. "If Sarastro and the priesthood were to find me here, they would surely put me to death, for I have no power in this place."

"I will not let them hurt you," Pamina said staunchly. "No one here will harm me, Mother, and if I come with you, they will not dare to touch you either." She swallowed hard. "Mother, let us escape together from this place." Kind as Sarastro had been, now, at the feet of the Starqueen, she felt like a little girl again;

her mother would protect and care for her, but first they must leave Sarastro's house.

"It is too late for that," the Starqueen said, and reached into the folds of her robe. "Take this."

She thrust a dagger into Pamina's hands.

"With this," she said, "you will approach Sarastro at the rites; and with it, you will kill him."

"What?" Pamina cried in horror. "Kill my father? Mother, you cannot mean it!"

"Silence!" cried the Starqueen. "For years I have endured the contempt of the priesthood of the Sun and of Sarastro! Now I have determined that you shall avenge me. As you are my daughter, Pamina, as the tie of blood binds mother to daughter, you will kill Sarastro before the sun rises, or never again look upon my face or think to call me Mother! Hear and attend, and obey me, Pamina, or never again be acknowledged daughter of mine!"

"But—Mother, no! Mother, I beg you, listen to me—"

"Not a word!" The lightning glare played for a moment around the Starqueen as she stood over Pamina, her face like stone. Then, in a thunderclap, she was gone, and only the silent moonlight played on the room. Pamina stared around her wildly.

"Mother—" she whispered. Had it been a dream? But no; clasped in her fingers she held the hilt of a dagger.

"No," she whispered, still disbelieving. "Kill my father?" She knew the Starqueen hated Sarastro; she herself had hated him by her mother's influence. She could understand that they might well disagree over matters of religion and the like, which as yet meant little to Pamina. But certainly it was enough that they should each dwell apart and rule each in their own realm. Murder? Her whole soul rebelled at the idea.

I cannot kill—no, no, not even for my mother, not even if she should cast me out, she thought wildly, and burst into tears. Would her mother truly cast her off? And then another mad thought occurred to her. It was possible that this was only one of the Ordeals, and that she had simply been tested, to see if she would continue to behave in accordance with conscience.

And yet she had been brought up to believe in the absolute rightness of the will of the Starqueen. Could it possibly be true that she had failed? Surely the Starqueen could do no wrong, and if she demanded that Sarastro should die, did not Sarastro then deserve death? Could she fail her mother, to save the life of the man the Starqueen hated? What was Sarastro to her, what was an unknown father against the mother who had loved and cherished and cared for her all her life?

Yet Sarastro's kindly eyes remained before her; she had demanded, "Are you my father?" angrily and in scorn, and he had answered her so gently. How could she kill him? What had he done to deserve death? She did not know. If her mother truly believed that her father deserved death, she thought despairingly, she should kill him herself and not try to make me judge!

There was a small sound in the room and she realized that Monostatos was still crouched in a corner. He got up slowly and came toward her.

She gripped the dagger between her hands. At least, while she held it, he would not force himself upon her. "Don't come near me," she said, hearing her own voice tremble and hating it, but not knowing how to keep it from shaking.

"Is it me that you fear, Pamina? Am I so frightful to you? Or is it the murder you hold in your heart?" Monostatos asked. "I am, after all, no common Halfling, but the son of the Great Serpent; and I know all that befalls here. I can save you and your mother; but you know my price, Pamina."

She raised the dagger quickly. "My mother would not accept such a price! Nor will I!"

"Are you sure of that?" he asked, advancing toward her. "You had better give me that dagger—"

He put out his hand to take it. In the next moment there was a blaze of light, and Sarastro himself stood in the room.

He said to Monostatos only, "Go!" and the Halfling, head down like some scuttling rodent, hurried through the door.

"Father—!" she cried.

"Hush, my dear, don't be frightened," he said gently. "I know everything."

"Father," she begged, "I implore you, do not punish my poor mother! Whatever she has done, I know now she cannot harm you, and—and—" her throat closed and she feared that she would cry again. She determined that she would not weep before him.

"But, I beg you, don't revenge yourself on her. She is so distressed because she has lost me—"

Sarastro put out his hand gently and drew her close. "Don't cry, my child," he admonished. "Revenge is no part of our religion here. She may do her worst; and while I cannot protect her from the causes she herself has set in motion, rest assured I will not lift my hand against her. If for no other reason, she is the mother of my daughter, and for that alone, her person and dignity are sacred to me. And for your sake, also, Pamina, I could forgive her much. Do you not know that this was one of the first of your Ordeals, that you should show compassion even under such testing as this." He kissed her gently on the forehead.

She asked, with a faint curl of her lip, "Was it also

one of the Ordeals that I must fight off Monostatos, or submit to being raped by him?"

"My dear child—" Sarastro said, sighing. "No, of course not, I promise you that; and I promise you further that he shall never touch you again. I am sorry beyond words that you had to endure that; I admit that I misjudged him and trusted him too far. I am sorry to punish him; his father was my friend, and a good and trustworthy man. He was also the consort of your mother before ever I knew her. I thought better of his son. Well, there is no help for it." He sighed again, and looked at the silken garment she had put on at her mother's request, and at the torn linen on the floor.

"Your servants have been sent away until the conclusion of the Ordeals. I will send a priestess to attend you properly and dress you as is fitting. I should tell you that Papagena, too, has been admitted to the Ordeals; she has served you faithfully, and I have destined her for a husband who will suit her."

"Papageno?"

"Yes, child. He has been good and faithful, and he has a good heart."

Pamina smiled, nervously. She said, "Papagena— she is a bird halfling; she is not very intelligent, Father. What will happen to her if she does not succeed at the Ordeals? She will not be hurt? She is so easily frightened—"

"Don't worry about Papagena, my daughter; the Ordeals for a Halfling are different than they are for you. If she behaves as is fitting under the circumstances, nothing more is asked. To you, born a princess, as more has been given, so more is demanded. Now I will send a priestess, to dress you properly. Do not be afraid, my child—" and then he paused, smiled down at her and patted her shoulder encouragingly.

"No. I will not tell you not to be afraid, for during

the trials you may know much fear. But I will say this, daughter; face your fears bravely. You have begun well; continue with courage, and listen to the voice of your heart, and you will certainly overcome every Ordeal you may face."

CHAPTER TWELVE

*P*APAGENO *was still lying on the floor, still treating* himself to the luxury of a fainting fit. Tamino yawned. Outside the high windows, he could just discern that the dawn was beginning to break. He had not been able to sleep after the invasion of the Starqueen's three ladies—if, indeed, "ladies" was the proper word to apply to them. "Harpies" might have been better.

It had been a long night and he had had plenty of time to think, to doubt himself and his motives, his power to endure the mysterious Ordeals, and if Pamina could possibly come to care for a man she had seen only for a few moments. There had been intervals in the long night when he had wished that he had never left his father's court.

It had been the first time that he had had leisure to doubt. The journey had been demanding, but it had been rewarding too. From the moment he had encountered the dragon in the Changing Lands, events had been moving so swiftly that he had had no leisure to think about them at all.

By the time the sun made its first appearance through the tall narrow apertures—they were above his eye height so that he could not see anything at all outside— he was feeling thoroughly downhearted. He wished that they had returned the magical flute; once before, when he had played it, it had given him considerable consolation. At least it would give him something to do except sit here and worry about his fate.

But would they really give it back to him? After all, it had come to him in the Starqueen's realm, and if he knew nothing else about Sarastro's kingdom, it was that the Starqueen was not well regarded here. And if, as they said, it had been given by one who had no right to bestow it—he assumed they had meant the Messengers, but probably they had intended to accuse the Starqueen—perhaps they would not return it to him at all. What, after all, had he done to earn such a powerful magical weapon as that?

As the light grew, Tamino could see that Papageno was asleep on the patterned stone floor. The line of sunshine extended, and when it crawled across the Halfling's eyes, he began to stir sleepily.

"Prince Tamino?"

"I am here, friend Papageno, just the same as you."

The Halfling sat up, rubbing his back. "Well, they certainly don't believe in comfortable guest beds around this place, do they? Tell me, were the three—were they really here, or was it some kind of bad dream?"

Tamino had been wondering a little about that himself.

"I'm not sure, Papageno. If it was a bad dream, then I had it too."

The Halfling shook his feathered crest. "It's hard to believe. I tell myself, looking at the light, that I ought to be out setting my traps for birds, and then I look round and I'm in this place. Me, Papageno, and I'm supposed to be undertaking the Ordeals of the priests. Me. Ordeals."

He sounded absolutely disbelieving. "It's as if they said that I was going to be a priest or something. What am I doing here?"

Tamino was not sure whether Papageno was asking him, or whether he was demanding an answer of the silent heavens. But the Halfling kept looking up at him as if he was sure that Tamino could provide an answer. Should he confess to the Halfling that he shared Papageno's own puzzlement, or should he, as a prince certainly ought to do to a subject, encourage the bird-man to persist, to show courage as he had been told to do?

Something the priests said, when they had been questioning him about his qualifications for the Brotherhood, came back to him: *Are you prepared to treat all men as brothers, whatever their qualifications of rank?* He was not sure whether or not that applied to Halflings, whether or not they were even men.

Well, if it came to that, he would rather have Papageno for a brother, human or not, than some of the men he had met around his father's court. At least the little Halfling was kindhearted and good-tempered.

He said, "I sometimes wonder that myself—what I'm doing here, I mean. In general" he spoke slowly, discovering each word as he said it—"I suppose, I'm going where my destiny takes me. I never thought about it, either, no more than you did, and that's true."

Papageno sounded disappointed. He said, "You're a prince. I thought, for sure, you'd know what you were doing. You mean you just go along, doing what you're told? Like me?"

"A prince is only a man, Papageno." And, he thought, if I had ever had any illusions otherwise, this journey will have taught me better. "And my father is the Emperor of the West, and all men are bound to obey him. Even his sons. Especially his sons, to give an example to other men."

"Oh." He could see that this was a new idea to Papageno. "I thought princes were different. What's the good of being a prince, if you have to obey just like everybody else?"

It was, Tamino thought, a perfectly good question. But he was surprised that it came from Papageno. He had been all too ready to dismiss the Halfling as stupid. The bird-man was naive, but when it came to serious matters, he was certainly no fool, and he had an uncanny ability to ask the right questions.

"I don't know that either, Papageno. Maybe there isn't any." He was relieved when, instead of pursuing this line of questioning, Papageno shook the feathery crest on his head and inquired:

"I wonder what time they serve breakfast in this place?"

That, at least, was predictable.

"I don't know that either, Papageno. Maybe part of the Ordeals includes fasting."

"I knew they weren't for the likes of me," Papageno grumbled. "The food's good around here, but the mealtimes don't come around half often enough."

"Well, don't lose hope yet," Tamino admonished, laughing. "By the look of the sky, they can't be back from sunrise observances yet; maybe after that, they'll decide we're entitled to breakfast. But if not, I'm sure they'll feed us sooner or later. You couldn't be that hungry yet."

"Oh no? I always get hungry when I'm frightened," Papageno grumbled.

But of course there was nothing to do except wait; there Tamino and the Halfling were in the same situation. The light grew. Clouds covered the face of the sun and after a time Tamino could hear the rattle and rumble of thunder and see the flash of lightning. It made him remember how the Starqueen's ladies had vanished with a thunderclap. The rain poured heavily down.

Papageno muttered, "They've forgotten all about us!"

"Oh, I wouldn't think so," said Tamino soothingly. "They'll get around to us sooner or later."

"Probably later," Papageno said under his breath, and ostentatiously whistled a little tune on his birdcall.

But the clouds had cleared away and the sun had begun to glare across the stone floor again before they heard approaching footsteps.

"We're in luck," said Papageno. "Maybe it's breakfast."

Instead, the figure that entered was bent, shrouded in veils. Ignoring Tamino, it went directly to Papageno and said in a sweet, fluting voice, "I have been sent to return to you your magical bells."

And what about my flute? Tamino thought, and was about to ask the messenger. But before he could get a word out, the shrouded figure suddenly threw back the black veil and stood revealed as a woman. The face was wrinkled, the mouth toothless, the body withered and crookbacked.

Nevertheless, Tamino thought, she is a woman and by the laws of the Ordeals I may not speak to her.

Papageno took the magical chimes. "I'm glad to have it," he said truculently. "With all the dangers there are around this place, I might have needed it sooner."

"But they tell me you are very brave," the old woman said in her wavering voice.

"Oh, yes," Papageno said.

Tamino flinched; the silly fellow was going to start bragging again and break his oath! He said in a low, commanding whisper, "Hush, Papageno. You broke your oath before and spoke to the Queen's ladies; but they are giving you another chance! Be careful."

"I didn't break my oath at all," Papageno said vehemently! "You didn't think they were *women*, did you? No, sir, those ladies of the Starqueen are fiends right out of hell, they're demons, that's what they are, and the priests didn't say one thing about talking to demons!"

Tamino could not help but laugh. Papageno had an answer for everything. It would probably be his downfall, but Papageno was what he was and must meet his own destiny.

The old woman said, "Is there anything I can do for you, my darling fellow?"

"Well, I could do with some breakfast," Papageno said. "Or even a glass of wine."

"Oh, if that's what you want, nothing is easier," said the old woman, and pulled out a wineskin from under her cloak. She poured Papageno a glass and extended it to him.

"Ah—and do you serve as cupbearer to all the heroes who go through the Ordeals?"

"Oh, no, not at all," said the woman. "I only came here because my promised husband is somewhere here."

"Oh, you have a lover, do you, granny?" Papageno asked.

"Oh, indeed I do." Her voice was sweet; Tamino would have sworn that beneath the hood was a young girl, yet she had the hideous impact of death's-head, of extreme, crippling old age.

"And what else do you do here?"

"Oh, I sing, and I play on the flute, and the bells, and the harp, and I dance, and I juggle—"

"You juggle?" Tamino heard Papageno gulp. "Now that must be something to see, granny."

"If you'd like to see it—" the old woman snatched up the bells and promptly began to juggle the bells, the wineskin, and one of Papageno's boots which he had taken off when he lay down to rest. Tamino was amazed at her skill; she was as deft as any apprentice of fifteen.

"How old are you, granny?" Papageno asked.

She giggled. Again, the voice was a young girl's voice.

"Just twenty years, and one day."

"That," Papageno observed, "must have been a very long day."

"Oh, it was, it was. But my lover is so sweet and charming, he won't mind." She gathered up the wine-skin and handed the set of bells back to Papageno. After a minute she picked up the boot and flipped it to him with a merry little gesture.

"That lover of yours, he must be a fine fellow in deed," Papageno said. "Is he as young and charming as you, granny?"

"Oh, no. They tell me he's older," she said. "Almost ten years older than I am."

"I'm sure you make a delightful couple." Papageno had forgotten the wine in his hand; now he lifted it to his lips. "I haven't many acquaintances in these parts, but one can never tell. What's his name?"

"Papageno," she said clearly, and Papageno choked and sputtered wine all down his shirt.

"What?" he demanded. "What kind of joke is this?"

"No joke at all; Sarastro has promised you to me as my husband. You see, I am your Papagena."

Papageno gulped. "This is some kind of trick," he mumbled, then blinked and looked straight at the old woman.

"Well, I asked for a friend and companion. I didn't say she had to be young or pretty. He told me—well, I trust him. If he says you are the wife he promised me, I suppose he knows what he's doing. Pleased to meet you, gran—er—Papagena," he said bravely, and held out his hand.

"You are a darling fellow, as they promised," said the young girl's voice softly. The figure under the black veil shimmered a little, and the old woman was gone. Where she had stood there was the slender form of a girl.

She was like Papageno, to the green and yellow feathery crest on her head, but younger. She did not seem pretty to Tamino; the nose was too sharply beaked, the eyes too glittery and piercing. But Papageno stood as if enchanted.

"Papagena!" he cried, and abruptly the room was plunged into darkness and his cry turned into a howl of despair.

CHAPTER THIRTEEN

IT was, from the appearance of the sky, late in the *morning or early midday.* Tamino was beginning to feel hungry himself, but his long journey had accustomed him to fasting, and he was prepared, if he must, to ignore his hunger as long as the Masters of the Ordeals should require. Papageno sat on the floor, sunk in despair, and silent willingly for the first time since Tamino had known him. He did not touch the magical bells; he had not even troubled to put on his other boot. Tamino was beginning to be worried about him, when the door opened at last and the two priests came in.

"How is it with you, Prince Tamino? Are you still determined to persevere?"

"As yet, I have seen nothing to change my mind," Tamino said quietly.

"And you, friend Papageno?" asked the other. "What has happened to you in this long night?"

Papageno sat with his head down. He said, "I'm sure you know just as well as I do, everything that happened. I don't suppose that I passed your Ordeals. I'm just a chattering fool, after all. I did the best I could, but my best just isn't very good." Then he lifted his head and looked right at the priest.

"It's your fault, you know. For expecting me to do

what I'm just not built to do. I used to catch and tame birds for the Starqueen, and I taught some of them to talk, too. I was pretty good at that. But after I taught them to talk, I couldn't go back and teach them not to, and I couldn't teach them to talk at the right time and say the right things, and be quiet when it was time to be quiet. I guess I'm sort of like those birds. Once I was taught to talk, I don't know how not to. I never said I wanted to be tested this way, and I told you, you remember, that I wouldn't be any good at it."

"So you did, my son," said the priest, and his voice was gentle. "I have not found fault with you. Will you tell me, then, since you feel yourself unfit for the Ordeals, what it is that you want out of life?"

"Right now? Right now, I'd like some breakfast. All I had was a cup of wine, and I suppose it's made me a little silly or I wouldn't be talking like this to you, Reverend Father. If I've offended you—"

The priest put a hand on his shoulder. "You cannot offend me here, little brother, not when I ask for truth and you give me what I have asked. Breakfast you shall have, at once." He made a signal, and a young priest appeared with a laden tray which smelled very good: hot honeycakes and cakes crusted with sticky nuts. He set it before Papageno.

"Satisfy your hunger, little brother. But tell me, have you no other wish?"

"Not just now," Papageno said, "but I know myself well enough to know that before very long, I'll have a dozen. Why? What good does it do to talk about that? Thank you for the breakfast, Reverend Father. Then I suppose, considering that I didn't pass your Ordeals, I'll have to go back to my little hut in the forest. But that's not a bad place. Only—" he stopped, and swallowed, and put aside the piece of nut cake he had started to eat. Tamino saw that his eyes were full of tears.

"Tell me what troubles you, Papageno, my boy."

"Well," Papageno said in a rush, "I'm sick and tired of being tormented by those fiends in the shape of pretty ladies. I don't mind working hard, but I'd like to do it in peace and quiet and know they wouldn't hurt me when I've done my best. And I do wish I could have Papagena with me. I'd even take the old lady, if you couldn't arrange to let me have the young girl. She's a jolly companion and a friend, at least. I suppose, because I didn't pass your test of not speaking to the young lady, I really don't deserve her. But why don't you ask her—Papagena, I mean—what *she* wants? Shouldn't she have a chance too?" He stared intensely at the priest, the nut cake forgotten in his hand.

"Papagena has had her chance, as you have, and she has chosen you," said the priest. "Continue to have courage, and she may still be yours. But"—his voice was severe again as he warned—"the joys of wisdom, known to the Initiated, may never be yours."

"Oh, well—" Papageno looked up, shyly. "I don't want to say anything rude about the life you've chosen, sir, but that's really perfectly all right with me."

"Very well; so be it," said the priest, and smiled at Papageno. "Have courage; there may be other tests before you. But at his point it is fitting that those who have chosen the ordinary things of this world shall be separated from those who have chosen to seek wisdom. Prince Tamino, bid farewell to your companion."

"Now, look here," said Tamino, "what's going to happen to him? I'm responsible for him; I got him into this."

Tamino's priest said gently, "Do you trust Sarastro, my brother?" Suddenly Tamino realized that this was another test, and was again pleased with himself for recognizing it.

"Papageno—" he held out his hand and clasped the small dry hand of the Halfling, which was more like a set of talons than a human hand. "I'm sure they'll look after you properly. When I'm finished with the Ordeals, if the gods let me survive them"—for he was sure that before very long they would grow much more serious than this—"I'll look you up and find out how you're getting along. Take care, little brother, and the gods keep you."

Papageno looked up at him skeptically. "I think you're going to need their help a good deal more than I do, my prince." Impulsively he flung his arms around Tamino. "Don't you let them scare you or hurt you. And if you need me, just—" after a minute he ripped the birdcall off his neck and handed it to Tamino. "Just whistle on this, and I'll come and do anything I can to help you. I'm not any good with dragons, maybe, but if you want somebody to talk to, I'll be right there."

Deeply touched—it seemed to be the Halfling's only possession except for the coarse clothes he wore—Tamino took the little whistle. He said, "I'll see you at least to return it to you, little friend."

When the priests had taken Papageno away, Tamino nibbled without much interest on one of the honey-cakes left on the tray, and wondered when, if ever, the real trials would begin. The day was well along when the door opened again, and Pamina, clad in a simple white robe very much like his own, came into the vaulted room. She looked about curiously, blinking a little as her eyes fell on the skulls, the symbols of ancient deaths, but when she saw Tamino, her eyes brightened.

"My prince, they have sent me to return to you the

magic flute." And she held it out to him, wrapped in a silken cloth.

Overjoyed, Tamino remembered that they had sent Papagena to return to Papageno his magical bells. This must mean that she had been chosen for him, as Papagena for the bird-man. At least they were not testing him with any idiotic disguises, but, unlike the silly fellow, Tamino fully intended to keep his promise not to speak. Since she was wearing a neophyte's robe, she too must understand the purpose of this testing, and why he would not speak to her. In fact, since she was Sarastro's daughter, she probably understood it far better than he did himself.

He took the flute, avoiding her eyes—he did not want to be surprised into a careless word, and he knew if he looked at her he probably could not keep from pouring out all his delight at seeing her. And especially that she should bring him the flute.

He had been trying to understand the symbolism of the flute. The old priest appointed as his guide had told him that he would be tested by Earth, Water, Air, and Fire. Possibly the night spent in the crypt, with the symbols of death and mortality all about him, served to commemorate the element of Earth, from which they had all come and to which they must return? He was not sure, but he supposed that someday the priest-guide would explain it to him, when the proper time should come.

Perhaps his love for Pamina was the test of Fire? He felt a desperate longing for her, to be with her, to speak to her, to ask her if she felt for him anything like what he felt for her. Or was she simply accepting him because it was the will of both her parents? Did he want her that way, or did he in fact want her under any circumstances?

He felt a soft touch on his arm.

"Tamino," Pamina said gently, "please talk to me."

He shook his head, still trying not to look at her, but he could not stop a glimpse through the corner of his eyes. When he had seen her before she had been clad in silken robes, and her hair had been braided with jewels: a princess, his equal in rank, daughter of the Starqueen and of the powerful priest Sarastro. Now, like himself, she wore a robe of coarse white linen, unadorned; her long fair hair was combed straight down her back, hanging loose and without a single ornament, almost to her waist. Again they had been made equals before the Mysteries, he thought, and silently smiled at her, shaking his head.

"But you are making fun of me," Pamina implored. "We must speak, we have so much to talk about. I need to know whether you truly want this marriage, or whether it is only that my father has chosen you and you accept because I am the daughter of the powerful priest. Did you even know that Sarastro is more than a priest, he is the Sun-king of all of Atlas-Alamesios? Is it that you wish to marry me, or that you wish to inherit this city and all its possessions?"

Her tone was pitiable; Tamino opened his mouth to reassure her at once. Inherit the kingdom of Atlas-Alamesios? What could he, a son of the Emperor of the West, possibly care for her inheritance? Pamina was what he wanted, Pamina...

But no. As the ladies of the Starqueen had done to frighten them, as Papagena had tested Papageno, Pamina was trying to play on his emotions and test him. He would not be caught that way. He would not lose Pamina by foolishly breaking the rules they had laid down for the Ordeals. He took the flute, bent his head to it and began to play.

The sweet tone of the flute stole through the quiet room and the flecks of sunlight illuminating the skulls on the high pillars. As he played, peace stole through him; he tried to play all his love for Pamina, his trust, the knowledge that only through this obedience could they come together. And as the sound seemed to spread quiet through the sunlit room, it flashed upon him that perhaps this was the testing of the element of Air.

For it was through the air of their breathing that they would speak to one another, and when speech was forbidden or forgone for the moment, surely only for the moment, then he could carry his love and concern for her through the magical medium of the air, speaking in the music of the flute.

Magical flute, speak for me. Sing to her of my love, say she must trust me until these Ordeals are safely behind us and then, be the gods willing, we will walk together in this place.

"Tamino!" It was such a cry of pain that he stopped his music to look at her. "Please, put away the flute, look at me, talk to me, I can't bear it when you don't even look at me! I thought you loved me. Was it only because that was what you thought I wanted to hear? Was it a joke, a lie?"

Her eyes filled slowly with tears, and Tamino, seeing them rise and stand in the liquid depths, felt deeply troubled. Had they not told her of the test? How he wished he could put the flute aside, explain it all to her. He could see himself taking her in his arms, holding her like something very frail and very precious, a jewel he had found by chance on this strange and unexpected road he had come here to travel, and telling her, reassuring her of his love and begging her to trust him.

But he must not. And if they had not told her of the nature of the test, well, she was a priest's daughter too, they must have prepared her for at least this Ordeal of trust.

He saw that she was crying. He had never realized that a woman's tears could tear like this at his heart. Perhaps, after all, this was the Ordeal of Fire, for watching Pamina weep he felt a burning spear of pain at his throat. He had been taught in his father's court that he should meet all trials calmly and without undue, undignified emotion, but for a moment he felt he could not do anything but fling down the flute, crush Pamina in his arms and kiss her until she stopped crying and listened to his reasons for refusing to speak....

And then I should lose her, as Papageno lost Papagena— He could still hear in his mind Papageno's wail of despair as the Halfling girl vanished. He kept on fingering the flute, his head bent over the instrument, not daring to raise his eyes to hers. Surely she must hear it in the music, he thought in despair. She must know without words. Why must there be words between us?

"Tamino, don't you love me anymore?" The words were heartbreaking. He bit his lip and tasted blood. Even if she did not know this was a test, surely this had gone too far. How could he endure to listen to her suffering?

Yet if the test had been easy, what was the use of it? He blinked away tears and went on playing, resolutely refusing to meet her eyes.

"Tamino!" This time it was a cry of anguish, and he felt her small hands on his arm, trying to wrench away the flute. He let it fall to the floor—he would not struggle against her, would not try to take it from her.

They only said I must not speak to her. They did not say I could not kiss her— He fought the temptation to do just that, his breathing ragged, but he heard the words of the old priest, you may not touch her or speak to her. With an effort that made him gasp with agony, he tore himself free of her hands and turned his back on her. He heard her wild sob of mingled anger and pain, then a rush of footsteps and a slamming door.

Then he fell to the floor and wept.

CHAPTER FOURTEEN

*P*AMINA *rushed from the vaulted building, sob-*
bing wildly. It felt like the end of all her dreams.
She could not trust Tamino; he had rejected her.
She could no longer trust Sarastro; it was he who had
sent her to take the flute to Tamino, exposing her to
this deathly cruelty of rejection.

She had begun to love him. She had begun to trust
him. Now what was there for her?

What can I do now? Go back to my mother's kingdom? she wondered. But her mother had cast her off,
had demanded of her that she must kill Sarastro or be
forever disowned.

She cannot mean it, Pamina thought. Would she cast
off her own daughter, the one she had chosen as her
own successor and heir? But the memory of her mother's cold fierce stare was icy in her mind.

My poor mother. Hatred and the thought of revenge
have driven her quite mad. Still, Pamina was afraid to
face the Starqueen unless she came to her with
Sarastro's blood on the dagger...and Pamina knew
that she would never raise her hand to her father.

She still had the dagger, tucked under the bloused
top of the neophyte's robe. She had been afraid to leave
it in her rooms for someone to find. She looked at it
bitterly. Perhaps she should turn it on herself.

If only her mother had been willing that they should escape Sarastro's realm together. She might now be safe again in the house where she had been born.

She could not go on like this, aimlessly wandering through the unfamiliar gardens of Sarastro's Temple. She had not been outside the walls since she had been here, she was not even sure of the way back to her mother's home. She was in a garden filled with palm trees, some of them loaded with ripe dates; the walls of buildings were blindingly white in the sun, dazzling her eyes—or were her eyes full of tears? She wiped them on the coarse linen of her robe, and looked around.

She saw a staircase, leading up and up to one of the highest roofs. Perhaps she could look out over the wall, find her way back to her mother's castle. Surely her mother could not mean murder. She would not cast off her youngest child for refusing to murder her own father. No. Her mother could never be so cruel or unjust. But the dagger, now in her hand—that was real, and surely she had not mistaken the words she had heard her mother say.

She thought, either hate and revenge have driven my mother mad, or I shall go mad from thinking about it. The staircase was narrow and steep, angling dizzily against the sheer wall, and Pamina, afraid to look down, leaned her whole body against the wall as she climbed, averting her eyes from the outside edge and keeping them turned on the placement of each foot. At last there were no more stairs and Pamina stepped out onto the roof.

She had chosen her vantage point well. The roof was evidently intended as a place of refuge from the worst of the heat, for shrubbery in pots stood about, shadowing divans and low seats, and at the center a small, cool fountain played. A high outer wall partially barricaded the view; but there was a step which, when climbed, afforded a view of the whole city, and Pamina, standing there, could clearly identify her mother's palace. It was not even so very far away, though it stood on the edge of this city of Atlas-Alamesios.

But she could easily reach it from here. . . .

She knew that she should descend at once from the roof, make her way to the nearest gate, and go along that one long, wide street whose route she traced as she stood there. But she stood, delaying.

Surely now her father would not compel her to remain, now that Tamino had rejected her and she was no longer of use to him to be given in marriage to the Prince of the West. In any case, the plain white linen she wore made her only an anonymous novice priestess, and she could come and go around the enclosure as little noticed as any one of them on some unknown duty.

From where she stood, high up, she could see a long procession winding through the streets near her mother's palace. Pamina marked it with surprise, and then counted on her fingers. Yes, the new moon was upon them and with them, the sacrifices. Horns were braying, there were the ritual cries from the mourners, all of them stupefied with the smoke of the sacred herbs, and there were her mother's sacrificial priests with their great knives. Surely all this was right and proper, it was the way the world had been ordered. When she had first come here she had asked Sarastro, at what hour were the sacrifices, and had been shocked when he told her there were none. Her mother had, after all, told her that Sarastro was an impious devil, and this had proved it to her, that he neglected what she had been taught was the prime duty of Humankind, in thankfulness that she had not been made Halfling—to offer up abundant sacrifices.

She knew now that when Sarastro had answered

her, it had been the first time she had ever thought about anything for herself, instead of taking the word of the Starqueen as the word of the very gods. What had he said?

Pamina, my child, why should the gods who created both men and Halflings need us to sacrifice the Halflings to them? If the gods gave the Halflings life, could they not give death to as many of them as they desired, too? Halflings do not live nearly as long as Mankind; why should we further shorten their lives? We make no sacrifices in this temple, daughter, neither of Man nor Halfling, but we honor the gods in prayer and praise, and by making the most virtuous use of the life they have given us.

This had been a shocking idea to Pamina. And yet, as she watched the procession winding along the street, priests and mourners and the manacled victims—tiny as little dolls from this height—she felt lonesome for a familiar thing. She could see, riding on the high cart, a dark-robed figure which could have been one of her half sisters.

But they were Halflings too. Why should they take pleasure in sacrificing those who were like themselves but less fortunate?

Pamina's head ached—was it from the burning light in the streets, or with tears and perplexity? Suddenly she found herself, for the first time in many years, remembering the night Rawa had disappeared.

Her mother had promised that Rawa should not be sent to the stables as rat-catcher. She had always thought that her mother had sent the dog-woman away to another assignment, somewhere outside the palace, but because her mother had given her a promise, Pamina had not troubled to inquire further. Now she supposed that she must have always known the truth: Rawa had been taken for sacrifice in Papagena's place.

How could she have been so blind to what had been so obvious? But she had always been blind, "the foolish child," Disa thought her. After seven years it was useless even to cry for Rawa. She had not even known that there had been a choice, Rawa for Papagena. Papagena was dear to her, but Rawa—in a very real sense Rawa had mothered her, and she had had no other mother at all. The Starqueen—except in the very limited physical sense—had never been a mother. So why did Pamina feel this terrible sense of loss, remembering in pain the moment when her mother's arms had tightened, so briefly, around her?

The procession had passed out of sight now, but she followed it painfully, in thought, through the portal doors, and inside to the altar of blood. The daily sacrifice, spilled on the altar at high noon—she had been taught that this fed the sun, enabled it further to shine...what folly, what a foolish tale for deluded children, yet she had never questioned it. Had the army of priests and sacrificers somehow failed in their duties, Pamina would have willingly taken up the knife to keep the daily sacrifices in their appointed courses; so she had been taught.

And now she knew that was foolishness, she had been shown pictures of the sun and the worlds that moved round it, the sun was no more than a huge ball of fire in the sky that would keep burning whatever Mankind or Halflings did or did not do, and the true gods, so Sarastro said, were no more than the forces of Order that kept the suns and moon and stars all burning in their appointed places. What a foolish child she had been! What a foolish child she was still!

No more place, then, in her mother's house. But since Tamino had rejected her, none in Sarastro's Temple, either. What life could there be, now, for her? What place anywhere?

She stayed at the wall, looking out into the city. Why, she wondered, should Sarastro's people have kept this outlook into the city whose manners and customs they had rejected? Surely they must turn away with abhorrence from the daily holocaust among the Halflings? How was it that they could dwell here, actually overlooking these dreadful things and make no effort to prevent them? The city blurred before her eyes, was it really as close as it seemed?

Outside the compound she could hear a rowdy barking sound. A dog-halfling, a young male, was shouting and running in a little alley; she heard a soft encouraging whine, and saw a young Halfling bitch, watching him. The male turned and with a returning whine, grabbed the female and hauled her down in the dust. No greetings; no preliminaries; they sniffed one another, pranced a little, and then they were barking and grunting together on the ground. A passerby on some errand cursed them for blocking the street, and tried to kick them out of the way, but, locked together, they were completely oblivious.

Of course. This was, Pamina had been taught, simply the way dog-halflings behaved, and lucky too, for it assured swarms of Halflings, unclaimed and the property of no one, for sacrifices, and what would they ever do if the supply was to dwindle? It was impious, she had been taught, to bridle the breeding of Halflings; this was to deprive the gods of their just dues in sacrifice.

But if the gods had no need of sacrifices—Pamina felt her brain would burst with all this. And for some reason, now, she felt ashamed for the female Halfling. Should they not have taught her better than this, to be rolled, rutting, in the dirt of an alley? Surely she must be of more use than this to someone or something. And her sister, Kamala—Pamina had heard her bragging once about the unquenchable lust of ox-halflings, though sometimes they had to be beaten to keep them in fear, so they would do what was wanted. At the time she had felt revulsion, and had resolved that she would never be guilty of such tasteless private sports, but not until this moment had she felt agonizing shame for her sister.

It was like this that Monostatos had grabbed at her—roughly, without caring whether she consented, without caring about anything but what he wanted at the moment. And then Pamina felt her cheeks redden and shame stealing through her.

Was this what she had expected or wanted of Tamino?

She saw him again in her mind, wearing the white neophyte's robe like her own, resolutely avoiding her eyes and playing on the flute she had been instructed to give him, as if he felt the sound could communicate something to her. Why had she not guessed at once? The neophyte's robe should have told her, this was some form of test or challenge set to him; he had been, no doubt, forbidden to speak to her or touch her, and he was obedient to the task he had been set. Now, his face clearly before her eyes in memory, she could see the pain there, and knew that he had been imploring her to trust him. And she had failed him.

And, no doubt, failed another test for herself, and perhaps she had lost him forever. How could she have been so foolish? Her hand tightened on the dagger in her hand. She had lost everything—everything but this.

"No," said a voice behind her, "you do not need that, either. Have you seen what you came up here to see, my daughter, and do you understand?"

Pamina turned, to see Sarastro standing at her side.

"Oh, Father, why have I never seen any of this before? And why—" Reason suddenly overcame what lay before her eyes. "Why is my mother's city so close? Why when I dwelled there, did I never see the Temple of Light from her dwelling or when I walked through the streets with the processions?"

"In part, because you were not looking for it," Sarastro said, smiling, and reached out his hand for the dagger. "No, you will not use it now, I think, neither on yourself nor on me, but it came from your mother's realm of delusion, and that is why you see things which are not there. But because you see from the light we serve here, you see truth, and no longer see only what she allowed you to see. Give me the dagger, Pamina, which bears the evil magic of the Starqueen's realm, and see the city as it truly is."

She dropped it obediently into Sarastro's hand. And as she let it go, it was as if a mist had cleared away from her eyes. Around the wall of Sarastro's compound, for many leagues, the forest stretched away, barren and uninhabited. Very far away, on the edge of the horizon, the towers of a city rose, a familiar skyline Pamina knew well, for she had seen it every day of her life until she came here.

"But how—why did it seem so near?" she stammered.

"It showed you what was in your own mind; what you had not learned how to see," Sarastro said quietly. "With this in your hand, Pamina, had it been your true will, you could have stepped from these walls almost into your mother's house. But since the viewpoint where you stood was in the realm of Truth, you saw only that truth. I will not ask what you saw." He looked briefly out over the forest where, a few minutes ago, Pamina had seen the sacrificers leading their unlucky victims through the streets of the Starqueen's city, and there was pain in his eyes. Then he thrust the dagger out of sight in a fold of his clothing and sighed.

"You need not tell me what you saw, child. Remember, once I loved her too," he said. "I thought she was as good as she is beautiful, and for many years I could not bear to test her in the clear light of Truth." Again he sighed, and turned his back on the view of forest—or was it the city of the Starqueen? Pamina would not look again to see.

"Come, my daughter," he said kindly. "One of the first lessons here is not to think of the mistakes of the past, unless it is possible to take action to remedy them; and that time, if it will ever come, has not yet come. Tamino has successfully completed the first of his Ordeals. Come and speak to him, for the remaining Ordeals, if your lives are truly to be joined, you must face together. And he is longing for the sight of your face."

With his hand on her shoulder, Sarastro led Pamina toward the narrow stairs.

CHAPTER FIFTEEN

"*I*N one thing at least you were correct,*" said* Sarastro, "the first tests you have overcome were tests of basic character: of restraint, of compassion, of endurance, and, not least, of obedience and willingness to follow orders. In themselves they were of no very great significance; except for this. If you had been discovered lacking in these qualities, you would have been determined unfit for the more serious Ordeals to follow."

He looked soberly at Tamino, over the remains of a simple meal which strewed the table before them. Tamino tried to keep his mind on what Sarastro was saying. It was not easy when Pamina was seated on a third side of the table, next to her father, her eyes seldom meeting his, but her face rosy with blushing. He wished they had been permitted at least a single embrace.

But, in a sense, it seemed right that they had not. As the Emperor's son, no woman, however trivial or fleeting his interest in her, had ever been denied to him. Pamina was something wholly different from this. He was not sure why, but he knew that he was willing—no; he firmly *intended*—to spend the rest of his life with her. They could wait a little while for kisses and embraces and pledges of love. He looked at a dimple at the corner of her mouth, thought briefly of how much it looked like the center of a cluster of rose petals and of how much he would like to kiss it, and firmly turned his attention back to the priest.

Pamina asked, "And what about Papageno?"

Sarastro smiled. "I think it is clear that the higher levels of wisdom are not for him. Yet he has demonstrated character and a certain strength of purpose. I think he will come through undamaged, with Papagena at his side. I truly hope so."

"I too," said Pamina firmly, "because I love Papagena and I have learned to value Papageno too."

"And I," said Tamino. "It took more courage, I think, for him to face the Starqueen's ladies and defy them, than for me to face a dragon."

"Of course—they were the dragons of his mind and imagination," said Sarastro.

"Were they really here, or was this an illusion for the purpose of the Ordeals?" Tamino asked.

Sarastro's lips curved in a faint smile. "My son, you are not yet qualified to inquire into the secrets of the Brotherhood," he rebuked mildly. Though the reproof was mild, it was an obvious rebuke, and Tamino lowered his head and stared at the crumbs and fruit skins on the table. But Sarastro's smile reassured him.

Pamina asked, "And Monostatos—?"

"Has been dismissed from the Ordeals, and may not enter here again on pain of death," Sarastro said, and he look sad. "I am sorry; as I told you, his father was my friend, and I thought better of the young man. This is the very first of the Ordeals for a Halfling. I do not think he failed it as Papageno might have done, out of sheer impulsiveness and inability to stop and think— I think Monostatos is very intelligent. Halfling or no, he is more intelligent than many men. And yet he behaved with no more restraint that the dog-halflings I saw you watching, Pamina."

"I am not sure I understand," said Pamina, and Tamino too looked puzzled.

"Since you have both passed this particular Ordeal, that of Earth," said Sarastro gravely, "I may discuss it with you. And it is relevant to your marriage. The first test for humanity, that which distinguishes the human form from the animal—and this is true for Man and Halfling alike—is the rational mind, which controls the animal impulse. To the Dog-folk at that moment, Pamina, nothing mattered but the instinct to mate, and they had never been taught to bring it under rational control or to consider suitable time or place. I do not think Monostatos is lacking in that rational control; but the circumstances were designed to tempt him, and he failed. Failed, as miserably as the simple dog-halflings whom he despises as much as you—"

"I don't despise them," Pamina interrupted, "I am sorry for them. But they have never been taught any better; how can you expect anything else from them?"

Sarastro looked sad. "That is the basis of my quarrel with your mother, Pamina; that in her realm they are taught no better. Monostatos, as I said, had the intelligence for more. But his pride made him incapable of forethought, so that he reacted like a base animal. Pride—he thought himself destined to be my heir and your consort, and so he failed." Sarastro sighed. "Even Papageno, with half his intelligence, passed that first of Ordeals. I was not sure that he could keep his hands off Papagena, nor trust her when she did not appear as he wanted her to be. Yet he displayed rational thought, good sense and at least some obedience. Humility served him where Monostatos, who thought he could not fail, yielded to pride."

"What will become of Monostatos?" Pamina asked.

"Or is that a secret of your Brotherhood into which I am forbidden to inquire, my father?"

"I have no control, now that I have banished him, over his fate. Yet I am troubled. He will return to your mother's realm, and I suppose, when the Great Serpent dies, he will inherit his father's kingdom and inheritance, which is not small. Having failed to pass the Ordeals, with the higher Wisdom forever denied him, I fear he will work ruin there. Yet his father's influence may still have some power over him; he may yet learn discipline and restraint. I do not know what now befalls in the land of the Great Serpent; he lives under the darkness the Starqueen has thrown over the lands, and I cannot see under that shadow. I can only say that there was a time when the Great Serpent was wise and courageous, and could even enter upon the Changing Lands without fear. Since then I have seen little of him."

"In a land where a Halfling rules," said Pamina, "I would think he would educate and teach them, so that they would be no less than men."

"So I too, once, believed of him," Sarastro said, "before he came under your mother's influence, Pamina. I think this may have been what the Makers had in mind—that Mankind should be diverse, that the Bird-kind and the Serpent-folk and even the more simple ones should each be educated and taught wisdom, each as he is able. But alas, they did not see it that way. To your mother, and to the one called the Great Serpent, the Halflings had been created by the Makers to be slaves, and no more. They can see it no otherwise."

"But he is Halfling himself!" Pamina cried.

Sarastro sighed and quoted softly, " 'In the beginning was the Serpent, and it is said that it was their hands which aided the Makers in the making of Humankind.'

To him, Pamina, there are two kinds of man: our folk and the Serpent-kin. All others are but base animals, made for no purpose but to serve the true humans. To them, any attempt to promote the welfare of the Half-lings is sentimental folly—hypocritical folly, since they cannot imagine I do not mean somehow to profit by it. But enough of them," he added firmly. "All these things you will learn at the proper time. Now we should speak of the Ordeals which lie before you. That of Earth lies behind you, the trial of the rational mind, which may be stated thus: *'I am in command of the animal within. It is a partner in my life, but I am master, not slave.'*"

"Is it permitted to inquire about the nature of these Ordeals?" asked Tamino.

"Only that you must demonstrate mastery of the Elements of Air and Fire and Water," Sarastro said. "You have been entrusted with a very powerful magical weapon in the flute. More than this I may not say." He pushed away the flimsy little table and rose to his full height.

"At moonrise you will be taken to the place of test-ing. Since you have committed yourselves, one to the other, it has been determined that you may undertake the Ordeals together. Each of you has strengths which may complement the other's weaknesses." He clasped Tamino's hand in a strong grip; bent briefly to kiss Pamina's cheek. "Courage, my children. You shall have my prayers; I wish it were permitted me to give you more help than that."

He was about to leave the room; abruptly he turned and strode back toward them. He said, in a voice trem-bling with almost visible emotion, "Pamina. Beware. Your mother may stop at nothing to keep you from your victory. I beg of you, do not underestimate her, nor let pity make you careless. She was the first, and until now, the only woman to be allowed to enter upon the higher Ordeals. I—" for a moment, though his lips moved, Pamina could not hear what he was saying.

At last she made it out.

"—I made an almost fatal mistake; I underestimated her pride in that accomplishment. She may—" he broke off. "I should not say this. Forgive me. Her person is sacred to me. But if she should try to harm you—"

Pamina opened her mouth to protest, then thought better of it. She could sense the tremendous struggle within Sarastro, and for a moment she did not know which of her parents she most pitied.

Tamino found himself, for some reason, remembering Papageno's question: *What good is it to be a prince, if you have to obey orders like anyone else?* Sarastro was a priest-king, the highest Adept of this Brotherhood of guardian wisdom. Yet in spite of all this, and in spite of his heroic attempts to conceal it, he was torn with conflicting passions and loyalties like any other mortal. Like Papageno, he was ready to ask what purpose lay behind it all, if the successful attainment of the Wisdom resting in the Ordeals left the Adept no wiser than before in ruling his own passions.

But he had learned much since he came here. Perhaps he, where he stood, was no wiser than Papageno compared with the man who stood before him. He bowed his head, not wanting to look at the misery in Sarastro's eyes. When he looked up again, the priest-king was gone, and the priest he had learned to call his guide was standing before him.

"Prince Tamino," said the guide formally, "are you prepared to continue with the Ordeals?"

"I am."

"My lady Pamina," the guide continued formally, "I am instructed to say to you that there is no obligation upon you to complete these Ordeals. You have been

made free of the Path of Earth, and no more is required
of women within this Temple. You may still turn back
in honor, and may be called priestess and princess.
But this is the last point where you may turn back. If
you persist for a single step further, then you are committed to the remainder of the Ordeals, and you may
not be released till you have conquered or met death
upon these Paths."

She looked up at Tamino for a moment, and he saw
her swallow, her throat moving just a little under the
white linen. Then she said in a quaint, formal tone,
"Priest, where my lord and my promised husband goes,
those Paths I will tread also, though they lead even to
my death."

"So be it; none may deny you that right, noble one,"
said the priest. "Tamino, do you accept Pamina, then,
to walk these Paths at your side?"

Pamina's hand was in his, very small, the fingers
trembling a little. One part of Tamino, remembering
how foolish the Ordeals had seemed so far, wondered
if this was simply another test of willingness, obedience, and courage, pretended obstacles which would
vanish if he faced them bravely. Yet something in the
memory of Sarastro's face, his obvious fear, told him
that what he had seen so far was no more than preliminary to the real testing. He wanted to beg Pamina to
let him undertake these Ordeals alone, while she remained in safety. Surely women were not required to
face death for Wisdom, and what did they need of it
anyhow? Yes, the Starqueen had undergone these Ordeals, but was she any the better for them? Only her
pride had profited, it seemed.

And Pamina was the Starqueen's daughter. Would
it not be safer if her pride should remain unawakened
and unchallenged? He said, "Pamina—" and stopped.
Did he trust her or not, did he love her? Or did he,

beneath the surface which inspired him to love and trust her, fear her because she was daughter to the Starqueen?

He said, and felt his breathing trip up and stumble as if he had been running too fast, "It is for Pamina to choose. She is my promised wife, not my slave, and I have no right to impose my will upon her. Whatever choice she makes is good in my eyes. But if she chooses to turn back here I swear I will never reproach her."

He felt her fingers tighten in his hand. She said firmly, "I have made my choice."

"So be it, then," said the priest. "Join hands, Tamino and Pamina." He smiled, as if he could see perfectly well that their hands were already joined.

"I commit you, then, to the Ordeal of the element of Air. May the Lord Guardians of the Winds protect you."

He struck his hands sharply together, and the impact was a thunderclap. Suddenly the room was gone. Pamina's hand was still clasped in his; but all around him, the wind tore at his garments, pulled his hair awry, freezing currents of air rode a tornado round them. He reached, on desperate instinct, for Pamina, feeling that the wind would tear her away from him.

"Pamina! Hold fast to me," he cried, but felt the winds drown out his voice. Through the battering of the winds, he felt her arms go round him and cling tightly as they were whirled, battered, thrust violently in one direction after another. In the darkness of storm-clouds they could see nothing, dark mist wrapped them tight.

For a moment the stormclouds cleared from their vision; they were standing, clasped tight in each other's arms, against the battering wind, high above the mountains, in a narrow cleft in the high bluffs where winds thrust and whirled at them. Even as they tried to recover a precarious balance by leaning against the cliff, the wind snatched Pamina's outer garment and whirled it away, flapping like the wings of some monstrous white bird, flinging it far out of reach across the storm-tossed sky so that she stood in her knee-length chemise, shivering. With every gust of wind it seemed as if they would be ripped from where they stood and flung into the abyss of jagged rocks they could see far below.

"Where are we?" Pamina shrieked, directly into his ear, but even so he could hardly hear over the howling of the gale. "What has happened?"

The Ordeal of the Winds, Tamino thought. And what was the Ordeal? To get out of here alive before they were blown off the cliff?

CHAPTER SIXTEEN

*D*AWN *was breaking. Papageno had wandered* half the night, after the priests had come and taken away Tamino, half expecting to encounter Papagena at every turn in the gardens. At last, disconsolate, hopeless, he had found a large sheltering tree and curled up in the dry leaves under it. He wished he were in his little hut in the woods. What did he want with wisdom and that sort of thing?

What right did he have to expect Sarastro to keep his word? The Starqueen's ladies never had. They had promised him all kinds of things, but he was no better off than before. And he hadn't even been able to keep his own promise. They had warned him not to speak to any women, and despite his brave words to Tamino about the Starqueen's ladies not being women but demons, he knew he had not done as well as he should have. He had laughed and made jokes with the old lady who had suddenly turned into his very own Papagena, and then, because he had broken the laws and talked to her, they had snatched her away and probably he would never see her again.

Anyway, he was only a Halfling, only fit for a slave. They had given him a chance and he had not been worthy of it, and what right did he have to complain? He had a chance to accompany Tamino on a real adventure, and he couldn't measure up. He twisted his small body into a depression in the dead leaves, and at last he fell asleep.

When he woke, day was breaking. He saw a pair of young priests sweeping a path, and wondered why they didn't have Halfling servants to do it for them. He wondered if they would like to have a good faithful servant. It was all he knew how to do, and he supposed the Starqueen wouldn't have him back even if he dared to go. He had hoped the prince would put in a good word for him, but Prince Tamino had gone off on his own business and was probably looking for wisdom somewhere, without a thought to spare for Papageno, who had never wanted to come here in the first place. He felt very dusty, very tired and bruised from his hard bed under the bush, and very hungry.

He got up and shook himself, ruffling the feathered crest of his head. What would the prince do? Not that the prince cared about things like food and shelter, but if he did, what would he do? He was on his own here; he might as well make the best of it. He stole out from the shelter of the bushes. The two young priests had finished sweeping the path, and vanished. Papageno doused his head in the waters of the fountain, and felt better for it; as he shook the drops of water from his crest, he smoothed down his tunic, and found, slung at his waist, the magical bells he had been given.

I can't have failed as badly as all that, he thought, or they'd never have left this magical thing with me.

He sat down cross-legged on the grass and took it off, examining the carved frame, the silver of the bells and the filigree wire on which they were strung. He remembered how Monostatos and his cohorts had been driven away when he played it. And when he played it before, the Messengers or angels, or whatever they were had appeared and given him food. No, that had been when the flute was played.

But maybe they came when certain music was played. They might even be willing to tell him what he ought to do next, whether he should return to the Starqueen, or whether they thought Sarastro and the priests had any use for an honest working man. His fingers hovered hesitantly over the bells; then he began trying to play the tune he remembered Tamino drawing from the flute.

If they didn't want me to use this, they wouldn't have given it to me.

The bells rang out, still with a cheerful jingling sound. They made Papageno want to dance, too. He began to think that they only played as they chose, not as he tried to make them play. Then a little rushing breeze whirled up from the ground. Papageno's eyes were briefly dazzled by the sun; in the golden light, the three Messengers suddenly appeared before him.

"You who are Master of the element of Earth, brother Halfling," said one of them—or was their curious speech a blend of unison song? As usual he could not see them clearly because their forms seemed to shift and change. "We are here, your brothers of the element of Air, to render you such help as we may."

Papageno scratched his head. "What did you call me?" he asked, bewildered.

"You have mastered the element of Earth," said the Messengers, "and thus, within reason, you may command whatever belongs to the earthly realms. What would you have?"

Papageno blinked and considered that. Then he said, "I guess food is just about as earthy as you can find. How about some of that? I really like fruits better, but if all I can have is vegetables that grow in the earth, I like yams and carrots and ground nuts about as well as anything. And do you suppose you could stretch that enough to include a cup of the element of Water, friends? I mean, springs and wells are included in the earth, aren't they?"

He thought for a moment that it was the wind jangling the magical bells; then he realized that they were laughing at him. But not as the ladies of the Starqueen had laughed, they were not making fun of his ignorance. Rather, their laughter included awareness that everything on the plane of existence was a subject for good humor and laughter.

"We will start there," said the Messengers. "For food and drink are the life of the body, and the body pertains to the element of Earth, little brother. But you have shown yourself master, in that your mind proclaims you human, master of the animal within. Give that animal just dues, Papageno. Would you not rather share your meal with the comrade you have won by your mastery?"

Papageno said, swallowing hard, "I don't know what you mean."

"You have demonstrated mastery over the first element," said the Messengers, in that voice that was like song, "and so you have earned the right to human speech and more than human speech. Papageno, do you know who we are?"

"You told us you were Messengers. I think myself that you're angels," said Papageno.

"Like yourself, we are Halflings," said one of the Messengers, and to Papageno it seemed that the speaker was a half-grown boy, with feathers like his own. "We are spirits of the Air, but we could not master the element of Earth, nor could we fly, because our wings would not bear us." The wavering golden form turned, to display long trailing wings, which hung, trailing and useless, behind his body; and he drooped as he spoke.

"Of all useless Halflings we were the least; so Sarastro with his magic made us free of the Air, so that we could bear messages and master magical song. It is the element of Air which carries music and desire. Tell us, little brother, have you no other desire than for food and drink?"

Papageno blinked. He supposed that they were taunting him too, as the Starqueen's ladies had done, after all. His eyes blurred with tears.

"Well, yes, I do. But there's no good talking about it, because I know I can't have it. I broke all the rules, didn't I, and I suppose I'll never see her again."

The laughter was like his own golden bells, and suddenly Papageno realized that once again, they were not laughing at him but sharing laughter.

"Little brother, you are a fool," said one of the Messengers. "What is the good of having human speech, if you do not use it to ask for what you desire? The element of Air rules not only music, but human speech and song. You have not been given what you most desire because in your humility, little brother, you have not asked for it. Now play on your magic bells, Papageno, and see who will come to bring you the banquet which celebrates not only eating and drinking, but the fullness of life."

Papageno took up the bells and began to play a tune upon them; first improvising from the sound of his birdcall, then ringing them out gaily through the morning. He did not at first notice that the Messengers had vanished, till he heard a cheery little whistle like his own. Papagena stood before him.

All disguise had vanished. She was wearing a simple green tunic; and in the feathery crest of her hair was a garland of white flowers.

She said softly, "Papageno—"

And now Papageno understood; he saw her through

a blur of tears. He stammered at her, "Pa-pa-pa-gena?"

She mocked him gently, with a smile, "Pa-pa-pa-pageno?" And then held out her hand.

"I have some of the wine you didn't have a chance to drink," she said softly, "and fruits, and nuts, in my little house here. And the priestess has told me that I may bring you there, and that it will be our little nest." She smiled up shyly at him.

"Do you want to come?"

But she did not have to wait for his answer. She held out her hand, and he clasped it; and they ran together through the woods.

CHAPTER SEVENTEEN

*E*VEN *as she clung to Tamino, battered by the* winds that threatened to sweep them both off the cliff face and into the abyss to be smashed on the rocks below, Pamina was aware that this was their first embrace. Before this she had felt only the briefest and most respectful touch of his lips against her hand. And, she thought in terror, it might well be their last embrace in this world.

Father warned me that these Ordeals might lead to my death. At least, if I die, I will die in Tamino's arms. But I would rather live in his arms.

She clung tightly against the winds, bracing herself against the wall of the cliff behind them. In a momentary lull she felt Tamino carefully pushing her into a little niche in the rocks.

"The flute," she cried, trying to get her head close enough to his ear so that she could be heard over the wild roaring of the winds. "The flute—magical weapon of Air—play the flute, Tamino!"

She could see from his face that he did not believe her. But nevertheless he braced himself against the rocks with one hand and struggled to unwrap the silks in which the flute was tied at his waist. As soon as the cloth was loosened the wind seized it and away it flew down the vast canyon between the cliffs, sailing like a bird, the long ends flapping and beating. He had to struggle to bring the flute to his lips because the gusts threatened to tear it from his hands. He flattened his body out against the rocks, spread-eagled there, pressing his shoulders against the wall with all his strength. Pamina dared not remain there in the safety of the niche; she crawled out, not daring to look down, trying to give him the small shelter of her body so that he could raise the flute and blow into it. He gestured angrily at her, signaling imperatively that she should get back to the relative shelter of the rock without delay, but Pamina ignored that.

"Play! Play the flute!"

Even with the shelter of her body it was not easy for him to get the flute to his lips, and Pamina, trembling, shivering, felt the agonizing slowness of every movement. The wind sucked the breath from their lungs with its freezing cold, and his first tentative breath into the flute produced only a small thin sound, vanishing in the winds.

But at last a soft, peaceful melody, so quiet that it could be heard only in snatches over the furious roar of the storm, began to sound. As Tamino played on, pressing himself to the wall with fierce concentration, Pamina began to hear the flute's melody, first momentarily, then for longer and longer intervals at a time as the winds began to die.

And after a time the sound of the flute began to dominate the winds; the tearing hurricane died to soft airs and at last Tamino relaxed and lowered the flute. Pamina drew a deep breath and looked round.

They stood on a high narrow ledge. Below them, a sheer cliff fell away thousands of feet to where, almost invisible below, the pale shimmer of a trickle of river could just be seen. A few feet ahead of them the ledge cracked and fell away into rubble. Above them the mountainside rose to impassable peaks. Gusty winds still careened down the ledge, though they were not strong enough now to dislodge the two who stood there.

Tamino said, "Now what?"

Pamina's voice was shaky. "We seem to have mastered at least a part of the element of Air. But how are we any better off for it?"

Tamino crept carefully to the very edge of the narrow pathway against the rock, knelt and peered over, while Pamina held her breath.

"There's no way down," he said at last. "I don't think we can climb it, either way. I thought there was a path over that way—" he pointed, leaning over so far that Pamina's breath caught in her throat. "But even if there was, we'd have to get down there first. There's no room to jump down, and no way to climb—the cliff face is almost like glass."

"There must be some way," Pamina said. "I know the Ordeals are dangerous. Yet there are many among the Brotherhood who have passed them, and so did my own mother. Dangerous, yes; life-threatening, as we have seen. But they would not make the Ordeals impossible; what would be the point of that? If they are possible for others, there must be some way for us."

Tamino considered that for a moment. "I'm sure you are right," he said, "but it's hard to imagine what choice we have. Are we supposed to grow wings and fly down to demonstrate our mastery of the element of Air? If so, I fear Sarastro has overestimated my abilities, for I was not born of sorcerer kin, and I never heard that anyone in my family had any magical powers whatever."

"If they expected us to display any magical powers," Pamina said, "it's hard to believe they wouldn't have taught us first how to use them."

Tamino was thinking, the flute in his hand. He said at last, "The last thing Sarastro said to me was that the flute was a very powerful magical weapon. And it did control the winds and probably kept us from being blown from this place altogether. I suppose I could play it again and see what happens. It has saved us already once, and we were not told that we could use it once only. If it is the weapon of the element of Air, and we were given no other—perhaps we are intended to use it to master this."

He put the flute to his lips and began to play. First he played a slow, stately dance, while Pamina looked upward over the peaks, remembering the garment which had flown away like a bird. To be a bird, it seemed, was the only way to get out of here. Trapped high in these elemental cliffs, what other escape could there be?

Tamino had said his folk had no magical powers, that none of his kin were of wizard-kind. But she was daughter to the Starqueen, and her father the most powerful sorcerer of Atlas-Alamesios.

The music of the flute had shifted. It seemed to be answering the spiraling currents over the peaks, shifting and changing with the airs that Pamina could see, floating, almost visible. She stretched out her arms and was not at all surprised to see long pinion feathers sprouting from the fingers. Her body seemed clothed in black feathers; her talons clung to the rock. Tamino recoiled as she stretched her talons toward him.

She looked out over the almost visible airs, the columns of wind, the updrafts of warm air, the scattered flying clouds over the peaks. *Now I can fly free, and why should I burden myself with a weaker?* In her mind she lifted and soared; the wind lifted her free of the ledge and she was off down the wind, with the dizzying joy of mastering the Air. *If he could not fol-*

low, that was his misfortune, but he would not be the first to fail the Ordeals.

And then a purely human memory struck at her.

I pledged myself to walk these Paths at his side, and he has not forsaken me. A memory was in the bird-mind: Tamino, thrusting her frail human form into the safety of the niche, so that she would not be blown to the distant rocks, and smashed living into fragments.

Yet her mind was filled with the fickle ecstasy of the winds, her wings ached for the freedom of the sky. She knew she must act quickly, or the mind of the bird-form she had taken would overpower her human memory and she would not be able to remember Tamino. She opened her lips—her beak?—but all that came out was a high eagle scream. She flapped her wings in frustration. She had lost the power of human speech. She opened her talons to clutch at him and he moved back in sudden terror, so that she feared he would fall off the ledge. They could not communicate in this form, and the ledge certainly was not large enough for both of them for more than a moment.

If he would only remember to trust the flute again . . .

Almost as if in answer, Tamino raised it to his lips and began to play. To her sharpened senses it seemed very loud; and then, astonished, she heard words in the sounds. But she should not be surprised, she thought; the flute was the magical weapon of the element of Air.

"Pamina, my beloved, is it you, really you? Fly to safety, then, my love. I have no such magical powers, but at least, if I must attempt that terrible climb down the rocks, I need not be hindered by fears for your safety. And perhaps you should take the flute; if I do not come safely to ground, at least the flute will not fall with me and be destroyed."

"No!" It came out in a long shrieking cry. She dared

not flap her wings again or she might startle him right off the ledge. She stretched her wings, felt them grow longer, longer, felt her body swelling, and with all her heart, in a fury of frustration she *willed* the words toward him.

"Tamino! Hold me, clasp me round the neck, tightly."

Did the words reach him? He was bending, tearing a strip from his tunic; like herself, he had lost his cloak to the winds. Quickly he knotted it round the flute and tied it securely at his belt. Then, although he looked frightened, he stepped toward Pamina and clutched her around the neck. She could not feel his hands through her feathers, but when she judged he was securely holding her, she stretched out her long wings and raised herself into the sky.

He was heavier than she had believed. She felt herself sinking down, down, and frantically flapped her wings to gain height. Then a current of air caught them in an updraft and they soared higher and higher, clearing the peaks. She looked down for a moment and with monstrously amplified vision, saw all of the countryside of Atlas-Alamesios lying spread out before her. It lay there, from her mother's city to the Temple of Sarastro, to the burning deserts of the Changing Lands where she had never gone.

At first she thought it was cloud which lay across the sky, a long, dark cloud like trailing wings. She flew toward the cloud which lay stretched across the city of Sarastro like some long vulturine shadow, now almost heedless of the weight of Tamino clinging to her throat. And then she heard the voice.

"Pamina, Pamina, my darling child . . ."

Her mother's voice; and now she saw that the cloud was like a dark robe stretched that away behind the paler nimbus that was formed into the well-loved features; that her mother was flying beside her. They flew side by side.

"You have learned to fly; you have taken up your heritage as my daughter and my heir, my most precious one. Come, together we will fly to my city."

Long habit of obedience made Pamina turn her wings in that direction.

"What is that wretched burden you carry round your neck? Drop it now, my child, you will not need it in my city. But give me the flute first. It was mine; I was tricked into giving it to that false young man who swore to rescue you and restore you to me. Sarastro has no shadow of right to it."

"No? But he fashioned it, Mother, as the magical weapon it is. And it was you who stole it from his temple when you departed." She did not question how she had come to know this. She heard an eagle scream, but it was her mother's voice, filled with rage, and the next thing she knew, she had turned and was fleeing down the wind, cowering in the shadow of the monstrous cloud-bird which followed on the wings of the storm. Tamino's weight still clung to her body, weighing her down, and she could not move and fly as freely as she would because of that weight.

"Pamina, let him go! Let him fall! This is between us now, mother and daughter, he has no part in our quarrel—"

"But he is my promised husband," she tried to say, and heard the words only in the eerie birdlike scream. She could not face and fight her mother in the Star-queen's own realm of the Air. She must somehow carry herself to safety.

Swiftly she turned, fleeing back into the shadow of the cliffs, trying to take shelter there. Down, down into the gorge between the mountains, seeking landmarks which would carry her into Sarastro's realm, with her mother's despairing voice in her ears.

"Pamina, Pamina, my darling, why have you betrayed me?"

Her wings were tiring, beat upon beat, with every movement sending stabs of pain through her heart. Tamino's weight was an agonizing burden, and there seemed something else. The flute which weighed her down, the flute—giving off painful sparkles of light—heavy, heavy, a stone, heavier than all of Tamino's body. She shook herself in pain, and heard Tamino's cry of terror. No, she dared not try to free herself, she must bear this burden which would weigh her down, that she would fall like a stone into the sea. She could see the sea below her; would she fall there and drown with Tamino in the depths?

Now she flew in the shadow of the long cloud which had borne her mother's face, a dark cloud darkening her eyes and she saw little flecks of pale light inside her eyes and brain. But a light shone before her, the light of Sarastro's temple. Her wings beat with desperation; the shadow was almost covering her fleeing form, and she knew that if she came wholly within that shadow she would never escape again. The shadow stooped over her, poised to pounce on her. She flew over the band of light, and suddenly the shadow was gone.

She flew down and her talons touched the rooftop where she had stood once with her mother's dagger in her hand and looked down on the sacrificial processions in the Starqueen's city. The bird-form dissolved, and Pamina slumped down on the roof, strengthless, Tamino's body cushioning her fall. She did not even feel the priest's hands catching her, lifting her up.

CHAPTER EIGHTEEN

*T*HEY had rested and recovered from the Ordeal. Tamino was half afraid to face Pamina now; in his mind he saw again the terrifying change that had come over her, when she spread her wings and became the great bird, changing again, larger and larger, till she was large enough to sweep him away, carry him down the cliffs to safety. At this very moment he did not know how he had had courage to cling fast to her during those dreadful moments when he clung, not to Pamina's body, but the terrifying shape of the mighty raptor.

Looking at her now, it was impossible to think of her in that frightful way. As masters of two of the four elements, they had been told, they were no longer required to wear the robes of neophytes, and Pamina had bathed and been dressed in a heavy garment of coarse white silk, belted with a plaited cord of brown woven with blue; colors which, he had been told when the priest girdled his waist with similar colors, were those appointed to the elements of Earth and Air. Her fair hair had been brushed and braided into a single plait; she looked very young, her soft features still childish. Yet, faced with the Ordeal of the Air, she had shown herself a powerful sorceress.

"I didn't know that you could do that—turn yourself into a bird," he said, uneasily.

Her smile was so faint it was almost imperceptible. "Neither did I."

"I think you must have passed that Ordeal and I failed it, Pamina. You rescued me, when there was nothing I could do."

Her fingers strayed to the cord at her waist, identical with his own. She said, "I don't think so. I couldn't have done anything, except for the flute when you played it. Without that, I would have died there with you. We came through the Ordeal together. As was right for us."

He felt humble before the innocent blue eyes. She was a mighty sorceress; and what was he? For a moment he wondered if he should be afraid of her, the daughter of the mighty Starqueen, and herself bearing these formidable powers. He had had no idea that she possessed such strength, such sorcery.

Nevertheless she was the Pamina with whom he had fallen in love before ever he laid eyes on the living girl. And if it meant that he must somehow acquire magical or wizardly powers before he was worthy of her, well, the Ordeals were the first step to that goal.

But he was frightened. The first Ordeal, that of Earth, had been so simple; but the Ordeal of Air had brought them closer to death than he had ever thought he could be and still survive. He was afraid as he had not been since he faced the dragon in the Changing Lands.

He looked at Pamina. She looked calm, but he remembered how she had trembled, in the bird-form, when he clung to her. He, at least, had been reared as a prince, taught to hunt and to fight and to face danger, and she was a gently reared young woman who, until this moment, had never had to endure even a pinprick of fear or danger. His whole heart ached with the wish to protect her.

He had offered her the chance to turn back, with the promise that he would never reproach her, and she had refused. She must, then, take her own way, and they would face the Ordeals together. He was not, after all, sorry that he would have her at his side.

He wished he dared embrace her. He had done so, to protect her against the battering winds, and again, without inhibition, when she bore him in bird-form down from the ledge. Even now the thought of that dizzying flight terrified him, borne out sickeningly over the abyss of empty space, clouds and mountaintops wheeling vertiginously below. He had clutched at her—he had an insane tactual memory of his hands filled with feathers and quills as he touched her, he wished that he could reach out and touch her warm body, her soft breast, just to reassure himself that it had been illusion, that she still possessed, in truth, the warm body of the real woman Pamina that he loved.

"What next?" he wondered aloud, and as if the question had been heard somewhere—who knows, he thought, perhaps it was—the door opened and the guide came in.

"Are you recovered, my children? You may have a little more time if you require it; it is nowhere demanded of you that you face further Ordeals until you have recovered from the last."

Tamino felt a shiver run down his spine. What further testing awaited them? Whatever it was, it would grow no easier with delay.

"If Pamina is ready, I am prepared."

He intercepted a quick glance as she raised her eyes, and saw fear in them. She had displayed so much strength and power in the most recent of the Ordeals that it had not occurred to him that she was frightened

too. She had at least been able to act; he had really
done nothing. He had never considered that perhaps
her action had not been based in strength and confidence, but in the desperation of terror.

But her voice was as steady as his own.

"It will grow no easier with delay. I am ready."

"Then, be it so." The priest raised his hands in
brief invocation. "I consign you to the Ordeal of the
Waters."

Tamino tried hard not to flinch as the guide struck
his hands together. But this time there was no thunderclap; only silence and a very soft sound which,
hours later and in retrospect, Tamino identified as the
music of falling rain.

This time he half expected it; he was floundering,
awash, choked with water in his eyes, in his mouth,
stunned and deafened by the battering noise of surf.
Of course. The Ordeal of Air had dumped them, unprepared, to assault by winds tearing at the cliffs. Salt-
water filled his mouth, and in the reflex of shock he
gasped some of it into his mouth, his lungs, and choked.

He kicked out, and was swimming. Beside him Pamina floundered, fighting the crashing noise of the waves;
by sheer reflex he reached out and dragged her head
above water. She gasped, coughed, managed to kick
out, then was swimming beside him. Her dank hair
flopped into her eyes, and she shook it, hard, to clear
it away so that she could see.

"It is only fair to warn you," she said, coughing,
and he wondered, even then, that he could hear her
clear voice so strongly over the noise of the waves,
"that even if you play the flute, I will not turn into a
fish and carry you to land!"

Tamino found himself laughing, spluttering water
out of his mouth.

"It would seem to be my turn, at that, but I'm afraid

I never mastered the arts of shape-changing. What is the test here? Are we to swim to shore?"

"What shore? Tamino, you know as much about it as I do. I really do wish that they would let us know what they are testing us to learn or to do!" Pamina coughed again—evidently she too had swallowed some water in those first frightening moments. "I cannot imagine that it matters to our spiritual progress whether or not we have learned to swim. Have you the flute?"

Tamino fumbled with one hand at his waist.

"It's there. But it's wet." Cautiously, turning over to float on his back, he managed to get it free. "But I thought it was the magical weapon of Air; what good would it be in the midst of the Waters?"

"I don't know. But if it wasn't intended that we should have it," she said, "we wouldn't have been allowed to bring it with us."

That, he supposed, made a certain amount of sense. But how could he play it, floating on the waters, and what would happen if he did? He hesitated, unwilling to attempt the wrong thing. Like Pamina, he could not believe in a simple test of swimming, any more than he believed that their Ordeal on the cliffs had been a test of their ability to climb mountains. Therefore there must be something more than that to this Ordeal. He could not imagine what it could be.

"But you can swim?" he asked. "Not that it matters to me if you cannot," he added, his free hand still beneath her chin, "but if in fact you can swim, it will give us a little more time to think about what it is that we are expected to do."

"Oh, yes, I can swim. When I was very little I had a dog-halfling for nurse, and she taught me almost before I could walk properly. Poor Rawa," she added, and Tamino, perceiving sadness in her face, wished that he could share her thoughts. "You don't need to hold me up, Tamino, I swim as well as any otter-half-ling or any of the Sea-folk."

He let her go, a little reluctant to take his hand away from even this fleeting and tangential contact with her body. His own mother had died before he was able to remember holding her hand when he was afraid, but he felt that some comforting communication was being denied him.

Nevertheless, if they survived this Ordeal and the others, they would have a lifetime together to share their memories. The flute, in his hand, must somehow be the key. Once or twice, when he had used it, the Messengers had appeared. Perhaps the test of this Ordeal was merely to know when they were out of their depth—and how literally that was true just now! and when to ask for help.

He tried to tread water, to get enough freedom from the all-pervading waves which kept breaking over him, to put the flute to his lips. As he blew across it there was a wet, bubbling sound, and he thought it was about as far from a magical invocation as any sound he had ever heard.

But he did manage to get it to him and after a fashion, to play, not even a melody, a few disjointed notes which, after a time, became a wavering little tune.

For a few minutes nothing happened. He felt very foolish, treading water and blowing into a flute out here in the middle of the ocean. The waves kept breaking over his chin, and every third one or so dunked the flute beneath the surface of the water, so that the tune was drowned in a gurgling sound.

Then, very far away, over the sound of the waves which kept breaking over him and his flute, he heard something else, a distant sound almost like voices. Singing. A whistling sound almost like Papageno's little birdcall whistle, but somehow, subtly, different. Then there was a splash and a face broke water not more than two arm-lengths away from him. A broad face, bewhiskered almost like a cat's, and softly furred except for the snub nose and the large, liquid dark eyes layered with dark and beautiful lashes.

Pamina whispered, "A seal-halfling."

And aloud she said to it, "Can you guide us to land, sister of the Sea?"

Tamino had no idea how she could tell that the sea-creature was female. Some intuition, he supposed, better than his own. The half-human woman backed away suspiciously, treading water and blinking it out of her large and lovely eyes.

"Land? On the land they make slaves of us, but you Human-folk have left us in peace here in the middle of the ocean. What are you doing out here, where none of your kind has ever come?"

"I am not one of the people who would make slaves of you," Tamino said, but he saw that the eyes of the seal-woman were fixed suspiciously on the flute.

"You called us with that and I had no choice but to come."

And suddenly Tamino remembered how, when he had played the flute on the doorstep of the temple, all manner of Halflings had stolen out to listen. The flute had power then over the Halflings, as did Papageno's magical bells.

So what was the test then? To demonstrate his power to command the Halflings of this element? He suspected that if he played the flute, and demanded of this seal-woman that she take them to the land, she would not be able to refuse. Pamina was tiring, he could see that. She swam uncomplaining at his side, but her eyes showed strain, and her movements were sluggish.

"I can swim," he said, "but I do not know where

the land lies. Nevertheless—" and he stopped to think.
What was expected of him now? The seal-woman had
withdrawn and was swimming in circles a little way
from him. Just beyond her, a head just poked from the
water; a face like her own, but larger, broader, more
heavily bewhiskered. With a sudden shudder, Tamino
remembered that male seals were four times the size
of the females, and perhaps male seal-halflings were
in the same proportion. He clutched at the flute; if one
of them should attack him, could he perhaps protect
himself with the flute's music?

He heard the whistling song again. Then the water
broke in a clean splash, and three forms, sleek and
hairless and gray, broke the surface of the sea, leaped
high, and came down between himself and Pamina. A
male, he could see, for all three were naked, another
male, and a female, all three with smooth round eyes
and huge noses, gliding swiftly without apparent motion through the waves. They whistled shrilly to one
another, speech he could not understand. Then one of
the males said to the seal-woman, "Sister, who are
these people, and what do they want in the dominion
of the free people of the Sea?"

Tamino could hear the menace in the words. A Halfling, yes, a Halfling of the Dolphin-people. But this
one had never been subject to Humankind; that was
in the very set of his head, the arrogance with which
his hairless head crested the breeze.

"Human," he said, "there is an ancient warfare, and
an ancient compact, between your people and mine.
Remember? We won freedom from your people, that
we would no longer live in chains and stagnant water
in your land, bound by your evil whistles to bring jewels from the deep and pearls from the hidden fields in
the bottom of the sea. We pledged in return that we
would never eat of your food nor ask it of you, whether

in good seasons or bad; and we took from you a pledge that as we asked nothing of you, so you would ask nothing of us. Of our good will we have destroyed, when we found them, the great sharks that menaced your beaches, so that your children could swim in the oceans without danger, and also of our good will, we have shared with you all the fish in the sea for your food. Why now do you break this agreement with us, and come into our world? For you know well that we are still subject to what you carry in your hand; play on it, and none of the people of the Sea may resist your commands."

"I did not know this," Pamina said. "Believe me, we did not summon you with any desire to command." She wavered, grabbed at Tamino; he put out his hand to support her, clinging to the flute with the other hand.

"Why then did you come here?" demanded the great male dolphin. "You are in our territory, now, not we in yours." He swam swiftly and furiously at Tamino, who ducked under the nearest wave, then surfaced, blinking, trying to clear his eyes of water.

He saw, with sudden clarity, that Pamina was in difficulty. She was not nearly as strong a swimmer as he was himself. He put the flute to his lips. By their own admission, it still had the power to command them, and he could at least protect her with it. Angrily he justified himself; he wouldn't hurt them, but did they really think he was going to let them hurt Pamina?

The enormous male seal he had seen at a distance made a swift rush toward them. Tamino grabbed the flute, holding it for dear life, then swam toward Pamina and put an arm around her.

"Hang on. This could be very nasty. These Halflings are not like the ones in the city; they're not tame. I may have to try and control them by playing the flute. I don't want to do it. They're free people. But I can't let them hurt you. So hold on tight, because if they rush us again, I'm going to stop them, whatever I have to do."

He could tell that she too was scared and frightened. "What do we have to do with some old war between our people? Can't they see that all we want from them is a little help which wouldn't hurt them at all?"

He put the flute to his lips, and stopped, seeing seal-halflings and dolphins swimming in circles, not far from them. But far enough that he was no longer panicked.

He lowered the flute. Surely there must be a better way to handle it than this. Somehow, remembering Sarastro's words, he did not think they had been sent out here to recapture the Sea-folk as slaves. It sounded totally unlike everything he had heard among the priesthood in Sarastro's realm.

He said tentatively, "You have to obey the flute?"

"You know that, Son of the Ape," said the great male seal-halfling, his huge sad eyes filled with bitterness. "You hold our lives and our people at hostage. What can we say to defend ourselves, while you hold a weapon against which there is neither negotiation nor defense? Why do you ask when you have the power to command? How can we even run away, when you hold in your hand the power to summon us back again, like toys or playthings?"

Tamino said, "Believe it or not as you will, brother of the Sea; I knew nothing of this. I was brought here against my will, but there must be a better way than this. The flute is not mine; I am obliged by my oath to guard it. But I swear on my life I will command nothing of you..." he broke off, looking at Pamina who was now struggling to stay afloat. She was exhausted, and no wonder, she had borne the brunt of the Ordeal of Air, and he had done so little to help her.

He said, "As for myself, I would like nothing better

than to leave your realms as quickly as I can, and never return. If one of you will point me in the direction I should go, I will oblige you immediately."

He tightened his arms around Pamina. "I will try to carry my companion." Pamina had borne him, unaided, from the heights of Air; he would carry her through the Waters if he must. "But I do not know the way; might one of you guide me, at a distance if you will, to the closest land?"

The seal-woman who had surfaced first said guardedly, "Land lies there. Just over the horizon." She broke water, swimming swiftly in a direction Tamino could not identify; there were no signs whether it was north, south, east, or west. "An hour's swim, more or less, will bring you to the land."

An hour. Tamino's heart sank. Could he swim so far and carry Pamina as well? Was it right or fair that his very life, to say nothing of the mastery of the Ordeals, should depend on his ability to swim when he had never before in his life attempted to swim or float for more than a few minutes in a guarded pool? To add to his dread, he saw at a distance a thin narrow fin cutting the water. A shark? No, it was not fair or right. Yet he could command these creatures with the flute. And if he would not do it for himself, still it could not be wrong to do it for Pamina.

He tightened his arms around her. The seal-woman, swimming rapidly, was almost out of sight. He raised the flute to his lips, feeling that it was justified. It was not as if he intended them any harm, and when Pamina was safely on land again, he would release them at once.

"Tamino—" Pamina whispered, catching at his arm. "Are we lost? Do you even know the way to land? I don't. But these people do. I am sure this was why we were given the flute; a test of mastery over them, Human over Halfling."

Her grip on his arm was painful now; she looked so weary that Tamino was terrified for her. Her eyes were red and swollen with the salt, her face drawn with exhaustion and strain, and her weight heavy on his arm. Whatever the cost, even if he accepted failure in the Ordeals, he must get her safely to land and rest. If he must use the flute to command help from the Sea-people, then let it be so. He raised it to his lips and blew an experimental note. The Sea-creatures, the Seal-folk, the three Dolphin-people, stopped dead in the water, their great dark eyes staring at Tamino, with the flute in his hand.

Then, with a long sigh, a little muffled because at that moment a wave broke over his face, he lowered it again.

"How can I prove to you that I have no wish to command you? We are at your mercy, my brothers and my sisters. We need your help in reaching the land. Yet we implore it as a gift; I will not command it."

He felt Pamina twitch restlessly on his arm, and knew he had disappointed her. But if the price of success in the Ordeals was to become a tyrant over the Halflings, to treat them as the Starqueen's ladies had done, he wanted none of it. The Starqueen had passed through the Ordeals, and it had made her a no more worthy person.

The dolphin leader blew water from his pursed mouth and said, "Give us what you hold, and we will guide you to land, and I will myself carry your companion; I can see that she is weary."

"It is not mine to give," said Tamino, "but I will engage my honor not to play a single note upon it."

"Not good enough," said the huge, furred male seal-halfling. "What do we know of your honor? We have seen little enough of it among Humankind." He splashed with his flat splayed feet and dived deep. Pamina sighed and went heavy on Tamino's arm; she had fainted.

Tamino said to the dolphin-man, who seemed to be their leader, "I have no knowledge of your honor, either. I am entrusted with the care of the flute; it is not mine to give. How do I know that with it once in your hands, you would not swim away and leave us to die?"

"Do you think I am a Son of the Ape or of the Serpent, to speak what is not true?" demanded the dolphin-halfling. "You know me not, but my name is Rock-watcher, and never in the history of the Sea has any of my folk violated his word. If I should die halfway to land, or be eaten by a shark, all of my people would protect you at the risk of their lives, that my word might not fall through the waves and become Seafoam! Shall I call a hundred of the Sea-creatures to witness the truth of what I speak?"

"I do not know them any better than I know you," Tamino said, distracted, his whole heart concentrated on Pamina's limp body on his arm. "I am entrusted with the safety of this flute, but I will make you a bargain. Help us to land, and any one of your people whom you can trust may hold and carry the flute. Set it on land, and I will pledge my own honor as prince that it will remain untouched and unblown until all of your people are out of earshot again."

Rock-watcher whistled shrilly in disbelief. "Never have I or any of my forefathers trusted a Son of Apekind."

"Nevertheless," said Tamino, "you told me that the old compact between our peoples had remained unviolated till now. I may not give you the flute, for Sarastro trusted me with it, but in the name of the compact of which you spoke, will you not trust me as you yourself would wish to be trusted, brother-halfling?"

"Sarastro." Again the shrill whistle, then Rock-watcher said, "So be it. Wave-rider, come and take the flute, and bear it to land safe, for my pledged honor."

The female dolphin-creature swam to Tamino, holding out one stubby flipperlike arm for the flute. Tamino reluctantly let it go. He did not more than half trust the dolphin-creatures, for all their talk of honor. Yet there seemed no alternative. His eyes were stinging with the salt, and his arms and legs felt as if they weighed a ton apiece. Wave-rider grabbed the flute and immediately swam out of reach, bobbing on the waves and staring at him with her huge eyes. Tamino noticed her sleek nakedness, the small breasts, no more than nubs of nipples low on her belly, the hairless well-shaped head. She and the third dolphin swam close together, their movements barely stirring the water, and Tamino contrasted their effortless movements, gliding side by side, with his own heavy splashing progress. As they swam together their limbs intertwined and they rubbed, one against the other, with a perfect, innocent sensuality. Would he and Pamina ever arrive at such a closeness? Why was he thinking about that now, when the important question was would they survive to land at all?

Rock-watcher glided through the water to Tamino; held out his arms.

"Give her to me," he commanded, and slid his arms under Pamina's body. "Ugh, how those ornaments of yours drag through the water, how can you swim in such things?" He bent his head down and tugged with his teeth at Pamina's tunic and ripped it through, pulling it away. Tamino, shocked, averted his eyes and cried out in protest as the sleek naked dolphin-man held Pamina's bare white body against his own. Then the other dolphins, laughing, ringed Tamino round, nipping at his clothing, tearing it away.

"Now you can swim like us," they teased, and nudged him along in the water. Tamino twisted his head to stare at Pamina. What would she think, how frightened would she be when she recovered to find herself held naked in the arms of a strange halfling? The two other dolphins slid alongside him, pressing their bodies close to his, bearing him up.

"Don't struggle and splash so," said the female dolphin—was her name Wave-rider? "We won't let you fall, but try and swim as we do, letting the water carry you." She emphasized the words with a sensuous little wriggle which Tamino found intensely embarrassing. The other male dolphin, too, pressed round him in the water, close against him, bearing him up with a touch, moving along his naked body. He tried to keep his mind barriered against the awareness of all this nakedness, this intimate sensuality.

Innocent—they were innocent, but he was not, that was the trouble, he was all too aware of it. Yet they seemed to take it for granted; the female dolphin pressed her sleek soft cool coat against his, seeming to enjoy the contact completely. There was nothing he could do about it, and after a moment he stopped trying, enjoying the touch and giving himself up to the water. The two of them bore him along far more swiftly than he could possibly have swum by himself, and it helped that he was no longer burdened with Pamina's weight, but he was troubled by seeing her held close in Rock-watcher's arms, borne along like that. He twisted his head to try and see her, but the two dolphins on either side of him nuzzled him hard to keep his head in the right direction, whistled gleefully and ducked him under the next wave.

His feet scraped land. Wave-rider bent and nuzzled

along the whole length of his body, appreciatively, whistling laughter. Rock-watcher hauled himself out on the sand, Pamina in his arms, and gently let her fall. Tamino was cruelly startled to see how clumsy the dolphin-man appeared on land, after the incomparable grace he displayed in the sea.

Wave-rider still held the flute. She dashed into the surf, standing there, borne up and down by the waves, her sleek grayish body expressing defiance.

Rock-watcher dived toward her, nipped angrily at her hand, at her neck, at her breasts, till she let the flute fall from her hand. He took it in his mouth, with the same unself-consciousness with which a man would have held it in his fingers, and came to Tamino.

"It goes against my heart to return to you this instrument of slavery, yet what I have promised I shall perform. Take it." Scowling angrily, he gave it to Tamino.

Tamino said, blinking salt from his eyes, "I owe you thanks, Brother of the Sea."

"You owe me nothing; you could have commanded our help and willingly did forgo it," said Rock-watcher, scowling. "Never again shall I say of a Son of the Ape that they cannot speak with a straight tongue."

"For my part," Tamino said, suddenly conscious of his nakedness again—why should he be so aware of it when Rock-watcher bore his with splendid unconcern, "I pledge that the old compact between Mankind and the Sea-folk will never be broken by me."

"So be it," said Rock-watcher, and whistled a long shrill note. The three dolphins leaped high, broke the waves, and disappeared beneath them. Tamino stood watching them go, until a cry of distress from Pamina recalled him to himself.

"Tamino! What has happened?" And then he realized that they were alone on the shore, that they were both naked, and that for all he knew, they had both failed the Ordeal of Water. A furry head, with large lovely eyes, surfaced from the water. It was the seal-woman, and clenched in her hand, she held something which she extended toward Pamina.

"For you," she said softly, "because you kept your word to us, my Sister of the Land."

It was a large, shining pearl. Pamina flung her arms around the seal-woman and received a damp embrace. Then the seal-woman also embraced Tamino quickly, hurried down into the surf, and dove out of sight.

And suddenly it did not matter to Tamino that they were both naked, that they were alone on the shore and must somehow make their way back into Sarastro's realm. He had a feeling that they had passed the Ordeal of Water, after all; and with the flute which he still bore, and with the pearl in Pamina's hand, they were none the worse.

When he was reasonably sure that the Sea-folk were all out of earshot, and thus sure of his promise to them, he put the flute to his lips again. This time, as he had thought would happen, as the first notes quivered on the air, the three Messengers appeared shimmering against the light, all but invisible.

"What would you have, Masters of Water?" they demanded. "And what is the reason for your curious costume?"

Pamina cast down her eyes; but it was she who answered, before Tamino could collect himself to do so.

"We wear the clothing of the Sea-people," she said firmly, "but it is not suitable for the land. Bring us to our rooms in the temple, and find us suitable clothing."

"It shall be done at once, Masters of the element of Water," said the Messengers in their voices that were like blended song. "For the element of Air is yours to command." There was a soft sound like a great rushing of wings, and they were standing in the court of the temple. Tamino's guide was there, as was a priestess who covered Pamina at once with a great white robe laced with cords of blue and brown and a new color, green. The guide covered Tamino with a similar robe.

Pamina, clutching her pearl, was very pale.

"Reverend father, if the last of the Ordeals, the Ordeal of Fire, starts by dumping us into the crater of a volcano, or something like that, I intend to go no further with the Ordeals. And you may tell Sarastro so for me."

The guide laughed. After a moment, so did the priestess. "You need not worry about that," he said. "The last of the Ordeals, like the first, is metaphorical; it is only in symbol that you need face the fire. Come now, my brother and my sister; rest and refresh yourselves, for tomorrow you must face the Changing Lands. And when you are done with that Ordeal, I doubt not, you will feel it would have been the lesser trial to be faced with the fire of that volcano you fear."

CHAPTER NINETEEN

"*THE essence of an Ordeal,*" *the guide said,* is that it invariably takes place in a wasteland. The Ordeal of Earth required you to face yourselves within reasonably familiar surroundings, while the later Ordeals placed you in unfamiliar and frightening circumstances. The Ordeal of Fire takes place within the ultimate wasteland of the Changing Lands. You cannot possibly return *unchanged*; you can only hope that the change will not be for the worse."

Tamino supposed it was something to have been reassured that they would not have to pass through literal fire. What frightened him most was that, while the magic flute was secured by a strip of linen to his belt, his bow and arrows had been returned to him and he had also been given a sword in a scabbard. Pamina had been given a small sharp dagger.

"May I ask a question, Holy Father?" Pamina asked. She had noticed that, of all the priests who wore different colored woven cords at their waists, he alone wore one of each of the four colors, brown and green and blue and the final strand of red.

"Certainly you may ask," he said serenely. "I cannot promise to answer if the question is not a proper one, but you may always ask."

"Why is it that, while we were thrust into the Ordeals of Air and Water completely unprepared, we are here given instructions?"

The guide smiled.

"That I may answer," he said. "You were thrust into them unprepared, because this is the nature of Air and Water. Life may seem perfectly certain and assured, and without the slightest warning, you will be thrust into a situation where your whole system of life, physical, spiritual, and moral, takes a turn so unexpected that you could not possibly foresee it. It is easy to adhere to ethical principles when all is going well, or when you have a chance to work out what is expected of you. If Monostatos, for instance, had been told that he was being tested specifically for the ability to restrain his lust, I have not the slightest doubt that he would have behaved to you as correctly as Sarastro himself. But we made him think that the essence of the test was otherwise; although we had admonished him, of course, that he must demonstrate his own best self at all times. Thus tested, given the opportunity to choose, you know his choice."

It would be a long time, Pamina supposed, before she could think of Monostatos without shivering revulsion.

Tamino took her hand. After she had carried him clutched to her breast, although as a bird of prey, and after they had both been borne naked through the waters by the innocent sensuality of the dolphins, it would be a foolish hypocrisy to pretend to the priest that they had no awareness of one another. The test of Earth had never been that he should not desire Pamina, only that he should prove himself in command of that desire until the proper time.

"I do not understand any of the Ordeals we have passed," he said, "but I do not suppose I am allowed to ask for an explanation."

"That is certainly your right, since you have passed the Ordeals in question," said the guide. Why did Tamino have the faint, but definite impression that he too was relieved to delay a little? "In the Ordeal of Air, you both discovered your own hidden qualities. Under the Sign of the Eagle, Pamina realized her own powers. And you, Tamino, found within yourself the willingness to be helped by someone you have always considered weaker than yourself. Where strength would not serve, you accepted that you could not always be in command or in control."

"And the Ordeal of Water?" Pamina asked. "I told myself at the time that it could not possibly matter in a testing of our spiritual abilities to know whether or not we could swim. Was it only a test of resourcefulness, or the ability to survive adversity, then?"

"Not quite," the guide answered. "The major test was whether you could restrain yourselves from the temptation to make use of the Halflings for your own personal purposes."

"Then it seems to me that we failed," Tamino said. "For they told us that they had no means of restraining us, and might as well help us willingly, since we could command their help if they did not give it willingly."

"It is permissible to negotiate or bargain," the guide said, "but even knowing that you were in a position of power, you bargained with a care for their dignity as human beings; you did not command them as slaves or humiliate them. When you let the flute pass out of your hands, rather than allow them to think you commanded where you should beg their assistance, Tamino, you triumphed."

Pamina hung her head. "I wanted him to use the flute to command," she said almost inaudibly. "I was so afraid—"

"But you allowed him to make that decision," the

guide said. "You are the daughter of the Starqueen, Pamina; it was always within the bounds of possibility that you would snatch the flute from his hands and yourself make the forbidden command."

"Then there must have been a time," said Pamina sorrowfully, "when even my mother resisted that temptation—"

But as she had half expected, the guide remained silent, shaking his head mournfully. She wondered if he had known and perhaps loved her mother as well. She would never know.

"To be tried in the Fire of the Changing Lands," the guide said, "it is enough to know that, as you have done in the previous tests, you must remain your best self at all times. And now I may delay you no longer."

He struck his hands together, and the temple vanished from sight.

They were standing together in a barren wasteland, their hands still clasped. Low rustling bushes surrounded them; high overhead the sun blazed with the blinding light of noonday. On the distant horizon, it seemed that ruins rose, ancient walls and pillars, but Tamino could not be sure whether or not it was a mirage.

Turning slowly, Pamina discovered in another quarter of the horizon the shadow of a city which might have been her mother's citadel; but she was not sure. The sand was hot even through the sandals she was wearing. She had never been here before; but she was sure that, as the guide had told them, they were in the Changing Lands. She had never ventured into them before. Her mother had forbidden it, and until she had been taken to Sarastro's palace it had never entered her mind that anyone would venture to disobey her mother's will.

"Well," she said to Tamino, with a little wavering smile, "no matter what he says, I still think it's better than being dumped into real fire."

Tamino was grateful that she could make a joke about it. For that matter, he too was grateful that the Ordeal of Fire did not begin, as Air and Water had begun, with a literal confrontation with the element in question.

He was not a coward—or at least until he had entered upon the Ordeals he had never thought himself one—but for him, at least, it was easier to know what to do when he was not struggling for his life. He supposed it was easier for everyone.

Nevertheless, under the blazing of the fierce sun, he realized that there was a literal, as well as a metaphorical, element to the Ordeal of Fire. In his original journey from his father's kingdom, he had dared the desert sun for a little too long and had been sunburned and half blinded in consequence. He said, "I'm just as well pleased it's not the real thing, but this sun is fire enough for me." He tore a strip from the edge of his robe and fastened it loosely over his head as a makeshift cowl to shade his eyes and offer some protection from the heat.

"That's not a bad idea. I should have thought of it." Pamina followed suit swiftly, looking out at him from under the hood. "This time, when there's no immediate danger, perhaps we can stop and think what we're being tested *for*. I knew it didn't matter whether we could swim, or for that matter whether we could climb down from cliffs. And I was right about that. Now he tells us what the truth is, that we discovered hidden qualities within ourselves—"

"You did," Tamino interrupted. "According to the guide I simply learned to let you take command when necessary." He managed a weak smile. "I was taught it was the business of a prince to look after all his subjects and always to take command. Perhaps it was only a test of my pride—"

Pamina said in a low voice, "I am more frightened of that than of anything else, Tamino. The test of pride. You know that the Starqueen—my mother—once passed all these Ordeals, the first and the last woman to do so. And look what has become of her? I am her daughter. I do not want to gain power, or to take command, if I must become like her, and end like *that*. And already I am far too much like her; Tamino, in the Ordeal of Water, I would have used the flute, or forced you to use it, to command the Dolphin-folk. I do not think I am fit for this Ordeal, Tamino."

"I do not think the priests would have let you undertake it if you were not fit, Pamina. It is their business to know such things."

"But they make mistakes. They must have made a mistake with my mother. Because she was heiress to the Kingdom of Night, hereditary Starqueen—so they must have certified her fit, and look what has happened?" Pamina lowered her eyes so he could not see, but Tamino thought there were tears on her face. "I believed in her. There must have been a time when my father believed in her. Must I be like her, Tamino? Do I have to be like that?"

"I cannot imagine that you ever could be."

Tamino wished, harder than he had ever wished anything in the world, that he could take her in his arms and comfort her. But something in him sensed that this was a very real part of her own Ordeal, to overcome this fear. And this she must face alone; if he tried to comfort or reassure her, she might never fully face whatever terrors arose in her. He had feared her, in the bird-form, almost as much as he feared her mother. If they were to be married, somehow he too would have to overcome that fear; he could not, or did not want to, imagine living in constant dread of her powers of sorcery.

He found himself wondering how Sarastro himself had managed to overcome that fear.

At last he said in a low voice, "Perhaps Sarastro loved your mother so much that he could not bear to refuse her anything. I love you too, Pamina. Perhaps that is part of the purpose of this Ordeal, for both of us, to help each other know when we may legitimately use power and when we should not. At the beginning of this, the priest said to us that each of us had strengths and weaknesses which would complement those of the other. I kept you from using the flute to command the Sea-halflings, and that turned out to be the right thing, so together we did what was right. Also, you dissuaded me from trying to climb down, and that was right too, so each of us kept the other from a dangerous and possibly fatal mistake. I am sure your mother and Sarastro could have done this for each other but for some reason they did not. We do not even know whether they were allowed to face the Ordeals together. But you and I *are* together, Pamina. Together we can make those decisions, and avoid disaster."

"I am sure you are right," she said, but she was almost crying. "But Sarastro loved my mother, too, and he did not manage to keep her from becoming— becoming what she is. What good is it, then, to love?"

"Sarastro loved your mother," Tamino said, wishing that he even dared to take her hand in his, "but we are not sure that your mother loved Sarastro. Judging how she spoke to me of him—and comparing it with the way Sarastro speaks of her—somehow I do not think she loved him, certainly not as much as he loved her." He thought, but did not say, that he did not believe the Starqueen loved anybody, or was capable of loving at all.

But it seemed to him that Pamina heard the unspoken words, that perhaps she would always know what he was thinking, and this was frightening to him too. He did not want to fear her; he wanted to love her. He wanted nothing to come before his love for her.

But now when he saw her wilting in the fierce heat, he realized that care for her, the need to protect her, would always come before anything else, certainly before his fear. He could not imagine anyone attempting to protect the Starqueen or the Starqueen allowing herself to be protected. Had there ever been a time when even she had been a vulnerable woman, as Pamina was now?

"We should try to find some shade," he said. "Even if this is a trial by fire, I doubt that we would be any good to the priesthood if we were broiled alive. Just as the Water Ordeal was not a test of whether we could swim, I am sure this is not a test of our ability to endure sunstroke."

She smiled faintly. "I would like nothing better than some shade," she said, "but where will we find it?"

He looked at the low line of trees on the horizon. "There must be shade somewhere. Certainly under those trees, if we could reach them. That is, if they are not a mirage. In any case there seems nowhere else worth trying to go. Shall we try and reach them, then?"

"That seems reasonable to me," Pamina agreed, and they set off in that direction.

It seemed that they walked for a long time, but as Tamino had half expected, the trees came no nearer. Pamina was pale and gasping with the heat; even more than shade, they needed water. And then he remembered the miraculous date palm that had appeared to him in his own need.

"We are in the Changing Lands," he said, "perhaps the test here is to see whether we can change them in a suitable way to our needs."

"It seems to me," Pamina argued, "that this would be something like using the magic flute to compel obedience from the dolphins—forbidden."

Tamino thought that over very carefully as he wiped sweat from his forehead. He said at last, "I can't believe it is so. We do not even know whether the Changing Lands are really like this, or whether we only see them this way. They were like this, a barren desert, when I first came into them. But as I traveled through them, they altered constantly, and I do not know which of the appearances is real, and which is an illusion to test us." He told her about the date palm, and about the antelope that had become, first a gazelle, then a squirrel.

"And I have wondered, since I began the Ordeals, did it change? Or was it a squirrel all along, and only showed itself to me as other animals for some reason of its own, or some law of the Changing Lands that we do not know?" Talking made his throat dry; but it was easier to bear that, than to bear the burden of all these thoughts unshared.

"I don't know the answer to your question," Pamina said, "but here at least is shade. We were looking in the wrong direction, that is all."

Tamino turned to see the bush, with its thick, dark green, spiny blades, so unlike ordinary leaves outside the desert. He would have sworn it had not been there a few minutes ago, but what else did he expect in the Changing Lands? Was it there, or an illusion? Did it matter? Would an illusion of shade protect them from the real sun? Together, parting its leaves, they crawled gratefully into the shelter of the thick, succulent blades.

Under the bush it was dark by contrast, and cool. Pamina lay back on the dry ground, wiping her face with the ample sleeves of her robe. He thought, Already she is weary and exhausted, and the Ordeal has barely begun.

She saw his eyes on her, and smiled faintly, sitting up.

"Look," she said, "we are not even alone here." She pointed to the sand.

A handful of little lizards, not more than a hand-span long, some of them no thicker than his thumb, scurried round and round the sand, climbed on the small rocks, fought, pounced on almost-invisible sand beetles, copulated, climbing unexpectedly atop one another for a moment or two, then falling off and scurrying again around the business of living; pouncing on sand beetles, fighting, crawling atop the nearest female for quick and unpremeditated sex, and starting all over again.

Pamina murmured, "They are like the dog-halflings. Or Monostatos."

"They are like many people I know in my father's kingdom, Pamina. I think perhaps most people are like that, outside the temple."

She said, and it occurred to him that she was very pale. "I hope not. That would be terrible, to live like that. That is the way my mother wants the Halflings to live. I think Sarastro wants them to be something more. To teach them what they are capable of. I hate to be disloyal to my mother. But"—he saw her stop and moisten her lips with her tongue—"I am afraid I think Sarastro is right, and so in any case my mother would have—would have cast me off."

They were very close under the bush, and Tamino

did what he had been wanting to do since first he saw her; he reached out his arms and pulled Pamina into them, holding her close to him. He did not honestly think he meant any more, at that moment, than to comfort her, to take away that awful desolation in her eyes.

But then it occurred to him that perhaps the time was right. Perhaps it was the right time to confirm to her that they would always be together, that they would make all decisions together, strengthened and comforted by their mutual love. And what better way to seal that love? She came willingly into his arms, and upturned her mouth to his for their first kiss.

For the first moment Pamina had been a little frightened; the memory of Monostatos's rough hands on her had created a reflex quiver when Tamino touched her, but as she felt the softness of his mouth, the slight roughness of his cheek so different from hers, she relaxed. This was right, this was nothing forced on her against her will. Tamino was even a little tentative, evidently afraid to press her further than she wished. She pressed herself close to him, opening her lips almost wildly to his kiss. And for a few moments, in that long-delayed bliss, they almost forgot where they were, or why, or what was threatening them both.

When at last they had to pause for breath and pull a little apart, Tamino said, almost in a whisper, "I cannot decide, Pamina, whether this is the final temptation, the final test of my resolution—"

"If so, it is a test for me too, Tamino," she said, looking up at him. "Only in the Ordeal of Earth was this forbidden to us. I have heard—not much, I have been kept away from such things—but I have heard people speak of love as a fire. Perhaps the test here is to know if we are courageous enough to accept it."

It was an incredible temptation to take her into his

arms again and forget the Ordeals, forget everything
but the slender strength of her body against his. Yet
he demurred.

"I can't believe this could be a part of the Ordeals."
He felt tender laughter bubbling up from some deep
wellspring inside himself. "They told us it would be so
dangerous we would in the end feel it would have been
simpler to be cast into the fire. Danger—here, from
you, my beloved? I cannot believe it."

"Ah, yes, there is danger," Pamina whispered,
throwing her head back and pulling his head down to
kiss her again. "I want to burn up in your fire."

"And I in yours," he murmured back, holding his
mouth close to the delicate scroll of her small ear. "And
yet—remember how the priests watched and knew
every word we had spoken in the far depths of the
ocean, or on the cliffs? They will be watching here
too."

"Let them watch, and envy us," Pamina said, pulling
him to her. "I am not ashamed. Are you?"

Was he? He wondered. It was not the custom of his
country to conduct such affairs in the open air, certainly not where other eyes were watching. He started
to say, *I would feel like one of your dog-halflings*, and
stopped himself. She was already a shy girl, shamefast;
now when she had overcome that shyness and was
ready to fling herself into his arms, was he to spoil her
perfect happiness in this coming together?

With shaking fingers he began to untie the braided
cord about her tunic. Papageno, who had refused the
further Ordeals, probably had enjoyed this moment
with his Papagena long ago, yet he and Pamina had
denied themselves. Why, and for how long? She smiled,
mimicking his movements with playful deliberation as
her fingers skillfully unknotted the colored braid of the
fastening.

Then he coughed and gasped. From nowhere a whirlwind, suddenly blazing across them, blasted through the shelter of the tree, stinging dust in his eyes, in his mouth. Pamina gasped, choked, turned her face swiftly away from the fury of the attacking wind. Tamino, tasting dust, feeling it sting his eyes, coughed and tried without success to spit sand from his mouth. The broad leaves of the succulent bush were ripped away one by one; the bush dwindled till it was no more than a small spiky plant half as high as his knee.

He had forgotten. They were in the Changing Lands.

Pamina was still hunched over, fighting the slashing sand from her eyes. She choked, scrubbing sand from her face with her sleeve. "Look, it made itself into a tiny plant to protect itself against the wind. Was it ever really a big bush at all?"

"I don't know, but whether it was or not, I wish it would come back," he said. Then he remembered the flute, still tied at his waist.

"This is a weapon of Air. It worked before," he said, and hunched himself over so that he could get at the mouthpiece without sand between his teeth. Where had it all come from? He could not even see the sun!

He began to play, trying to catch his breath between grit-laden gusts of thick air. He felt Pamina's hands, catching at him. He could not see her now for the sand, even if he dared open his eyes without imminent danger of being blinded. He could not put his arm round her; both hands were on the flute, and it seemed to him that he had to make that choice a great deal oftener than he liked. He hoped someday he could pay enough concentrated attention to her to induce her to forgive him for it.

He played. As he had expected—that wind had been no natural wind—almost from the first notes of the flute, the sandstorm began to die away. It had, he thought grimly, been no accident that it came when it did. His instinct had been right after all. He wanted more privacy for their bridal couch, and so, he was sure, would Pamina.

The wind died. In the Changing Lands it was abnormally still. The bush was gone, even in its shrunken form; only a few of the little lizards still scurried in their unending round on the rocks, fighting, pouncing on beetles, copulating, fighting.

Pamina released him. He could see her now, though her eyes were red and swollen from the grit, and he supposed his own were no better. She retied the cord of her tunic, looking up at him with shy laughter.

"You wondered if this was the right time. I think we were given our answer, and just at the moment. Imagine if it had come five minutes later!"

Her mirth was infectious, making him laugh, even through his dry and strained throat, at the picture of that wind striking them when they were naked, wholly defenseless, absorbed only in each other.

"The desert was bad enough," he said at last, "but the desert after a sandstorm? I will be afraid to do anything, I think, for fear of making it worse!"

Pamina said, with a skeptical look round the bleak wasteland that surrounded them, "I do not see how any change could be other than an improvement. If these are the Changing Lands, I wish I knew how to make them change!"

"Perhaps that is what we are required to do?" Tamino surmised. "If not to change them, to make them show their true substance, show themselves as they really are?"

Pamina sank to the ground. It looked to Tamino as if she were too weary to stand.

"I am tired of worrying about the purpose of this test or what we are supposed to do," she said in utter exhaustion. For a moment she had really believed she had found the purpose of the Ordeal of Fire, that it was to determine if she and Tamino had the courage to claim one another in the face of the Changing Lands. Could they change even love? She was terrified to find out.

"Maybe the flute could make them change."

"But the flute is the magical weapon of Air—"

"And it is through the means of Air that we communicate with all the elements," she said, and then remembered what the priest had told them. In the element of Air she had discovered hidden powers; in the element of Water, Tamino had learned that he could not *(need not?)* be always in command. As Tamino had conquered these Ordeals, so too had she, and she had untapped powers over the element of Water.

At her gesture of command, Tamino obediently lifted the flute to his lips and began softly to play. With the aid of the soft air of melody, Pamina began to think about the element of Water: hostile and angry, filling their mouths with salt spray, submerging and drowning them; healing and warm then. How she wished she could lie submerged in it, washing grit from her mouth and sand from her body, secret water, stealing through the land, even beneath a desert such as this, hidden far below the sandy wasteland, gushing forth from the rock. . . . Then it was time and she *knew*, and she quickly bent and slapped the rock.

"Water!" she commanded, in a voice she had never heard, feeling her throat ache with the word of Power.

It gushed up and struck her in the face. She bent and drank and drank, laughing and crying with relief. She splashed it in her sore eyes, stepped back a moment so Tamino could do the same, dampened the cowl of her robe as the spring spread into a little pool in the rock. Tamino drank and laved his gritty cheeks, rinsed sand from his teeth. They looked into each other's eyes, laughing in delight.

And then, as he stood close to her, about to bend forward—she sensed it—to kiss her again, this time not sensually but for pure delight and pride in the sorcerous powers that had again delivered them from peril, she saw his eyes change, grow cold. He dropped his hands from her shoulders, stepped back and quickly notched his bow. He drew it to full tension, gesturing her behind him.

She whirled about to see what menace was there, and gasped aloud. Monostatos stood there, his face drawn into a mask of implacable hatred, unflinching before Tamino's drawn bow.

"Do you think I am afraid of that toy?"

"Make but a single move," said Tamino, "and you shall know whether or not you have reason to fear it."

His lips curved just a little in a faint mocking smile.

"I am son to the Great Dragon," he said. "Do you think because Sarastro cast me out I have no sorcery at my command? Now you are in *my* realm, Prince of the West, not I in yours, and I say to you: "Go! Get hence!"

He did not move his hands. He made no move at all. But thunder lanced from the clear sky; Pamina felt herself flung into darkness, and Tamino was gone.

CHAPTER TWENTY

*D*ARKNESS. *Tamino was gone. Pamina was* fighting in the dark against an invisible enemy. Monostatos? No, Monostatos was human, Halfling at least, and this thing she fought was no way as human as that; it enfolded her with suffocating wings, leathery in texture; talons raked her face, and the creature's breath was nauseating, some dreadful stench of carrion and sewer.

Blindly, Pamina snatched at the dagger the priests had given her. They had known, then, that in this Ordeal they would face physical dangers as well. Once she had asked her father if Monostatos had been one of the trials she must face, and he had told her, no. But Monostatos had sent her into this darkness, and she thrust with her dagger as if she were fighting Monostatos himself.

How did she know that she was not? How did she know that he did not, like herself, have the power to transform himself into some alien and frightening shape? She slashed, and the thing screeched hideously, a sound that racked her ears. If only she could see it; but the leathery wings enfolded her face so completely that even if there had been light she could not have seen. Suffocating, coughing at the thing's foul breath, Pamina tried to stab into the body of the creature, but this time her dagger went through it as if there had been nothing there.

A talon raked the arm with the dagger and she felt it draw blood. She had never been seriously hurt before, and the pain almost paralyzed her. Almost worse than the pain was horror, the thought of that dreadful beak ripping at her eyes and ravaging them. She fought in a nightmare frenzy, as if every terror of her life was attacking her there, filth and suffocation and soft obscene touches in the dark, and again and again, as she thrust with the dagger, it seemed that the dagger went through it as if nothing was there. Yet the pain of talons and ripping beak, stabbing at her again and again, was very real.

In the Ordeal of Air we could have fallen to our deaths, or in that of Water we could have drowned, before we ever knew the real nature of the Ordeal. Yet the physical danger had nothing to do with the true testing. What was the real test here? Pamina's mind struggled as fiercely as her body fought the terrible thing that was tearing at her in the dark.

Nothing was real now but pain and horror and the nightmare of the obscene thing she fought in the darkness. Her dagger arm was beginning to tire, and the arm she held before her face to ward off the creature's assault was lacerated with many cuts and scratches. She backed away, felt her heel catch in something she could not see, and fell, losing the dagger as she sprawled headlong, and knew in a moment that it was upon her.

Think, Pamina, she admonished herself frantically. There must be something you can do. Think what you are supposed to do or this thing will kill you before ever you know the true nature of this ordeal!

She supposed she was supposed to use her newly discovered powers of sorcery against it. But how did she know that Monostatos, too, did not have the power to change himself into some unknown and incomprehensible shape? Once again, how did she know this was not Monostatos himself, terribly transfigured?

Whether Monostatos or another nightmare shape out of her innermost terrors, somehow she must conquer it. It was stabbing at her head now as she rolled herself into a little ball of terror to keep her eyes away, and without even the dagger, she still must free herself from its attack.

Tamino! Where was he, why had he forsaken her? Or was he, too, fighting some dreadful adversary alone? Frantically, Pamina sought to call upon the new powers she had discovered within herself. In the darkness, she rolled away from its beak, pulled herself swiftly to her feet, and as she had cried out for water beneath the bush, she cried out, "Light! Fire!"

Light exploded across her eyes like the glare of the sun. From *somewhere* she felt herself grasping the light, flinging it at the thing she could see clearly now in all its horror, grasping talons, stabbing brutal beak dripping with her own blood. The clotted fire struck it, blazing up like a torch. There was a horrible scream and the thing fluttered to the desert sand, ashes dropping as it fell. Then there was only a little stain of ash on the barren sand, and Pamina was alone in the desert.

And she fell like the bird, crumpling to the sand, between horror and relief.

She lay there for some time, numbed by the terror and its cessation. Finally, she raised her head and began to assess the damage. The sleeve of her tunic was in shreds and her arms stung with multiple scratches; there was a long, painful, blood-streaked gash on her cheek where the thing had come close to striking at her eye. She remembered how her dagger had gone through it as if there was nothing there. How could anything so insubstantial leave such material wounds?

She decided none of the wounds was serious. The one sleeve was so badly torn that she finally ripped it away; it had been hanging by a few threads, dirty and so clotted with her blood that she could not even use it to bandage up the other cuts. She wiped her face with the other sleeve and wished she could find a spring to bathe her hurts.

Where was Tamino? Was he, too, fighting some deadly battle against the dangers of the Changing Lands, alone, separated not by the priests but by Monostatos's wiles? How could they get on with the Ordeal of Fire, if that apostate from both worlds, that evil wretch, was allowed to interfere?

Or, in spite of what her father had said, was this simply a further testing? She could see now, even though her father told her that the lust of Monostatos had not been intended as one of her trials, that it had been a very real part of her testing, to face him and refuse to submit to him. It had strengthened her resolve.

In the previous Ordeals, she and Tamino had been together, and the priests, this time, had sent them out together. She blinked away fierce tears of regret when she remembered; only a little while ago—though she had no idea how long it had really been—she and Tamino had been lying together in the shelter of the bush. He had touched her, she had untied the cord about his waist—

And then had come the sandstorm, and the beginning of the real trials. It had not, then, been intended that they should consummate their love, not yet. Would that time ever come? Pamina did not know, now, if she even wanted it to come. There had been so many trials, so many tests. Would there ever be an end to them?

"Pamina," said a soft, beloved voice, "I've come to take you home, my darling."

She raised her eyes, and her mother stood before her.

Not now, the majesty and rage and terrible beauty of the Starqueen. This was the mother she remembered from her childhood, a little woman really, not as tall as Pamina herself, clad in a robe of soft gray silk that enwrapped her like a cloud. She wore no jewelry, not even the silver lamen of the moon coiled into the strands of the dark hair on her brows. Not even the tiny star at her throat, peeping out from the gray robe. The dark hair was silvered now, and Pamina saw lines of pain, as well as the first wrinkles of age, in her mother's face.

Her mother put out her hand tenderly to touch the long, still bloody slashes on Pamina's forearm and face.

"My poor darling," she whispered, and folded Pamina in her arms. "What has he done to you, that dreadful, evil man? Why have you let Sarastro torture you this way?" With her head on her mother's shoulder, held close in her arms, Pamina let herself give way to a great, shuddering fit of sobbing, like a child, and her mother held her close, as she had never done in Pamina's real childhood.

"There, there, my child, my little love, it's over, I won't let him hurt you anymore."

All her life she had longed to be held like this, comforted, cherished. Now at last her mother came to her, holding out all the comfort for which she had so longed, and it was too late. With pain like the claws of the creature tearing at her heart, Pamina drew herself free of her mother's arms.

The Starqueen drew her fingers gently along the

scratches on the abused arms, and the blood ceased to ooze from the wounds. The pain was gone, too. She touched the ugly wound beneath the eye, and it was soothed.

"I've come to take you home out of this terrible desert, my treasure. Remember, you are all I have, you are my heir, one day you will be Starqueen. Did you really think I would abandon you to Sarastro's sorcery? But it's all over now. Come, love, take my hand, and in a moment we will be in our own city again. Now you are no longer a child, but a woman to rule at my side." She held out her hand to Pamina, but Pamina hung back, hesitant, staring at her mother's extended hand. It was smooth, unwrinkled, quite unlike the gray weary-worn face; the hand not of the quiet little woman, her aging mother whom she had begun to pity, but the hand—she felt it, with a shudder that went right through her—of the Starqueen.

"Come, come," said her mother, with a touch of impatience. "Take my hand, child, or I cannot transport you from this desert. Don't you want to go home, my treasure, my darling?"

To go home—Pamina felt that never in her life had she wanted anything so much. But had it ever been home to her? Had any of it ever been more real than this image of her mother, the image which tugged at all her childhood memories—and was no more real than any of them? She had longed for these endearments; and when they came they were hollow, meaningless, she could sense and hear in her mother's voice that they were only tools to manipulate her into doing the Starqueen's will.

She said, hearing the trembling in her own voice, "You told me that you would disown me, never again call me daughter, unless I came to you with the blood of my father on my hands."

"I was angry, Pamina. Have you never known anger? Now that you are a woman do you not understand the power of rage?" She looked directly into Pamina's face, and again, seeing the pitiful lines of age and mourning in that face, Pamina was moved to tenderness; but she struggled against it, knowing that the Starqueen would use this, too, as a weapon against her.

"Then you will indeed take me back without harm to Sarastro?"

"Pamina," said her mother, "can it be that you have not yet guessed the truth? As you and Tamino are bound, so Sarastro and I are the two faces of power, Light and Darkness, Night and Day, Truth and Falsehood, Life and Death. I would have had you renounce him; he has bidden you to renounce me; both of us were testing you, and now you must rise above the false division between the darkness and the day." Again she stretched her hand to Pamina. "Come quickly, child, while still there is time to make the choice."

This was the most painful test of all; was not this what she wanted most to believe, that somehow she could choose to follow Sarastro's truth and yet not lose the mother she still painfully adored? How persuasive it seemed, that all this was one more complicated test, to see if she could know the ultimate truth; that her mother and Sarastro were two facets of the truth, the light and the darkness intertwined, and there was no need for these terrible choices.

"Quickly, Pamina. Take my hand."

But the hand of the Starqueen was still smooth, unwrinkled, giving the lie to the illusion of age and sorrow which she had put on—*yes, put on to beguile me*—and Pamina shrank back.

"Sarastro has told me nothing but what I can see for myself to be truth," she said, "and you have told me lie after lie. What of the sacrifices, Mother? Should I reign over a world drowned in blood? What—" Another memory she had deliberately put away, once more surfaced within her. "What of Rawa, Mother? Why did you send her to sacrifice, after promising me her safety?"

"Rawa?" The Starqueen frowned, and to Pamina this was even more dreadful, her mother did not even remember, among the thousands of sacrifices Rawa was just one more. "What are you talking about, child?"

"My nurse. When you gave me Papagena's life, you sent her away. I did not know then that it was to sacrifice."

"Oh. The Halfling bitch. She was Kamala's nurse too, I seem to remember. That one. I had forgotten her name." The Starqueen was quiet for a moment. "Why not? There are Halflings enough. I would have gotten you a dozen dog-halflings if I had known you wanted them."

Pamina started to say, But I loved her, and suddenly knew that to her mother the words would be meaningless. And that was worst of all. If the Starqueen could not understand that she had loved Rawa, of what worth were her own protestations of love?

Her mother was still facing her, that lying hand out stretched, and yet Pamina had not the courage to face her and refuse to come. In her mind already she could hear the furious cry, see the thunders of rage, the towering majesty of the Starqueen, and she shrank, shrank down. Never to have to see that fury again, never to hear the thunders of that wrath. Never to have to choose.

I can change myself; these are the Changing Lands indeed, and no one returns from them unchanged. She could change herself to the bird-form and fly free—

But once before she had escaped into flight, and her

mother had flown beside her, a great cloud-bird, entreating and cajoling her to abandon Tamino. She could not escape that way, into her mother's very realm.

She felt a sudden passion to become a tree; to feel her feet send out roots, stretching down into the good earth, to spread her arms and feel them sprouting branches and leaves; the birds, good and evil, might nest in her branches, but she need never listen to them nor hear any of their beguilements, need never know the terrible mystery of choice. Tentatively she dug her toes into the sand, feeling all through her body the tingle of growth as they spread into the desert sand, seeking out water. She spread out her arms, fiercely *willing* them to send out shoots, to put on bark and leaves. . . .

"Stay here, then!" cried the Starqueen, in that sudden fury which had been the torment of Pamina's childhood and girlhood, and suddenly she towered to the sky, thunder flaring from her voice and her spread hands. Pamina cowered among her leaves, trying to will herself deaf and dumb and passive, silent forever and immune to that pleading. . . .

Defeated, then. Numb. The Starqueen had won, and she had failed the test of Fire, retreating to frightened passivity, as she had always willed to do. Something in Pamina wanted that. Something in her had always wanted to be blind and deaf to her mother, but the real Pamina had fought back, as she had struggled in the darkness against the terrible creature. Was she to abandon the fight now and allow her mother's lies to triumph? In Sarastro's realm she had learned another way.

There was no retreat now into Earth; with regret, Pamina thrust out her hands, seeing her leaves drift sadly to the ground, wrenched her roots painfully from the earth and felt herself stand unconnected on her human feet. She drew a long breath, feeling the fire of defiance fill her lungs.

She cried out, "No! I love Tamino, and I will stay with him!"

Her mother was still towering over her, blazing with the gems and beauty of the Starqueen. Her laughter was like summer lightning, a fierce manic sound.

"Tamino! Do you think he wants anything of you except the power of a marriage to Sarastro's daughter? Why, you sorry little fool, he bargained with me for you, Pamina. Did you not know that he was in my kingdom and in my power, and it was I who sent him to rescue you from Sarastro? But when Sarastro offered him more power than I had—or so that fool Tamino thought—he abandoned me because he thought Sarastro could offer him more!"

"It isn't true," Pamina cried out in fury and terror. "It isn't true!"

Yet she should have known. She was her mother's daughter, tainted, evil throughout, what could Tamino possibly want of her except the power she held as Sarastro's daughter?

"You who talk so much of truth," said her mother scornfully, "still you fear it, I can see! Well, truth you shall have, Pamina. Keep silence now, and listen while I test your precious Tamino and you shall see how deep is this"—she paused, with the terrible smile Pamina remembered from her childhood—"this *love* of which you are so certain."

She gestured. Pamina, with her own newfound powers of sorcery, recognized the gesture just too late to move free of its influence. She stood in a bubble of darkness, hidden, powerless, and struggled in vain to move, to speak, to make herself known. And then, slowly dawning before her eyes, she saw Tamino.

CHAPTER TWENTY-ONE

EVEN as he realized, with a dreadful sense of apprehension, that Pamina had disappeared, and that he was alone with Monostatos, Tamino had his sword out and ready. For once he felt prepared for what was to come. His father's son had been extensively trained as a warrior, a fighter, and now that he had Monostatos before him, actually within sword reach, he had no fear. But where were the sorcerer's weapons? Monostatos stood before him, empty-handed and mocking. How could he strike an unarmed man? Confused again, Tamino hesitated, and Monostatos, with a little flash of light, moved to the edge of the little grove of bushes. Surely he could not have run so far? Holding his sword, Tamino ran after him, but mocking laughter filled the ruins, and once again Monostatos was standing a dozen feet away, taunting him from a distance.

"Stand and fight, coward!" Tamino yelled.

"With your weapons? You'd like that, wouldn't you?" Monostatos was shrieking with laughter. Out of nowhere a whip of fire lashed Tamino's forehead. Stung, he threw up his arms to shelter against it, hearing the jeering cries of the sorcerer.

"What have you done with Pamina?" he shouted.

"Wouldn't you like to know? Throw down your

sword, and perhaps I may tell you!" Another whip of fire descended, this time full across his face, barely missing his eyes. Shouting, furious with the burning pain, Tamino rushed blindly at Monostatos, flinging himself on the magician, eager to come to grips with him, but he stumbled over a bush and measured his full length on the sand. Wordless with fury, he howled, as whips of fire fell, one after another, lashing, burning the tunic from his back. He rolled into a ball to protect himself against them, thinking desperately that this was an Ordeal of Fire indeed—but was it the kind the priests had intended?

Slash after slash of fiery pain rained down on him. There must surely be something he could do against it. And Pamina, where was she, what trials of this kind was she facing alone? The thought of Pamina, helpless against this wicked man, or Halfling, or snake, or whatever he was, infuriated him more than his own pain.

He jerked himself to his feet, ran toward Monostatos, and caught him unawares; this time the sorcerer barely managed to escape in his sudden flash of light. Tamino made a feint with the sword; the sword vanished in a burst of white-hot fire, burning Tamino's hand. But Tamino ignored the searing pain and grabbed a handful of Monostatos's hair. Somehow he knew that the sorcerer could not do his disappearing trick if Tamino was actually touching him.

His sword was gone. No matter. Now he actually had his hands on the vicious Monostatos, he did not need it. He jerked the man's head back, his other hand at the Halfling's throat. He could feel the dry, warm, not unpleasant scaliness there which marked the serpent-halfling.

"What have you done with Pamina? Speak, and I may spare your wretched life!"

Under his hand the scaled throat writhed, reared

upward; under his very touch a dragon roared, and Tamino recoiled as it reared above him.

He had a swift and terrible sense of *déjà vu*. Surely he had been here before, when first he came into these Lands and the dragon had come against him. Had that too been Monostatos? In that flashing moment of memory he had a quick impression of the man in the ruins: taller than Monostatos, and with a noble and melancholy face... not Monostatos, then. These were the Changing Lands, and for a moment Tamino, before the crawling terror in his veins, the atavistic horror of the Serpent felt by all children of the Ape, longed to shrink down into something tiny, too tiny for a dragon to see or kill....

Instead, suddenly feeling the flaring fire in his hand and the power of fire bursting through him, he opened himself to that power, crying out—he never knew what; but the pain that seared his hand made him aware that the sword was in it again. It had not been burned up in white fire. That was illusion, as the dragon itself must be partly illusion. He struck down hard with the sword where Monostatos would have been most exposed, breast unshielded against the sword, and saw the flash of light. Monostatos, in human-form again, was standing at the edge of the ruins. Then he vanished.

Tamino slowly lowered the sword. On some deep level of awareness he knew that he had not conquered Monostatos; he had only driven him away on the physical plane. The sword in his hand bore long silvery streaks, as if the metal had melted and been somehow reforged. He shuddered as he looked at it. Ordeal by Fire indeed; and as he looked at the still raw, seared, throbbing wound in his palm, he knew it was only beginning.

In the tension and fury of the battle with Monostatos, he had not been fully aware of the agony of the burn. Now he gripped his wrist with his other hand, as if somehow the very pressure could ease the dreadful burning pain. He heard himself moaning aloud in the agony of it, and plunged toward the spring which Pamina had commanded from the rock to wash the grime of the sandstorm from their bodies. Pamina. Where was Pamina? He wanted to cry aloud for her in his despair, as he remembered—surely it had been in another life, a million million years ago—Papageno howling Papagena's name. There was nothing in the world but this pain and deprivation, the screaming pain in his hand. He plunged toward the spring, thrust out his hand, and sand raked the burn, with a pain that made all that had gone before seem like pleasure.

He cried out, as he had called to his sword, as Pamina had cried out striking the sand: *"Water!"*

There was time for a moment of despair, a moment of silent agony and dread—would he die here in the Changing Lands, burned to a crisp by dragonfire?— before he felt it flooding over his hand, cooling and soothing the pain: cold water, icy cold. But not the desert spring Pamina had commanded from the rock. He was lying in the water full-length, as it soothed his burned hand and the scars of the fiery whips on face and neck and back, and, lying near him in the pool was the otter-woman.

Then it was not Pamina, alone, who had developed the powers of sorcery. He himself was a sorcerer, a sorcerer like Monostatos. And for a moment he felt revulsion at what he had become. He had been afraid of Pamina, when first he had seen her transformed magically into a great eagle. Now he feared himself. For a moment he wished that he was in his father's lands, that he had never come into this world of deviltry and wizard's powers. It was corrupting him too. What had he become? Would he be no better then than Monostatos?

He had never asked for these sorcerous powers. He could not believe that they were anything but evil. He had been given them, unbidden, unasked. The words of Sarastro and of the guide rang with wicked irony in his mind, *"Nothing is asked of you but that you shall remain your best self at all times."*

Was this then his best self, that he should call down fire to burn his enemy as he had himself been burned? It was a frightening riddle.

His soaked garments were weighing him down in the pool as they had weighed him down in the sea among the dolphins, and he supposed the remedy was the same. He dragged himself wearily to the verge and sat on the grass, pulling off his drenched tunic and trousers.

As he fumbled with the wet clothing, his fingers lingered a moment on the cord at his waist. Only a little while ago—yet how long ago it seemed!—Pamina had playfully untied this cord. That had started everything that had happened.

No, to be fair, it had started when he had begun to desire her. Damn these Ordeals, which aroused desire within a man's loins and punished him for yielding to that desire! Unfair, he thought bitterly, it was unfair as everything that had happened to him in Sarastro's kingdom was unfair.

He untangled the wet cord. Water and Fire had burned away all but memory of that desire. Would he ever feel a man's desire again without the terror of what had come between them? Tied to the cord was the magic flute.

He looked at it, bitterly. Was he supposed to play it again and yell for help from magical Messengers once more? He was tired of being acted upon; he wanted to act for once on his own and in his own name. The guide had told him: in the Ordeals of Air and Water, he had learned that he could not always be in control. Was he never to be in control again? He laid the flute down by his side, and turned his attention to spreading the wet garments on the grass to dry.

Where had the grass come from? They had been in the sand desert, and now he was in the jungly rain forest where he had seen the otter-woman. She was submerged in the pool, only her eyes and her sleek dark hair visible, but her intent dark gaze made him uneasy.

How dare she look at him like that, anyhow? He was a man, and he had been stared at quite enough by Halflings in the last few days. Monostatos, arrogant brute, had dared to lash him with whips of fire in a sorcerer's duel in which Tamino had never intended to engage, and had provoked him into retaliating in kind. He felt used, bruised, burned, naked before the eyes of the Halfling woman.

He said roughly, "Why are you staring at me?"

She ducked beneath the water, and before her fear something ugly stirred in the back of his mind. These Halflings who continually bested him, chivied him about, Monostatos with his whips of fire, the dolphins who had forced him to give way and abase himself...he was a man, he was finished with being harried about by these Halflings.

She was a woman. The Ordeals had surely not been intended to deprive him of manhood, and the test here, perhaps, was more subtle than he had thought. The simplest of the metaphors of Fire was simply sexual; and now, feeling it rising again within him, he took up the flute and played a single note.

It has power over the Halflings. I can make her

come to me. Perhaps the test was only this, that where everything seemed to conspire against him to rob him of manhood, of power, of the will or desire, to take the initiative, at that point he should assert his own strength and prove the power of Human over Halfling. Then indeed would he prove dominion over the final element of Fire, the lust he felt burning in his body.

He blew another tentative note on the flute and a third. The otter-woman, her eyes fixed on his, slowly crawled up from the water as the separate notes merged into a little tune. Why was she looking at him like that? She was of the miserable Halfling-kind, like Monostatos she would outrage and attack him if he did not maintain his power with the flute. He kept playing while she moved, slowly and with obvious reluctance, up the bank. She was naked. Good—now she had paid for his humiliation before the dolphins. She lay passive, spread out before him. Her body was not a woman's body, not quite, but it was female and as raging lust stirred in him, he did not care. The fire was burning in him, a fire of rage. She was not Pamina....

Pamina. To protect Pamina he had been willing to play the flute, to exploit the Halflings; even for that it had been forbidden, and now he would misuse it this way? With a cry of despair he flung the flute aside and covered his face with his hands. What had he done, after all this time, to fail at the last like this? The otter-halfling woman still lay, spread-eagled numb and passive, her eyes wide with terror. He gestured to her, without turning, to go. He muttered, "I won't hurt you. Go! Go—" and, remembering what the Dolphin-kin had said to him—"go, sister."

He stared in horror at the flute. What had it almost led him to do? He had been told it was a very powerful magical weapon. Now it had turned in his hand and almost betrayed him. At the moment, if he had not been afraid to touch it again, he would have flung it into the pool.

His clothing, blood-soaked and scorched from the fiery whips, still lay in damp wads on the grass, but he struggled into it anyway. How vulnerable and mean his nakedness now seemed to him. From the far side of the pool he could still see the otter-woman watching him distrustfully. He did not blame her. He wouldn't trust himself either. He had never felt so miserable and ashamed in his life. He tied the woven three-colored cord about his waist, struggling with the clumsy wet strands. He didn't deserve them.

His hand still throbbed, though the cold water had alleviated the pain of the whip-wounds a little. He fastened his sword to his belt. At least he had not disgraced that weapon as he had disgraced the flute entrusted to him. He looked at it, wondering if it would bring Pamina back; it had helped them earlier, but that had been before he had so grossly violated the trust placed in him. If only he had had the sense to play the flute and ask the magical Messengers to help bring Pamina back to him. If only he had Papageno's innocence!

He lay on the grassy bank, castigating himself over and over. Time crawled by, and he heard the otter-woman's furry babies splashing and chittering heedlessly in the pool, but he paid no attention to them. He remembered the otter-creatures who had bathed him in the Starqueen's palace, and that seemed very long ago, as if he had been then only a boy, a long ago innocence.

To go so far along the Ordeals, and fail at the end, on the very level of Earth where once he had triumphed! Pride and overconfidence had brought him low. Had he failed forever? Was that why he could not recall

Pamina to his side even with his newfound and unwanted powers of sorcery?

He lay there for a long time until, in the burning sun, a shadow crossed his vision and lay dark on the grass. Had Monostatos returned to taunt him further? He opened his eyes and saw the Starqueen standing beside him.

There was now no touch of majesty or grandeur, no thunder, no train of stars. She was only a small, stooped, aging woman, shrouded in a misty gray mantle the color of raincloud, a veil covering her graying hair as was seemly for a matron no longer young. He scrambled warily to his feet, backing away and bowing to her.

"Are you afraid of me, my son?" she asked reproachfully.

He had not the faintest idea what he ought to say to her. There was a long silence.

"So you too have betrayed me," she said at last. "Did I not beg you to rescue my daughter Pamina? And did you not swear to me faithfully that you would do so, even if it should cause your death?"

Tamino bowed his head. "I did," he said, stifled.

"I believed you my friend. Did I not have reason to believe you were sworn to be my friend, Prince Tamino?"

What could he say to her? He had indeed promised, and no sooner had he reached Sarastro's realms than he had been won over by the priest-king. He no longer knew just why he had come to mistrust her, or why he had been false to his promise to rescue her daughter. Why had he not rescued Pamina? Why had he suddenly decided that she did not need rescuing?

He could no longer remember.

"You were seduced by Sarastro, as all my friends have been seduced by that wicked man," she said. "All this land of Atlas-Alamesios lies under his tyranny, a tyranny which perverts and seduces the very mind, which would set up the rule of the Halflings over us, and throw down all the wisdom of the Makers. But it is not yet too late, my son, to renounce your allegiance to this greatest of tyrants. Do you not yet see how he has lied to you, used you, bribed you with the thought of Pamina's hand in marriage? But it can be set right. Renounce Sarastro, and I shall be your friend."

Tamino's eyes suddenly strayed to the magic flute where it lay on the grass. He had not had the heart to tie it again to his belt. But it was as if a voice he could not recognize—Pamina's voice? he could not tell—was crying to him in the darkness:

"The flute, Tamino. Play the flute. It is the magical weapon of truth, and no lies can be spoken in its presence."

He looked away from the Starqueen. How could he account for interrupting what she was saying by bending down to pick up the flute? What made him think that it was very important to get it into his hands, to play it, before she saw it?

"Tamino, look at me, my son. Listen to my voice. Sarastro has bewitched you, worked upon your pride. Pamina has returned to me; she knows the truth now, and knows how Sarastro has lied to you both."

"Tamino. Get the flute. Play the flute."

It was surely Pamina's voice. He made a little side-step, bent down and snatched it up, but he could not interrupt her by suddenly beginning to play the flute. Nevertheless, he felt better with it in his hand.

"Well, Tamino, have you nothing to say to me? Will you not come with me to my palace, where Pamina is awaiting you? Sarastro cannot now give you her hand; she has renounced him," the Queen said gently. "But if you will come with me, you shall be reunited. Here are her sisters; they shall take you to her. Did you not know they were Pamina's sisters, my dear son?"

Now he saw them in the shadows behind her, the three women—he remembered their names now, he thought with wild irrelevance: Disa, Zeshi, and Kamala, who had told him as a warrior that the flute was a weapon for which she would give sword and spear and bow. Why did Kamala have her spear poised? They wore dark garments like stormclouds, darker than the Starqueen's.

"Come with me, my dear son. I have promised you Pamina's hand, and you and my daughter shall reign with me over all this land, and in the end throw Sarastro down."

"I would want to hear that from Pamina's own lips," said Tamino.

"But do you not know," said the Starqueen's soft cajoling voice, "that I am Pamina, as I am all women?" And before his amazed eyes, the bent and shrouded figure straightened, the dark hair silvered with gray became pale gold, just waving, and Pamina's lovely face smiled up into his.

"My beloved," she whispered, "I am with you again, you see, and together we will throw down that great tyrant. Come, take my hand, my only love, and together we will conquer."

She stretched out her hand to him. "Take my hand," she said. "Forget the wiles of other sorcerers. We are together again."

Could he believe this? Pamina had appeared to him before this, altered beyond recognition by her magical arts, and he had believed that. What was the truth? Was it all a magical charade, playing upon his innocence, his credulity?

"Take my hand," she commanded, a little more

harshly this time, "and once again we shall be united—"

Tamino started to stretch out his hand to her. Surely it was Pamina. Had it been the Starqueen all along? He began to stretch out his hand to her. But then he discovered that in his hand, he already held the magic flute.

"In every Ordeal before this, I have asked you to play it, to bring us aid and comfort in our difficulties. Tamino, play the flute."

He looked at Pamina before him. He did not think she had spoken. But surely it had been her voice. He hesitated, and Pamina said in a rage, "Make haste! Take my hand, while I can still avert your fate!"

Behind her it seemed that stormclouds raced across the sky, that darkness was about to fall.

Then there was a thunderclap, followed by a flash of lightning.

"Who speaks of betrayal?" It was the voice of Monostatos. "It was to *me* you promised Pamina! To me! And now you are again making overtures to this wretched outlander from the west, this plaything of Sarastro! Pamina is mine, so you swore to me, and now again you have lied, as you lied to my father's self—"

Pamina's body flickered, her face faded; it was the Starqueen, towering high in majesty over them both.

"You, Monostatos? You—Halfling?" She said it, and spat disdainfully into his face.

Monostatos wiped his face deliberately. His sallow features were pale with rage.

"Lady," he said, "not even the Starqueen can play these games with the son of the Great Serpent!"

The Starqueen shrugged disdainfully. And at that moment there was a great roar and where Monostatos had stood, the dragon once again reared upward, and the breath of flame swept over them. Tamino had seen the transformation before. This time it did not terrify him; but the Starqueen reacted with rage and dismay. She gestured at the three ladies hovering in the background.

"Kill him!" she cried. "Kill him, quickly!"

There was a great cry of anguish and despair from Disa.

"She betrayed us too! Our father! Our father, and we never knew!" And suddenly it flashed upon Tamino just what were the depths of the Starqueen's treachery.

Not once, but twice before Tamino had seen this man-to-dragon metamorphosis, this terrifying transformation. Once it had been Monostatos; but the time before that, when he had first come into this country, he had battled a dragon and the three ladies, he now knew, had killed it to save his life. . . .

That had not been Monostatos, but the Great Dragon. For reasons of her own, the Starqueen had bidden her daughters to slay the one who had been her consort, who had fathered those daughters. In doubled rage now, Monostatos in dragon-form loomed over the Queen; but Tamino still saw some trace of Pamina's features there, and threw himself, sword in hand, between the Starqueen and the dragon.

"Monostatos," he shouted, "don't fight with women! I have enough of a quarrel with you that I will not spare you to fight with the Starqueen; turn on me, I tell you, and I will fight you!"

He raised his sword and heard behind him the laughter of the Starqueen.

"Ah, gallantry! What a fool! As if I feared him, in dragon- or human-form, *Halfling*!" Again the word was a searing whip of sarcasm. She turned on her three daughters. "What are you waiting for? Your spears are mine, foolish girls: kill him!"

Yet they hung back, and Disa cried out in pain.

"For you we slew our father. Should we kill our father's son as well, Lady?"

"Tamino! Play the flute! For the last time, I implore you!"

Tamino put it to his lips and began to play.

The Starqueen cried out, "Take it from him! Take it, it was stolen from me, it is mine—" But Tamino played on. This had power over Halflings and for all his dragon-form, for all his sorceries, Monostatos was Halfling. The music of the flute stole through the Changing Lands. From the pool the otter-woman crawled up again, her small fuzzy rounded-headed babies behind her, but this time Tamino did not even look at her. Monostatos, rearing up in dragon-form, slowly dwindled till he stood no higher than the Queen.

Then Pamina was standing beside the Queen, covering her eyes as if the light hurt them. It was the real Pamina this time, in the sand-grimed tunic, the braided cord he had himself untied.

She pointed her finger at Monostatos.

"Son of the Serpent," she cried out, "in the sound of Truth, be now what you truly are! I command you!"

For a moment Monostatos the man stood before them, his face contorted in a grimace of terror. Then he began to dwindle down and down, shrinking further and further. No longer a man, no longer a dragon, he slumped forward on all fours, grew smaller, smaller still. The scales grew rougher, larger as he grew smaller, until before them a little lizard scampered in circles, and while they watched, climbed on another lizard, briefly copulated, climbed down, ran away and began to fight with another lizard.

Pamina's face was pale with horror, but she looked up at Tamino, tearless.

"He has found his true shape," she whispered. "As was his soul, now so is his body."

Tamino shuddered. So swiftly had Monostatos's fate come on him that the Starqueen still stood motionless.

At last she said to Pamina, "I would never have let him harm you." But the words rang hollow, and Pamina looked at her mother with a face like stone.

"You lied to me and you lied to Tamino. Have you ever told the truth?"

The Starqueen's voice was scornful. "Truth? You are a fool, Pamina. I have done what I must, and I make no apology. Shall it be war between us too, then, Pamina?" She gestured to the three ladies.

"Take her to the palace, while I deal with this fool!"

But they stood motionless.

"You have lied to us too," said Zeshi at last. "All our lives you have lied to us. We have served you loyally; and all your love and care has been for Pamina. To you we are no more than servants to be exploited for the sake of our sister."

"How can you say so? You have stood always at my right hand and shared my power," said the Starqueen. "And as for this futile fool with her dreams, I renounce her too. Kamala! Your weapons have been always ready to serve me—"

"But never again," whispered Kamala. "Pamina— sister—I have not been a good sister to you, but I beseech you, help me."

Pamina whispered, "Sister, be what you would be—"

For a moment Kamala was still. Then, as Pamina watched in horror, Kamala began to shrink downward. Her clothes slid to the ground, empty; her legs were already half sunken in the sand, and Pamina, remembering the moment when she had put out roots, shuddered in sympathy. Kamala's arms, very tiny now, stretched out, grew green, thrust out the vicious spines of a desert cactus. She shivered once and was forever still, surrounded with the useless weapons she had forsworn.

Only a moment the paralysis of horror lasted. Then there was a thunderclap, a cry of fury, and the Starqueen, in all her rage, bent over them, ready to destroy.

"You at least are still in my power!" she cried. Frozen, Tamino watched her stoop down from a giant height, and her hands were a giant's hands, ready to crush them like dust.

But Pamina gestured, and cried out in a voice that seemed to fill the whole sky, the whole universe. "No! Let the Makers judge between us! Once you were mistress of Earth, Water, Air, and Fire, as I am now. Tamino! Play the flute!" And as Tamino put it to his lips and began to play again, Pamina cried out, "In the name of Truth! You too, Lady, show us your true form. *Be what you are!*"

For a moment gray wings hovered, huge, terrible, great claws swooping down to snatch, and Tamino quailed. Then a wind ruffled the Changing Lands, and an owl rose and flapped away in the dusk, hooting a mournful, repetitious tone. Pamina swallowed, but to Tamino the sound was a muffled sob.

"Bird of Night," Pamina whispered, sobbing, "fly in the dark, cry out your lies to any who will listen, until some greater predator comes along....Oh, Tamino, Tamino, she's gone!" She collapsed, sobbing, in his arms. "It's over, and she's gone, and she was the Starqueen ...and she was my mother, and I loved her, and if she had ever loved me, if she had ever loved *anyone*—"

Tamino held her in his arms, with no word to say that could ease her pain. After a time he began to play on the flute again, knowing that this time it would bring the Messengers who would take them back to the city in triumph. But for Pamina, as well as for him, the triumph would be bitter and barren for a long time.

As he played, he could see, with a curious double-sight, what would happen afterward. He could see Pamina reclaiming from Papageno the magical bells, and could even hear what Papageno would say when she begged his pardon for taking them from him.

"That's all right, Lady, I'd rather have my birdcall, magical things aren't for the likes of me. Papagena and me, we don't need such things."

He could see the magical procession through the Starqueen's city, he playing on the flute and Pamina playing on the magical bells, to proclaim to the Half-lings that the sacrifices were at an end forever. Some of them would flee the city and find homes for themselves in the wilderness, where they would live, free of all men, till Atlas-Alamesios sank beneath the waves in a final earthquake. Others would remain, dependent on Mankind to shelter and care for them, a burden Man must bear, and he, Tamino, would bear that burden when Sarastro was gone.

The Messengers were before them with their sweet musical magical song. They were hailing him as Master of Earth, Air, Water, and Fire. As Pamina gravely saluted them, he managed to find a smile for Pamina. After all, it was their wedding day.

"But what are we to do?" Zeshi demanded. "I do not want to die, like Kamala—"

Pamina said gravely, "You are free to do as you will, sister."

Disa looked up in horror at the sky where the Starqueen had gone, and threw herself at Pamina's feet.

"Sister! Sister! Don't change me into a bird or anything terrible, please, oh, please—"

"I will not hurt you." Pamina sighed. "What do you want to do?"

"You—you have become so powerful—" Disa whispered. "If I come to Sarastro's temple, may I enter upon the Ordeals?"

Pamina looked helplessly at the Messengers.

"I don't know. May she?"

The Messengers spoke as one. "The Ordeals are open to all who will undertake them. Not since the Great Dragon has any Halfling passed through all four of the Ordeals in triumph; but so far as she may go, she will. Enter, Halfling woman, where Papageno entered before you."

Pamina reached out silently and took her sister's hand. She knew that if Disa entered upon the Ordeals seeking power, she would not get very far, no further than Monostatos. Yet how did she know? Disa might prove stronger than Pamina guessed; she was, after all, eldest daughter of the Starqueen.

Pamina looked around the Changing Lands, and wondered if she would ever come here again. Her heart was empty of the old adoration, and there was a raw and gaping wound where her mother had once been. But on this day of triumph she would not take away from Tamino's joy.

She took his hand and awaited the Messengers to bear them back in triumph to the Temple of Sarastro, there to inherit the reign as priest-king and queen of Atlas-Alamesios.

"We have not been through the volcano, dearest," she whispered, "but your clothes are as burned as if you had been set on fire. What do you think the guide will say to that?"

And with great thankfulness, she heard him laugh.

AUTHOR'S NOTE

On Night's Daughter *and Mozart's*
The Magic Flute:

*T*HE *first performance of the opera* The Magic Flute *was in 1791,* a collaboration between the composer and his librettist, a popular clown and performer in the "Kasperl" tradition of comedy in Vienna. From the time of the first performance it was recognized that into the fairy-tale scenario a serious meaning and allegory had been inserted. Ever since then, for the last two hundred years, thoughtful people have been asking, "What does it mean?"

I fell under the spell of the magic flute when still a child. (In fact, as a teenage science-fiction writer, I adopted for a short time the pen name of *Astrafiammunte*, after the Queen of the Night, and though I soon outgrew it, first abridging it simply to *Astra* and then dropping it entirely, no one who was a fan at that time has ever let me forget it. I still get teased about it at science-fiction conventions.)

I have spent most of my adult life as a writer of fantasy and science fiction; I see the story, of course, in that light.

In this re-creation, I have of necessity used many sources. I have, of course, read commentaries about the "Masonic" symbolism of the opera—Mozart and Shikaneder were both Masons—and seen the Ingmar Bergman film which made a superstar of Haakon Hagegaard as Papageno. I might as well say at once that I adopted from Bergman only one idea: that Pamina was the daughter of the Queen of the Night *by Sarastro*. This makes good sense of the whole tangle of relationships, even to the rivalry between the Priest-King and the Lady, otherwise inexplicable.

Other influences on my version include the persistent legend that an ancient civilization before our own was destroyed by its misuse of certain sciences, and that one of these was a blasphemous attempt to interbreed man and animal. In the light of current research into recombinant DNA that is not nearly as fantastic as it sounded when I first read about it.

I mentioned science fiction fandom above; there is a commonplace, facetious remark that "reality is a crutch for people unable to handle science fiction." Some people, desperate for their preferred reading to be treated as "respectable"—that is, on a par with popular fiction about adultery in the suburbs—grow very angry when it's quoted at them. But my favored reader is one who can read with his full awareness and does not need to be pacified by familiar settings or such characters as can be found on the street corner or in the soap opera of the mundane world.

So I like to go one step further and say that science fiction is itself a crutch for people unable to handle fantasy. As science fiction forces people to imagine the technology and cultures of the future, without the crutch of the here and now—tales of adultery in the suburbs, the familiar "hairdryer novel"—so fantasy forces the reader to confront his or her own archetypes, the images which move within the human subconscious, without even the "imagined future" binding us to our own mundane world. Here we move directly among our own psychological archetypes, the inward needs of our minds and spirit. In the words of Michael

Straight, commenting on J. R. R. Tolkien, "Fantasy does not obscure, but illuminates, the inner nature of reality." Such creatures of eternal imagination as the bird-man Papageno, or the Queen of the Night, do not need to be explained by such commonplace imaginings of mundane life as recombinant DNA; like the Cheshire Cat and the Wicked Stepmother, they exist within the collective imagination, if not of the human race, at least of the English-speaking universe.

Is this, then, fantasy, science fiction, parable, allegory, or simply a fairy tale to feed the child within us all?

That answer is for the reader. As a writer I only stand here with my magic flute and play you a magical tune.

—Marion Zimmer Bradley,
Berkeley, California,
December, 1983

About the Author

Marion Zimmer Bradley has been a professional writer for more than twenty-five years. She is best known for her novels of exotic fantasy adventure, particularly her best-selling *Darkover* series. Ms. Bradley lives in Berkeley, California, with her two younger children.